# HART OF VENGEANCE

## THE HART SERIES

## S.B. ALEXANDER

RAVEN WING PUBLISHING

# 1

## DENIM

The prison walls were closing in on me. Six fucking years behind bars were enough to make a man go batshit crazy. What was more maddening was the fact that I was innocent. I swore if I found out who'd set me up, I would slice and dice the fucker.

A chair scraped along the floor in the library. A big-ass-dude carried a book to a shelf while a guard stood watch at the door. It wasn't as if any of us would break out of the library and use books as weapons. Then again, inmates hid shivs in books.

Rubbing my eyes, I flopped my head back, taking in the smell of old and worn books. For the last hour, I'd been trying to prepare a speech for my parole hearing. On the advice of my lawyer, I should be ready to paint a pretty picture of what my future looked like if they granted me parole. Unfortunately, my brain wasn't working.

*Just tell them how you reformed. College classes. A model prisoner.*

I pulled on my shoulder-length blond hair as I righted my head and squinted at the blank notepad. I'd torn up about ten sheets of paper after starting and stopping several times.

I snagged the pen and tried to *say what I felt.*

*Dear Parole Board, I'm angry as fuck for spending six years in this hellhole for a murder I DID NOT commit.*

Maybe if I emphasized some words, they would get the message.

I crossed out my first sentence and tried again.

*Dear Parole Board, how can I reform for a crime I didn't commit?*

I could hear them answering with, "Mr. Hart, the jury found you guilty beyond a reasonable doubt."

I blamed the moronic court-appointed attorney who'd tried my case. He hadn't gone to bat for me. He'd given up before I'd even sat down in court.

"Your best bet is to plead guilty," he'd said. "Save the taxpayers' money."

I would've hired my own lawyer if I had the money.

*Asshole.*

Many times in the last six years, I'd dreamed of strangling him. I'd argued with the fucker until I'd been blue in the face.

"Do you think I'm stupid enough to leave the murder weapon at a crime scene? And in my backpack no less!" I'd shouted at the man.

I'd forgotten my backpack on the night in question when I'd left Hector Alvarez's apartment. More importantly, Hector had been alive and kicking when I left.

Regardless, murder wasn't my MO. Never in a million years would I shoot a person unless it was in self-defense, and Hector hadn't given me any reason to defend myself. He and I had gotten along great except when I was late turning in the loot after a night of drug sales. I had been late that night, which was what I'd explained in my statement to the cops.

Hector had yelled, but I'd taken my licks, and we'd moved on. *No need to kill him for reprimanding me.* Besides, Hector hadn't been a hothead like his younger brother, Tito. That fucker wouldn't think twice about shooting me if I pissed him off or he didn't get his way.

I tapped my pen on the pad, my nerves singing as I tried for the millionth time to figure out who had put the Glock used to kill Alvarez in my backpack—the same gun I'd seen sitting on the coffee table in front of Hector.

I growled low as a big-ass dude strutted by, snarling at me as though he wanted to snap my neck.

I ground my back teeth together. "What's your problem?" I'd never seen him around before, and I knew just about everyone in most cellblocks.

He backtracked then slapped his fat hands down on the table across from me, causing the stack of books next to me to bounce. "You."

I debated if I wanted to mitigate my frustration by knocking his crooked yellow teeth from his mouth, break his large nose, or squeeze his bulging eyes out of his pointed head.

I shucked the idea. The hole was the last place I wanted to go, and one fight could put my good behavior in jeopardy, which meant I might not get parole.

But my mouth impeded my brain. "Feeling's mutual."

He flared his nostrils.

I clenched my fists. I would like to believe I had the patience to walk away, but my brother Dillon was the only Hart brother who won that award with flying colors.

The big-ass dude growled. "I could plan for you and me to tango later."

I snorted. "I don't swing that way." I knew he was referring to a fistfight, but I couldn't help myself, although maybe he was one who liked men.

The guy leaned over the table, pressing his big gut on the top as his garlic breath burned the hairs inside my nose.

"If you're trying to pick me up, then you need some mouthwash."

His dark eyes narrowed to slits.

Stew, the guard, cleared his throat. He was what the inmates called a good egg. If we needed something or wanted to hide something, Stew was our man. "Costa, back off." Stew was also the guard we didn't want to cross. The man was built like a sumo wrestler.

Costa cocked his head. "We're talking."

Stew's uniform pants rubbed together as he came over. "Costa, back the fuck up."

Costa straightened, gnashing his teeth. "Watch your back, Hart."

If he thought he frightened me, he was mistaken. I was afraid of few things in my life, but the one thing that freaked me the fuck out was tiny, dark spaces. I'd learned that quickly when I'd been thrown into the hole, where light was a luxury and rats were my cellmates.

I pushed to my feet, curious as to how Costa knew my name. "Do we know each other?" I angled my head one way then the other. I didn't remember seeing him around, not even in the chow hall.

Stew stood next to Costa, ready to intervene if a fight broke out. "Go, Costa. Farley will take you back." He pointed to another broad-chested guard standing outside the library.

Smirking as though he knew a secret, Costa left without a backward glance.

"How did he know my name?" I asked Stew.

Stew shrugged. "He's new. He just came in yesterday."

"What cellblock?" I had a feeling Costa would be trouble.

Stew's radio crackled. "Hart has guests. Get his ass down to the visitors' center."

"Copy that," Stew said into his radio. "All right, Denim. It seems people love you after all."

I laughed. "I doubt that." The only person to visit me in the time I'd been locked up had been Dillon and his lawyer friend, Kelton Maxwell, who was now my lawyer.

My other family members didn't give a shit about me, and my girl-friend... well, I'd ditched her a long time ago. She didn't deserve to live in my world. She didn't deserve to look over her shoulder when-ever she went out alone. And she certainly didn't deserve an asshole like me who sold drugs, carried a gun, and fought whenever the need arose.

Still, I wasn't about to have a pity party. That wasn't me. Besides, my family was as dysfunctional as they came. My mom had taken off when I was eight. My old man was a drunk. My baby sister had disap-peared for years thanks to the Black Knights, a gang into sex traffick-ing. And my older brother, Duke, was being a dick.

I had no idea why he hadn't taken the time to visit me. I wasn't about to analyze the whys and why-nots. Maybe by some miracle or wake-up call, Duke had decided he wanted to see his baby brother, or maybe Dillon had lit a match under Duke's ass. But my guess was probably Dillon. He made a point to visit me every couple of months.

Locks and doors clicked open as we navigated the prison halls until Stew ushered me into the visitors' room a few minutes later. Cameras hung from the four corners. Walls that had once been white were now dull, almost yellowish. And empty tables were scattered around except for one.

Two men rose when I entered. Both were dressed in dark suits, white shirts, and black ties. One was shorter than the other. Both had government badges hanging around their necks.

*Ugh, great!* I had hoped that maybe Stew was right, and my guests were people who loved me. But then again, with the exception of Dillon, no one in my life loved me.

The shorter one with red hair stuck out his hand. "Denim Hart, I'm Special Agent Brock. This is my partner, Special Agent Travers."

I looked at Stew for answers, even though I knew he didn't have a clue why the FBI was here to see me. Maybe they'd found the real killer, and I was innocent and free to leave prison.

Hope bloomed quickly, like a spring day filled with the tulips, but I shut it down. I couldn't go down that path again. I'd gotten excited two years ago when Kelton Maxwell found evidence tampering in my case. As it turned out, though, the loophole was an administrative error that didn't make a dent in getting my case thrown out.

The news that day had hit me like a train barreling down the tracks at two hundred miles an hour, ramming me right in the gut. I'd feared I would die in prison. I'd come so fucking close a time or two. But after being thrown in the hole one too many times for fighting, I'd made it my mission to be the model prisoner. So far, I'd succeeded, and I prayed the parole board would agree.

Travers folded his lanky body into one of three metal chairs. "We would like your help."

The only way I could help the FBI was to be a narc, and no fucking way was that happening. If I spilled the beans about anyone in prison, I was a dead man. I knew a handful of secrets from inmates who had befriended me, but what went on inside the joint stayed inside. That was an unspoken rule, and those who'd defied it were buried six feet under.

I shook my head. "Sorry, I can't help you." I started for the door.

"Just hear us out." Travers's low baritone sent a chill down my spine. The agent's voice brought back memories I'd buried a long time ago—memories of my sperm donor who would rather suck on a bottle of booze than care for his children.

Stew raised an eyebrow as if asking, "What's the harm?"

He knew what the fucking harm would be. Costa instantly came to mind. I wasn't afraid of him, but a gang of inmates could do some damage.

"We want to make you an offer." Brock's voice was deep and scratchy, a chilling reminder of my bastard of an old man. "Can you give us the room?" he asked Stew.

Stew hesitated. As a guard, he had to ensure inmates didn't get out of hand. I wasn't one of the violent ones. Sure, I could talk with my fists, but he knew that as close as I was to becoming a free man, I wouldn't screw up my chances.

I gave Stew a slight nod only because I was curious about their offer.

When the three of us were alone, Travers waved to the empty chair across from him. "Sit."

I narrowed my eyes at the fucker. Maybe he was a good egg, but his voice and piercing green gaze made my skin crawl.

His partner stood with his arms folded over his chest, watching me.

One side of my mouth turned up.

"What's so funny?" Travers asked.

I waggled my finger between the two. "Are you about to play good cop, bad cop?"

"Sit down." Brock's tone permitted no argument.

I was fucking tired of the government telling me when to eat, sleep, shit, and sit. Since I didn't report to these two fuckers, I stood my ground. Then I realized they could affect my parole. *Well, fuck.*

I dropped into the chair. "Talk."

Brock's lips curled as though he'd won a medal. "We understand you're up for parole, and your stellar behavior for the last three years gives you a great chance of getting out."

Agent Travers cut in. "If you do, we would like you to help us infiltrate a large criminal organization in Boston."

"Why me?" My first thought was that they wanted me to involve myself with Alvarez and his drug business. After all, I'd worked for the man and knew the drug trade backward and forward.

Brock unbuttoned his suit jacket as he sat beside Travers. "You can get on the inside of your brother's business."

My eyebrows snapped together. "Duke? Oh, fuck and hell no." No matter how pissed I was at Duke, no amount of bribes or false promises would get me to snitch on my brother.

"Your brother Duke has built a massive empire," Brock said.

I shrugged. "Not my problem. Not my business."

Travers elaborated. "The guns he's selling are falling into the hands of gangs all over the city. Boston PD answers five or more calls a night for drive-by shootings. It's getting way out of control."

The laugh that was blaring in my head escaped and echoed throughout the room. "And you think I can stop my brother?" I'd never talked to Duke about his business, even before I was incarcerated. We had a rule—he stayed out of my way, and I stayed out of his.

Leaning in slightly, Travers clasped his hands together. "We can get your record expunged provided you get out on parole. You'll be free to live like a normal person without a record."

I straightened. My stomach did one of those butterfly flutters I'd gotten every time I had laid eyes on the most beautiful girl in high school. The same girl who still tortured me in my dreams. The one I would give anything to see.

"If I don't get out on parole?" As pissed as I was at my brother, I wouldn't give up Duke. Him not visiting me in prison was no reason for me to help put him behind bars, although I was curious to learn how desperate the FBI was.

"You'll get out." Brock bobbed his head, seeming quite sure of himself.

Maybe he knew something I didn't, or maybe these two were so desperate, they would say anything to convince me to help them. "You're certain I'll get parole?"

Travers relaxed back in his chair. He was also giving off a confident vibe. "The early release program is hardly questioned at a parole hearing, provided you don't fuck up between now and then."

I rose. "Find someone else to do your dirty work." I would clear my own name.

It would be a monumental task to find the person who'd set me up. The only witness, Hector's neighbor, had told police she'd seen a person wearing a hoodie leaving the building right after she'd heard the gunshot. I hadn't been wearing a hoodie that night. But the crux of my problem was that the neighbor had disappeared before my trial began.

*What if you can't find the neighbor? Even if you do, what then? Most people turned a blind eye, not wanting to put themselves in the middle of a murder investigation. That was probably why the neighbor had skipped town in the first place.*

Kelton thought she'd been spooked or bribed. Or maybe whoever killed Hector had murdered her too.

Travers studied me. "We're offering you an excellent opportunity. Having a murder charge under your belt will make it hard for you to get a job. You'll need money to live."

Six years in the joint had given me a wake-up call. I longed to clear my name, find a decent job, and maybe start a family. But blood was blood no matter what.

"Sorry, gents. I'll pass."

I was halfway to the door when Brock asked, "What if we told you we believe Duke might've had a hand in Alvarez's murder?"

I went ramrod straight as the blood running through my veins gelled.

# 2

## JADE

I smoothed a hand down my pencil skirt, the same skirt I couldn't afford but had bought anyway. I had to look sharp for my job interview.

I checked my appearance in the glass window of the tall building I was about to walk into. My red polka-dot blouse went well with my red skirt. My black hair was pin-straight, and my black heels complemented my outfit. In my mind, this interview was do or die.

I'd been let go recently from a low-paying receptionist job at a financial company in Boston due to downsizing. For me, money was scarce. After high school, I hadn't had the money to go to college. My dad had been working hard to save as much as he could to help my sister and me when the time came to pay for college tuition. But when he died, his plan was buried with him. Then again, even if he were alive, I suspected he would have been hard-pressed to afford to help one of us, let alone both of us.

Savannah and I had grown up in a loving household but with very little money. My parents couldn't afford to pay the high heating bills, and New England in the dead of winter had sucked. Mom had found cheap, moth-eaten blankets at the thrift store and piled them on Savannah and me as she'd tucked us into bed.

If I didn't get this job, I would be living on the streets. I didn't have enough money in my bank account to pay the next month's rent, not that it mattered. My apartment wasn't any better than the streets. My water barely came out of the faucet. The heat didn't work, and I had one window that didn't close all the way.

As much as I wouldn't want to live in a jail cell, I envied my sister. At least she had a warm bed, food in her belly, and she didn't have to worry about making ends meet.

I slid into a section of the revolving door. I actually hated revolving doors. My hand had gotten stuck in one last year at my former place of employment, and since I didn't care to repeat that move, I pushed on the glass to hurry it along even though the door was moving from others getting into their little carveouts.

Once inside, my phone rang. I found a quiet spot away from the elevators and traffic and plucked my phone out of my purse. I prayed that Mallory—my BFF, who had been instrumental in setting up the interview for me—wasn't calling to tell me the interview was canceled. I couldn't take another rejection or another "We need someone with more skills than you have, Ms. Kelly."

The words "No Caller ID" lit up my screen like a beacon in the night. The "No Caller ID" was usually my sister. Sighing heavily, I debated whether to answer or not. If I didn't, Savannah would bug me until the cows came home, and I didn't want to be interrupted during my interview.

"Hello." A knot formed in my stomach as it always did when I accepted a call from my sister in prison.

"Will you accept a collect call from Savannah Kelly?"

I swallowed thickly. "Yes."

"Jade." Savannah's voice was rushed. "I need your help."

The panic in her voice made me wince. I loved my younger sister. I'd been trying to take care of her since our parents died. But no amount of words or threats had gotten through to her. However, like a stupid sister, I always gave in to her.

"You're not stupid," Mallory had said. "But you need to know when to tell her no. She's a great liar and knows how to get you spun up."

It had taken a few years to learn to say no to Savannah. As Mallory had said, Savannah was a great liar, at least with me. I'd bought every excuse she'd given me about how she needed money until she drained me of our life savings.

I took full responsibility for my actions, and with her in prison, I was keeping my fingers crossed that she was learning from her mistakes. "Are you okay?"

She'd been in several fights in prison, which didn't surprise me. Savannah had been a bully in high school. Where she threw caution to the wind, I did as I was told.

"No. I'm not. You need to get ahold of Duke for me."

My blood ran cold. "Why? You're not dating him or working for him anymore." Savannah had said that before prison she'd tended bar in one of his clubs.

I refused to associate or speak to the devil, and Duke Hart was the devil incarnate. I blamed him for my sister's foothold in the criminal world, which made it too easy for her to get her hands on money, drugs, and booze.

"He owes me money, and I need it, or else I'm dead."

The word "dead" should've raised a red flag, but I was talking to a cunning person who was an expert in making me panic and feel sorry for her. Plus, she had a flare for the dramatic.

"Savannah, I don't have time to do your bidding. I've got an interview. Call Duke yourself."

"I tried, sis." Her tone was sickly sweet.

I rolled my eyes. "Listen, I can't help you." I didn't have time to ask her why she needed money. My guess was either gambling or drugs. Two things she was good at were snorting coke and playing poker.

The sugar in her tone evaporated. "You're my sister. Family. You're supposed to help."

"You should've thought harder before you robbed a convenience store."

Mallory, my best friend, and the only person in my life I could count on, glided toward me from the bank of elevators. If anyone was like a sister to me, it was Mallory. We'd been best friends since the fourth grade.

"Bitch," Savannah said.

My sister would drive me to drink. *Oh, wait. She already has.* I often got stinking drunk when she blew into my life, wanting help or money. I thought prison would stop all that. Boy, I was wrong.

Unsure if my words had registered, I said it again. "I have an interview. You know, a job to pay bills and put food in my belly."

Mallory angled her head, and a stray auburn lock fell out of her messy bun. "Savannah?" she mouthed.

"Yeah," I mouthed back.

She tapped her wrist where a watch would normally be.

Savannah was breathing heavily, or maybe she was crying.

I wasn't caving. "Savannah, I have to go. We'll talk soon, okay?"

She growled into the phone before the line went dead.

I took a huge breath, hoping to calm my nerves.

Mallory hooked her arm in mine. "We need to head upstairs."

"How did you know I was down here?"

"I was coming down to wait for you. You need a keycard to take the elevator." Mallory had been working for the law firm as a paralegal for the last two years, and she'd told me that very thing the night before.

But because of Savannah's call, my brain wasn't firing on all cylinders. Before I dumped my phone in my purse, I flicked the volume to silent. I didn't want to risk another call from my sister during my interview.

On the elevator ride up, Mallory asked, "What does Savannah want now?"

"She wants me to call Duke."

Mallory laughed. "Is she nuts? She knows you hate him."

"Desperation will drive anyone to get what they want," I mumbled.

"Forget Savannah," Mallory said. "Are you ready?"

I inhaled a long, deep breath and rolled back my shoulders. "A little nervous, but ready. He knows I don't have any paralegal experience?"

"He knows you have the basic receptionist skills. And remember, if you get the job, the firm will train you."

The job was too good to be true. If I did get the job, I would be making two times more than I did at my last receptionist job, and eventually more when I became a paralegal. Butterflies took flight as the elevator doors opened.

The scent of cologne or perfume immediately wafted over me as Mallory and I stepped out onto the eighteenth floor.

A blond receptionist sat behind a rich wooden desk up ahead. She smiled at both of us. "Hey, Mal, the conference room is ready."

"Thanks, Dina," Mallory said before escorting me down a long, carpeted hall.

We passed a large cubicle area with offices lined along the back wall. Phones rang, whispers floated in the air, and my pulse pounded in my ears. When we reached the end of the hall, Mallory stopped outside a large corner room that overlooked Boston's skyline.

"As I told you last night, sit up straight, don't let his looks rattle you, and sell yourself. Don't forget to ask for the job before you leave."

I wasn't a salesperson. That feat went to my BFF. "I'm not going to drool over his looks."

Her pink-painted lips curled. "You will. Mark my words."

I lifted a nail to my mouth. "I'll be fine." I wasn't there to drool over my potential boss. The last boy I'd pined for had broken my heart. I would like to believe I'd learned from my mistakes. Besides, my number one goal was getting the job. "Aside from Kelton Maxwell's great personality and good looks, what else should I know?"

She gently pulled on my wrist, her blue eyes appraising. "Be yourself and don't chew on your nails. I'll let him know you're here." She nudged me to go inside before she left.

I took in a few deep breaths, clearing my mind as I went into the imposing room bathed in rich cherrywood. It was furnished with tall leather chairs, a table bigger than my apartment, and a spectacular view of Boston.

Within a minute, a tall, dark-haired, blue-eyed man came strutting in, dressed in what I would guess was an expensive tailored suit with a light-blue shirt and patterned blue-and-yellow tie. He headed toward me with one hand outstretched while holding a folder in the other. "I'm Kelton Maxwell."

*And you're intimidating, confident, and stoic.* Oh, and handsome for sure.

Mallory had shown me pictures of Kelton from a recent office party. However, the pictures didn't do him justice, or maybe it was his cologne that was making me swoon.

I swallowed an elephant as he shook my hand, hard and firm. "I'm Jade Kelly. It's nice to meet you." I stared at him, unable to look away.

His ocean-blue eyes reminded me of someone I'd once known, someone I'd been trying to forget forever.

He waved his hand at the table, breaking my memory of the boy who had broken my heart. "Please, have a seat."

Once we were settled across from each other, he leaned back in his chair, studying me as though I were a witness for the prosecution.

My stomach churned, and the need to chew on a nail was stronger than ever. If he were grilling me on the stand, I would cave in a millisecond.

"Mallory has told me a lot about you. I only have one question for you, Jade."

I reared back as my eyebrows drew down. *Surely getting the job wasn't that easy.*

*You don't even know the question.*

I sat up straight.

"Would you represent a client guilty of a crime?" he asked.

I swallowed, feeling my eyebrows coming together. That wasn't the question I was expecting at all. It wasn't like I was applying for a lawyer's position. I scrambled to find an answer in the fogginess of my brain. Maybe his cologne was still interfering with my ability to think.

"You look puzzled," Kelton said.

I nodded. "With all due respect, I would expect that question if I was a lawyer."

He chuckled. "Fair enough. I like to know the person who's working for me. It tells me a little about his or her character."

I couldn't argue with him and didn't exactly want to either. "It depends."

He steepled his hands in front of him. "Oh? Tell me more."

"Honestly, I know little about the law. Well, that's not true. My sister is in prison." I'd researched unarmed robbery and how long her sentence could be. The judge had been lenient with her since she was a first-time offender, sending her to jail for three years.

His eyes twitched, but he said nothing.

"I believe everyone, guilty or innocent, deserves a fair trial and a good lawyer."

He was quick with a response. "What's your idea of a good lawyer?"

I couldn't tell from his blank expression if he liked my answer or not, but I was telling the truth. Savannah's court-appointed attorney had fought hard for her, and if it weren't for him, the judge might not have been as easy on her as he had been.

"A bulldog is the best term I can come up with. A lawyer should know the law inside and out, and whether or not the client is guilty, he or she deserves your best foot forward. At least then if the client goes to jail, they can say their attorney did all he could. Just my opinion."

His elbow rested on the arm of the chair as he pressed two fingers to his lips. "Of course." Then he opened the folder. "Jade, I lied. I do have another question for you. Why is your sister in prison?"

"She robbed a convenience store. But I want you to know I don't have a criminal record. I've never been arrested." The last part rushed out of me like a fast-moving river.

He was back to pressing two fingers against his lips, studying me.

I felt the need to squirm beneath his scrutiny. Instead I held my breath.

"Good to know. But the firm will do a background check on you nonetheless."

Mallory had mentioned that very thing, and aside from Savannah's indiscretions, which had nothing to do with me, I was squeaky-clean.

"Do you have any questions for me?" he asked.

"When can I start?" Mallory would be proud.

He regarded me for a long moment before removing his phone from his suit pocket.

*Please, please let me get the job.*

He tapped on the screen. "Let me look at my calendar to see when I'm in court."

Once again, I held my breath, not yet sure if that meant I got the job.

"I would like to be here when you start. How about Monday? A week from today?"

I had the urge to fly over the table and hug him. Instead, I smiled. "That works for me." Although I wanted to start sooner. Money was becoming tight.

Smoothing a hand over his tie, he stood. "Good. I'll have Mallory prepare the paperwork, and I'll see you on Monday."

He escorted me down to the reception area, where Mallory was talking to Dina.

I beamed at Mallory. The giddiness inside me was ready to explode. I couldn't believe it had been that easy. I almost pinched myself to make sure I wasn't dreaming.

"Mallory, can you get things set up for Jade?" Kelton asked. "She'll start on Monday."

Mallory's eyes popped wide. "Sure thing, sir. Anything else?" Mallory had also shared with me that she was filling in as Kelton's temporary assistant.

He flashed his blue eyes at her. "Yeah. I'm expecting Dillon Hart in a few minutes. Can you escort him to my office when he gets here?"

I sucked in a sharp breath.

Kelton angled his head toward me. "Something wrong?"

"Jade knows the Harts too." Mallory brushed it off as no big deal.

It wasn't a big deal for her. She hadn't been kicked to the curb by one of them.

Kelton deadpanned. "Well, Dillon should be here in a few. I have a call to make. Just buzz me when he arrives." He ambled back down the hall toward his office.

Mallory grabbed her iPad from the reception counter. "I'll walk you down to the lobby."

I was about to probe her on Kelton and how he knew Dillon when the elevator doors opened, and Dillon Hart strutted out. The man hadn't changed since high school. He was still tall, dark, and handsome. I didn't see a ring on his finger, but I was sure he didn't have trouble getting women.

His thick thighs were encased in worn, distressed jeans. A black button-up shirt was stretched over his broad chest. And if that weren't enough to make women drool, then the three-quarter sleeves he had rolled up showing off a rather large diver's watch had to set women's panties on fire.

But I wasn't into dark hair, dark-eyed men, no matter how delicious Dillon Hart was. My palate salivated for his younger brother—blond, blue-eyed, and a stud in bed.

*Stop it, Jade. You're getting wet and flustered, and Dillon is going to think you like him.*

Dillon pinned his dark gaze on me. "Jade Kelly, is that you? Wow."

My cheeks were burning.

He sized me up and wasn't in the least bit subtle about it either. "I need to tell Denim."

*Let him tell Denim you look hot. Let Denim suffer knowing how well you're doing.*

On that thought, I lifted my chest. It was a little more than a handful for most men. "It's nice to see you," I finally said.

Dillon slipped a hand into his jeans pocket. "Do you work here?"

Mallory gushed with pride. "She'll be working for Kelton Maxwell."

Dillon's dark eyebrows shot up. "For real? You know Kelton is Denim's lawyer."

"Is that true?" I asked Mallory.

*What's next? Denim getting out of prison?*

The latter couldn't be true. If I had my math right, Denim wasn't up for parole for another year or two.

Mallory's pretty features pinched. "To my knowledge, Denim isn't a client."

"Mm," Dillon said. "Then why is Kelton helping Denim prepare for his parole hearing?"

Nausea sat heavy in my stomach. If I worked for Kelton, I might see Denim. I wasn't sure I was ready for that. The problem was I needed the job.

3

___________

# DENIM

I couldn't move. I couldn't breathe. The intake of the stale air in the room burned my lungs.

"We thought that might resonate," Travers said at my back. His deep New England accent came through the derision in his words.

I fisted my hands at my sides. The urge to throttle the FBI agent vibrated in my bones. I didn't know what bothered me more, his voice or his cocky attitude.

Slowly, I pivoted on my heel, hoping with all hope I could burn him alive with just my glare. "What makes you believe Duke had a hand in the murder?" My muscles were rock-hard as I opened and closed my fists as though I had stress balls in them. I sure as hell could use a fucking stress ball at the moment. But my ire jumped from the agent and splattered on Duke. The brother I'd looked up to since I could walk could have set me up. I blinked, shaking the cobwebs from my brain.

"We have our informants," Brock chimed in.

*Liars for sure.* No fucking way had Duke had a hand in Hector's murder. He'd hated the guy, but he had no reason to kill him. "Bull-shit." My teeth clamped together hard. "My brother didn't even know Hector." He'd known of him but hadn't broken bread with the man.

Brock cocked an eyebrow. "Are you certain of that?"

*No.* Doubt pricked the base of my brain. During my trial, the prosecution's goal had been to put doubt in the minds of the jurors. "Convict beyond a reasonable doubt," the judge had firmly ordered.

The prosecuting attorney had been giddy when he'd told the jurors in his opening monologue, "By the time the defendant's trial is over, there will be no doubt in your mind that he is guilty."

The murder weapon in my backpack had been the glaring evidence. But my fingerprints weren't on the gun. The forensic analysis had only shown Hector's on the trigger. But that hadn't mattered. The prosecuting attorney had added the perp could've only done one thing—used gloves. That was the only obvious piece to support his claim. I'd had a pair of black gloves in the front pocket of my backpack.

The FBI was trying to put doubt in my mind, and they were succeeding.

*Motherfuckers.*

But I wasn't about to let them see me sweat. "Duke had no dealings with the Southside Creepers."

My brothers and I had been in a gang. But Duke had wanted no part of gangs after high school. He also hadn't been keen on selling drugs, which was the bread and butter for gangs like the Southside Creepers, the one I'd joined my senior year of high school. The gang that Duke, Dillon, and I had grown up in had been mild—fights and territorial crap. But maybe Duke had wanted to add to his empire, which was money laundering as far as I knew, not drugs and certainly not guns.

"You don't believe us?" Travers asked, seemingly appalled that I didn't. "Why don't you ask Duke yourself?"

I would put money on the fact that he was lying about Duke being at Hector's. Still, I suddenly felt suffocated, as though Travers had clamped his fat fingers around my throat.

I knocked on the window to get Stew's attention. "Don't worry. I will." I highly doubted Duke would confess to me, but that didn't mean I wasn't going to ask.

Stew opened the door.

Fresh air floated in, and I gobbled it up faster than the speed of light, hoofing it out of the room as fast I could as well, not acknowledging Travers, who was telling me they would be in touch.

*Fuck them. No way am I being a pawn in their scheme.*

"I need to use the phone," I said on a growl.

*Save your rage for Duke.*

He was lucky I was in prison.

"Sorry, man. I didn't mean to snarl." If any other guard besides Stew were with me, he wouldn't have had a problem shoving me into a wall. "So did you hear any of it?"

He swiped his badge over a panel at the door leading into the hub of the prison. "Bits and pieces."

The sound of the lock clicking open echoed, piercing my eardrums. When we were on the other side, I asked, "Do you think my brother would set me up for murder?"

"Can't say. But people do all sorts of unbelievable things to family." He sounded as though he'd experienced being burned by a family member.

Stew banked right, and I went left.

"Hart, no phone privileges. It's time to get back to your cell. We have a shift change in thirty minutes, and that means you need to be in your cellblock."

It was probably best. The prison phones were heavily monitored, and I had another idea anyway. So I followed Stew back to my cellblock.

Inmates—tall, short, fat, skinny, and in-between—lounged around on chairs and butted their bellies up to tables. Some played cards. Some read. Others talked and laughed.

I searched the room up and down until I spotted Rudy Brown. He was our cellblock's gang leader and quite savvy in finagling deals with contraband.

Rudy and four of his men were playing cards as I approached. The burly guy next to Rudy, who was famously known on the block as Munster, jumped up to block me.

I raised my hands. "Rudy, can we talk?"

Prison gangs were different than gangs on the outside—fiercer, dirtier in their fighting, and took no prisoners. It was easy to shoot a gun or aim it at someone as a threat. Inside, knives and shivs were by far more powerful and deadly than any gun I'd carried. A person didn't see a blade coming until it was carving through muscle and bone. I had a feeling Munster had one of those shivs on him somewhere.

"What the fuck do you want?" Munster asked with a snarl that would scare a cockroach.

Some old fuck who'd been in prison most of his adult life thought Henry Vasquez looked like Herman Munster from a TV show I was too young to know.

"I need to talk to Brown."

The buzz of voices in the high-ceiling room died. Even the men leaning on the rails outside their cells on the second floor turned their attention to us. Most of the men on our block didn't mess around with Rudy Brown. The main reason stemmed more from what he could get them rather than his arsenal of men.

I wouldn't be surprised if the guards on the third floor were watching us. A solid glass room surrounded two sides of the cellblock and was the epicenter in which the guards had a full view of the common room, either through the glass or via cameras positioned strategically in places that were hidden from view.

"Let him pass," Brown said.

*Damn straight.* The fucker owed me. I'd done my time for him in the hole for protecting his ass not long after I'd started my sentence. He owed me more than one favor too.

Munster moved out of my way, and I slipped into the chair he'd occupied.

Rudy waved his gnarly fingers at the other two at the table. They scattered like rats.

Once we were alone, I leaned in. "I need a cell phone."

Rudy set his brown gaze on me. "I sold them all."

"Bull. I know you always keep one hidden in your cell."

The other inmates returned to whatever they were doing, and the hum of chatter ensued.

Sitting back with the cards in his hand, Rudy kicked his long legs out. "It will cost you."

"Let's not forget you owe me, and I'm collecting on favor one."

He chewed on his toothpick like it was a juicy piece of meat. "I hear you're getting out."

I leaned my elbows on the table. "I have a parole hearing. Nothing is set in stone." I refused to get my hopes up, but no matter who I talked to, the consensus was a resounding yes—I was getting out.

"Why the need for a phone? No one loves you on the outside."

I stuck Rudy with the middle finger as I popped up. I had no patience for him. "Forget I asked."

Duke wouldn't answer anyway. If he did, I doubt he would corroborate what the agents had told me about him being at Hector's the night of the murder. Still, I had to know if the agents were blowing smoke up my ass or not.

*Good luck with that. The only way you'll know for sure is if you confront Duke in person.* That probably wouldn't work either. Duke was the master at keeping things close to his vest, in person or not. He was an expert at bluffing in a card game.

I shoved my fingers through my hair, ready to head toward my cell in the back corner of the main floor.

Rudy caught my arm. "Wait."

I backtracked two steps.

"Sit," he said evenly.

I was getting tired of people telling me to sit. I wasn't a fucking dog. Regardless, if my brother would answer the phone or my question, I had to try.

I dropped down once again in the chair.

Rudy's bald head glistened beneath the bright lights. "I hear we have some fresh meat. I also hear he wants you dead."

It took me a second to register his words. "Who?"

"Does the name Costa ring a bell?" Rudy glanced around as though Costa was close by.

I followed his lead, anxious to know if Costa was in fact living in the same block as me. My search came up empty unless Costa was in a cell on the second floor or had gone back to the library.

"Costa isn't in this block," Rudy said. "However, rumor is the warden is moving him into our cellblock. The others are packed to the gills."

"Just met the fucker in the library earlier. And let him try."

Rudy perceptibly flicked his head at Munster, who looked up to the glass tower—the epicenter of where the guards watched us with a keen eye.

Rudy was smart. When he wanted to talk without the guards reading his lips, he had Munster stand in front of the camera pointing at his face.

Munster did just that.

"So you don't know him?" Rudy asked.

"Fuck the dude. Are you going to give me a cell phone or not?" I whispered with a frustrated sigh.

"When the guards make the shift change, duck into my cell. You can make the call there. But be quick about it. You only have ten minutes max before head count."

Duke had better fucking answer. If not, I just might take the FBI up on their offer.

4

———

# DENIM

Rudy stood outside his cell while I dialed Duke's number, tapping my foot on the floor. I doubted he would answer or take my call, although I wasn't on the prison phones. Then again, a burner phone probably came up as "No Caller ID" as well.

Rudy was nervously darting his head around and then back at me. I couldn't blame him for being anxious. If we got caught, it was the hole for sure. As much as I despised small, dark places, I needed to talk to Duke. I needed to try to get him to talk to me. I had no clue why he'd been ignoring me, but that voice in my head was convincing me that just maybe the Feds were right.

The line rang and kept ringing. I was ready to launch the phone at the chipped cement wall when the line connected.

"Hello." The woman's voice was like a siren's, lulling me home on a dark and stormy night.

Rudy stuck his bald head in. "Hurry the fuck up."

"Is someone there?" she asked sweetly.

Blood rushed to my cock. I cleared my throat, adjusting my pants as I turned my back to Rudy. "Who's this?"

She giggled. "Who's this?"

Between her voice and her laugh, I was instantly hard.

*Fuck Duke. I'll take the minutes I have and talk to her.*

I looked at the phone to be sure I'd dialed the correct number and not some sex hotline, although the latter sounded like a fun thing to do.

"Hello." That time her voice wasn't as silvery, and I detected a hint of familiarity.

"Do I know you?"

"I doubt it. Are you looking for Duke?"

"Who is that?" Duke sounded sleepy.

Sexy woman. Sleepy voice. The fucker had probably just gotten done with a fantastic round of sex. What I wouldn't give to roll over and tangle my limbs around the soft and silky skin of a woman.

"Put him on," I said curtly.

Rudy poked his head in again. "Your ten just dropped to two minutes."

A growl was ready to erupt from the deep pit of my stomach. "Sweetheart, put my brother on the phone."

"It's for you," she said to Duke.

Rudy was bouncing on the balls of his feet.

"Hello," I said to the woman. "Put my brother—"

Rudy ripped the phone from my hand. "Get back to your cell. Guards are coming." Panic jumped off him in waves, which was a stark contrast to the calm, cool, and collected con man. Rudy had been pinched for armed robbery and was in year three of his five-year sentence. He would've been a candidate for the early release program if it weren't for the contraband he'd been caught with last year.

Grinding my molars together, I ducked out just as heavy footsteps filled the room. Guards piled in. Inmates scattered into their cells.

I eyed Rudy as I slipped into my cell three doors down. He looked relieved.

I was anything but. My pulse thumped a rapid beat in my ears. I'd learned over the years in prison to accept the things I couldn't control. If I hadn't, I would've gone mad in a split second. But I had a feeling I was going to be a crazy fucker and unleash my pent-up madness on

Duke if I got out. I had to reel it in. Otherwise, I was afraid I might do something to screw up my parole, thanks to the Feds.

*They're busting your balls, man. You can't believe them.*

The sad part was that I did, or at least a tiny part of me did. Coupled with Duke not showing his face in six years, I was beginning to believe the Feds were right. I was beginning to believe Duke had indeed had a hand in Hector's murder. Duke had set me up, and that was the sole reason he never visited me in prison.

The guards finished with their head count, and slowly the normal buzz of chatter returned to the cellblock.

I wanted one more shot to get Duke on the phone. But when I started for Rudy's cell, the sound in the room died. When I glanced at the main entrance to the cellblock, blood rushed to my head. I clenched my fists, grinding my back teeth, as I watched a guard escort Costa to a cell.

The burly fucker strutted in as though he were the head asshole in charge of the cellblock rather than Rudy. Costa searched high and low until he spotted me. Then those crooked yellow teeth shined like a spotlight.

Rudy sauntered over to me. "He wants to tear off your head."

"He can try." I was ready to feel my fists connect with bone. I was ready to taste blood and to draw blood.

Costa bore his lethal gaze into me as he settled into a cell with a short, squat inmate. *Poor guy.* I didn't feel bad for anyone in there, but I did now.

Once the guard left behind the ten-inch steel door, Rudy warned, "Careful, Hart. You might not get that freedom you salivate for."

"What are you, my father?" I bit out.

"I have to answer to the warden," he said.

I shoved my hands through my hair. "Sucks to be you."

Rudy had some deal with the warden to keep peace in the cellblock. I had no idea what type of deal and didn't care to know.

Munster strutted over. "We're going to have a problem."

*Let the fun begin.*

My money was on Munster. He was taller and bulkier than Costa, and he had a right hook that could knock a person's lights out in a flash. I'd seen him do just that in the yard when some newbie tried to piss off Rudy. Maybe I should just let Rudy's gang handle Costa.

Costa pushed off the doorjamb of his cell.

"Showtime," I mumbled.

Munster's mean glare at Costa said he wanted a piece of the dude. I would gladly give him his shot, but I wanted to know how Costa knew my name and why he had a hard-on for me.

But before I could open my mouth, Costa had his hands around my throat and was shoving me into my cell. I tried to pry his paws off me, but the fucker was strong. The room began to spin as darkness encroached from all sides.

Then he threw me, and my back landed against the stainless-steel sink, punching the air from my lungs. In that moment, I swore I was about to face my maker. I gulped down more and more air as intense pain careened up my spine.

A commotion followed with men egging on Costa, or maybe me. I couldn't exactly hear over the pounding in my head and the burn in my lungs.

*Don't engage. You'll land in the hole, and then your parole hearing will be compromised.*

*But it was too late. I couldn't let the fucker kill me. I had too much to do when I got out.*

*If you get out.*

I shook my head to stop the room from spinning when Costa launched into a series of left and right jabs. My head bounced back and forth like a tennis ball.

Bone connected with bone, sending warm liquid trickling out of my nose.

I wouldn't see freedom. After this, I would probably be waiting another few years to go before the parole board.

Maybe if I didn't engage, I still stood a chance for parole.

Costa rammed a punch to my gut.

I doubled over. "I have no beef with you. I don't even know what your problem is." My words came out strangled.

He bared his teeth. "Tito Alvarez wants you dead, and it's my job to do just that."

My body stiffened as I listed to one side. "Hector's brother?" I wasn't surprised the fucker would want me dead. The question, though, was why had he waited six years?

Guards rushed in. One of them had his Taser out, ready to shoot Costa.

Costa raised his hands over his head, smirking. "We're not done, Hart."

A guard cuffed him. "You're done for a long time."

I imagined he would be in the hole for at least thirty days. I'd served the same fate when I first arrived. I hadn't been trying to kill anyone when I'd gotten that punishment. But inmates who had been in for years were set in their ways, and newbies were put through a hazing of sorts to see what they were made of.

Costa's nostrils flared. "Watch your back, Hart. Whether in here or out there. There's a hefty contract on your head."

The guard dragged him out of my cell.

I held out my arms, ready for Stew to slap the cuffs on me. No matter who started a fight, it meant an automatic trip to solitary.

"The only place you're going is to medical. You need to get that eye checked."

I heard him, but my mind was still stuck on one question. *Why wait six years to retaliate?* I understood Tito's need for revenge. He was definitely an eye-for-an-eye kind of dude. I was sure he had friends in prison, even though I knew he didn't have anyone in my cellblock. But the prison had several cellblocks.

I wiped blood from my eye, nose, and face with my shirt. "Why not the hole?"

Sympathy washed over Stew as he grabbed my arm. "Medical first. Standard procedure."

I had the worst luck. It was as though someone didn't want me to get out of prison.

*Yeah, dude. That someone is the person who murdered Hector.*

Rudy whistled. "He did a number on you, man."

"I'll be fine. I guess I'll be staying for a while."

Rudy's lips turned down, his expression telling me he was sorry.

I didn't want his pity. But if I wasn't getting out, I might as well do whatever it took to protect myself.

5

**JADE**

Two weeks had passed since I'd interviewed with Kelton Maxwell. I'd settled into my new job, feeling a great sense of accomplishment, and I was making new friends with the other ladies in the office. Mallory was my mentor and trainer, but I could ask anyone in the office for help, and they would drop what they were doing to help me. Before long, I would be a paralegal, and that excited me more than anything. With that title came more money, and I could finally breathe for the first time in years.

Mallory's boss's office was next door to Kelton's, so her cubicle butted up to mine. It was nice to have someone I knew helping me. It took away most of my nerves, allowing me to concentrate better. According to Mallory, Kelton was a very demanding attorney, and his previous assistant couldn't handle the late nights or him. So far, I didn't feel as though Kelton was demanding. However, I was still new, and he was probably waiting for me to get up to speed. Regardless, I could handle whatever he threw my way. After all, it was my job to make sure he had everything he needed for his cases.

I typed as I listened to Kelton's deep voice in my headphones, transcribing his notes and filing them into the clients' respective folders.

I'd been hard at work for the last hour when someone touched my shoulder.

I jumped about a mile in the air before removing my earbuds. I usually didn't have both in my ears since I had to answer the phone, but Mallory had shown me how to set up the system so the phone would ring in my earbuds.

Kelton leaned against my desk, his bright white teeth flashing as he smiled. "Sorry to scare you. Meet me in my office in five minutes." Then he waltzed toward the restroom, or at least in that direction.

Ladies at their desks took notice. They always did when Kelton was around. It was hard not to notice my handsome boss. His stark blue eyes popped against his black hair. The expensive tailored suits he wore only enhanced his *GQ* look, making every woman in the office drool. I'd learned he had a girlfriend, so he was off-limits, not that I was interested.

Mallory peeked around her cubicle. "I think he wants you to accompany him to his meeting with Denim. He's preparing Denim on what to expect at his parole hearing."

The blood drained from me.

When Dillon had told Mallory and me that Kelton would be taking on Denim's case, I'd been surprised that Mallory hadn't known since she'd been filling in as Kelton's assistant.

"I didn't know," she'd said as she walked me out of the building after my interview that day. "Kelton doesn't tell me everything. Sometimes my own boss doesn't tell me much about a client until he firmly decides to represent him. Besides, Dillon and Kelton are good friends. So I had no reason to question why Dillon had shown up."

Mallory snapped her fingers, zapping the haze clouding my eyes. "You'll be fine."

My hands trembled. "I can't see Denim for the first time with my boss next to me." I kept my voice to a whisper as I rolled my chair closer to her. "I love this job. Kelton will fire me."

Mallory had informed me that Kelton's pet peeve was unprofessionalism. His last assistant had flirted with one of his clients. Granted, I knew one of my duties as Kelton's assistant would be to attend meetings and hearings with him outside the firm, however I wasn't ready for anything but work at my desk.

She giggled. The woman actually giggled. "He won't."

I sagged in my chair, pinning her with wide eyes. "I might not be in control of my actions with Denim." I hadn't seen him since high school. Since he'd broken up with me. Since he'd broken my heart.

I shivered as dread and excitement comingled in my stomach. I often wondered what he looked like, if his blond hair was still long and curled at the edges. Did he still have a baby face, or had he aged fast with the hard life he'd lived in the eight years since I'd seen him?

My BFF batted her blue eyes. "This is your chance to show Kelton how good you are. Plus, it will be a good learning experience."

A wild laugh broke out in my head. "What do you mean how good I am?" Mallory had never seen me in action at any of my jobs. Sure, I carried myself in a professional manner and greeted clients with a smile and polite conversation. But we were talking about Denim Hart. He wasn't a client to me. He was a man who could probably rattle me without even opening his mouth.

"You don't give yourself enough credit," Mallory said. "I see how you are with clients that come in. You're a natural. And I know you. You can tuck those feelings away for an hour. Remember when I was dating Noah? You wanted to punch him because he ditched me for a sporting event. Instead, you were sweet and kind to him when he showed up the next day."

"Because you asked me to be nice."

"This is no different," she returned. "This is your job, Jade. You're the face of Kelton and this law firm, and that means you leave your feelings at the door."

I sat up straighter. She was right.

"Look at it this way," she added. "He'll probably be in shackles and cuffs. It's not like he can throw himself at you."

But I could throw myself at him.

Kelton returned, tipping his head toward his office. "Jade."

"Good luck," Mallory whispered before rolling her chair around to her cubicle.

The sun glinted off the John Hancock Tower in the distance as I followed Kelton into his office with a pen and notepad.

He waved his hand to one of two chairs in front of his mahogany desk as he circled around it. "Please, have a seat." He shrugged out of his suit jacket then draped it over the back of his leather chair. "I understand from Dillon that you know the Hart family. Dillon tells me you and Denim dated in high school. I normally don't get involved in others' personal lives, but considering your past involvement with Denim and the fact that he's a client, should I be worried?"

*Absolutely.* "No, sir." My tone was small.

*Girl, you better talk with more vigor. Make your boss believe you.*

He sat down and picked up his pen. "Good. You'll be attending my meeting with Denim at the prison tomorrow. I'll be prepping him for his parole hearing. Your role is to take notes, listen, and learn. Understood?"

I hoped my features weren't displaying anything but confidence because my insides churned like a washing machine on the spin cycle. "Yes, sir." The words came out strong and firm. I gave myself a mental high five, despite the red flags waving around in my skull. Every fiber in me was screaming not to go. But if I wanted to keep my job, I had to dig deep to shield myself from whatever Denim would throw my way. I had to put on my big-girl panties.

Suddenly, a ton of questions flickered like neon signs in my head.

*How would I react when I saw him? Would I slap him? Would I scream at him? Would I even be able to speak? Does he still have his heart-stopping smile?*

*I repeated the word "professionalism" several times and made a mental note to use that as my safe word when I saw Denim.*

"Good," Kelton said. "If you'll be working for me, I want you to be top notch in your role as you work into the paralegal position. I want you to know the law backwards and forwards as much as I do. And what better way than to see how things are done in the field. We'll leave from here at nine a.m. sharp."

I rose on weak legs and smoothed a hand down my gray pants.

"Sir, why is Denim up for parole? I didn't think he would be eligible for another year."

One side of Kelton's mouth curled. "You've been following his case."

*Busted.* I lifted a shoulder but didn't say a word.

"Massachusetts has an early release program, and Denim's been the model inmate. He shaved off a year of his sentence."

Another round of shock and awe plagued me. The Denim I knew had always been reckless, rebellious, and carefree. Maybe prison had been good for him.

I rolled back my shoulders. "I'll be ready for tomorrow."

When I reached the door, Kelton's next question stopped me. "Jade, do you think Denim is a murderer?"

I often thought about that very question. Part of me thought justice had been served. The other part of me who knew the real Denim Hart didn't agree. Denim had several faults, but murder wasn't one of them. Sure, he was in a gang, he sold drugs, and if push came to shove, he would do what he had to do to defend himself and those he loved.

The only evidence brought up at trial had been the gun used to kill the victim. The facts had shown the gun was found in Denim's back-pack, but no prints were on it. Still, the prosecution had done a great job of convincing the jury that in Denim's haste to flee the scene, he'd forgotten his backpack. That could have been true, but Denim knew how to cover his tracks like a corrupt cop.

I pivoted on my heel. "The Denim I knew in high school, no. After high school, I couldn't say. I didn't see him after that." I'd heard through my sister that Denim had done well for himself as a drug dealer for the Southside Creepers.

All Kelton said was, "Mmm."

I'd often come close to hunting Denim down and giving him a piece of my mind. But my heart was always one beat away from shat-tering into pieces when I thought of him, so I couldn't risk it. Besides, Savannah was a great example of how dating a criminal could mess up a person. I would like to consider myself a strong person, but I wasn't, not when it came to Denim Hart.

"It's not that I don't love you," he'd said as we stood on the steps of our high school. "My life is not the place for a beautiful, smart, and caring girl. And my enemies would use you to get to me."

At the impressionable age of eighteen, I'd felt I couldn't live without the blond-haired, blue-eyed boy who always made me melt into a puddle of water. Hell, I would've followed him to the ends of the earth if he'd asked me.

Kelton tapped the pen against his lips. "He swears he's innocent, and he wants help in finding the real murderer."

"During his trial, I read that one witness or the neighbor in the building disappeared."

Kelton appeared pensive. "Dillon hired a PI to find the neighbor. But no such luck."

"Do *you* think he's guilty?" I asked.

Kelton lowered his pen. "My gut tells me he's not, and my gut is usually right. Well, tomorrow is nothing more than preparing him for his hearing."

In my mind, tomorrow was everything—nerves, nerves, and more nerves. I probably wouldn't eat that night, and I definitely wouldn't sleep.

**6**

———

# DENIM

A guard escorted me to my meeting with Kelton Maxwell. It had been two weeks since Costa had done a number on me, and my cuts and bruises were healing. The good news was the warden hadn't thrown me into the hole because Stew had gone to bat for me. I'd thanked him profusely.

"Don't thank me," Stew had said. "Witnesses said you didn't fight back."

While that was true, the warden was hardly ever lenient when someone broke his rules. Part of me believed the Feds had gotten wind of my brawl and talked to the warden. But Travers or Brock would probably never admit it. Or maybe they would and hold it over my head. Speaking of the Feds, I hadn't gotten another visit from them.

I hadn't seen Costa again either, which was fine by me. I was hoping I didn't have to deal with the fucker when he was released from solitary in another two weeks, although rumor was Costa wouldn't return to my cellblock. I wasn't surprised. The warden didn't like deaths on his résumé.

In the meantime, I tried to call Duke again using Rudy's phone, but no one answered, not even the chick with the siren's voice. Luck wasn't on my side. I'd been informed a day after my brawl with Costa that the parole board postponed my parole hearing because of a mix-up in scheduling or some fucking excuse.

*Fucking government.*

Farley nudged me. "Inside."

I snarled at the guard before I waltzed into the ten-by-ten room with a table, three chairs, and the same gray cement walls I'd come to hate over the years.

Kelton Maxwell's jaw dropped to the table when he saw me. But mine hit the fucking floor when my gaze rounded to the woman sitting next to him. Her silky black hair hung wild and free, and her shiny emerald-green eyes stared back at me. Her round tits appeared bigger than I remembered, and those lips were made to tempt any man, gay or straight.

Her red lips curled slightly, making my knees buckle.

*What is Jade Kelly doing here?*

My high school days came roaring back with a vengeance. The blood rushed south like a river swollen after a violent storm, causing my dick to throb.

Farley practically pushed me toward the table. "Sit your ass down."

That was probably a good idea since my dick was growing. I stumbled to the lone chair, not taking my eyes off Jade. My heart punched my ribs as hard as Costa had rammed his fists into my face and gut.

"What happened to you?" Kelton's voice was deep and commanding, but not enough to make me take my eyes off Jade, who looked everywhere but at me.

A halo shined around her, or maybe it was the light spilling in from the window. Either way, she was an angel. *My angel.* I'd often lain in my bunk at night, thinking of her, wondering if she was married, had kids, and if she still hated me.

I would give anything to know what was going through her head. The last time I'd seen her was a year before I'd gotten arrested. She'd been walking into a restaurant with her friend Mallory in Roxbury. I'd been in the area, making a drop to a client. I'd almost stopped to say hi, but she had seemed happy, and I couldn't shit on her happiness.

Kelton snapped his fingers. "Did you hear me? When did you get into a fight? And why didn't you tell me?"

Jade stared at her blank notepad as her mouthwatering chest rose and fell, drawing my attention to her voluptuous breasts.

I dropped into the chair while my brain wandered down memory lane, flashing through times when she and I had been naked.

*Motherfucker.*

Getting laid would be icing on a bare cake. I had a strong urge to kick Kelton out of the room until I could fuck Jade senseless.

"You're not listening." Kelton tried to get my attention for the third time.

Jade lifted her head and peeked at me through her long lashes. Desire flashed in her bright emerald orbs.

My dick jerked as I swallowed the sand coating the back of my throat.

"Farley, we're good," Kelton said.

No, we weren't. I wasn't. With Jade in the room, I wouldn't be able to concentrate.

*There goes my parole hearing.*

I mentally shook off images of my girl naked. If I couldn't get those thoughts out of my head, I would jack off and not care that Kelton and Jade were watching me.

Kelton cleared his throat. "Let's start again. What happened to you? This will not look good at your parole hearing on Friday."

The connection between Jade and me snapped. "Why did the parole board postpone?"

"It doesn't matter," Kelton said. "It's in three days, and I'm worried about your appearance."

"I'll borrow some makeup from one of the gumps."

A crease formed in between Jade's eyebrows. The woman was in for a treat if she wanted to hear about the gay men in prison. But she didn't need to hear about any of that. She was too pure and innocent.

"Denim." Kelton's voice hardened. "How do you expect to display good behavior when your face looks like you ran into an eighteen-wheeler? Is any of this going on your record? Again, why didn't you inform me?"

I interlocked my fingers in front of me. "No. The warden gave me a pass. And what could you have done if you knew? Besides, I'm healing. You should've seen me two weeks ago."

Jade fidgeted with her pen.

The butterflies inside my stomach were having a fucking party.

"So she works for you?" I asked Kelton.

Jade narrowed her eyes in my direction. Her ball-squeezing emerald eyes penetrated me as if she were trying to take a peek into my black soul. "I have a name." Her knuckles were white as her delicate fingers clenched her pen.

I'd always loved when she got feisty. Her cute nose twitched, and for some reason, that drove me insane with wanting to rip off her clothes.

"Since when do you like the law?" I asked Jade. "I thought you wanted to be a teacher?" She'd talked nonstop about teaching elementary school one day.

Kelton opened his leather binder. "We don't have time for reminiscing. Save that for if you get parole."

Jade swallowed, her throat working as she poised her pen over paper.

*Please write me a love note like you used to do in high school.* I'd always gotten off when she slipped me a note in class, particularly when she'd scribbled the words "I want to fuck you."

Grateful for the barrier of the table, I lowered my cuffed hands to my lap and adjusted my rock-hard cock.

"Dillon will be at your hearing," Kelton started. "You're allowed a family member to speak on your behalf. The board will ask you questions like why you think you should be paroled. Do you have living arrangements? How will you manage challenges? What does your future look like? Are you ready to answer those questions?"

After seeing Jade for the first time in years, I was ready to blow this pop stand because, suddenly, I had a newfound goal in mind. *Get out. Track down Jade. Rekindle our relationship.*

I spoke to my lawyer but still couldn't take my eyes off the beautiful woman in front of me. "You know, Kelton, Jade and I dated in high school."

"I'm well aware of that," he said in a pragmatic tone. "I want to do a dry run with you to see how prepared you are."

I was sure Dillon had told him about my relationship with Jade since he and Kelton were buds. Or maybe Jade had told him. It didn't matter. I didn't want to do a dry run either. I wanted to talk to Jade. I was dying to know if she believed I was guilty of murder. But Kelton was a persistent fuck, and I had to commend him for that. If I didn't get parole, then I wouldn't be able to see or talk to Jade.

With my new excitement to get the fuck out of there, I turned my attention to my lawyer.

"Why should you be paroled, Mr. Hart?" Kelton asked.

I cleared my mind as I thought about what I'd finally written down. "Aside from the fact that I'm innocent?"

Kelton pursed his lips. "If you start with that, it will diminish your chances. The parole hearing isn't a place to retry your case, Denim."

I pushed my tongue against my bottom teeth. "My first year in prison was challenging. Trying to understand the hierarchy of prison life put me into situations I'm not proud of. I was angry, frustrated, and feeling sorry for myself. I didn't want to live the rest of my life in prison. In my second year, I picked apart my life prior to prison. I wasn't a good person. I had no direction. I had no discipline at home. But being inside has taught me I can do better. I want to do better." The words spilled out freely. The more I fixated on Jade, the more hope I had that I would get out.

Jade's heart-shaped lips parted. "How can you do better?" She quickly looked at Kelton as though she'd spoken out of turn.

Kelton kept his expression neutral.

"I've gotten my associate's degree, and my plan is to get my four-year business degree. Eventually, I want to start a family." I had other words on the tip of my tongue like "with you, I could conquer the world." Or the cheesy line—"you could make me a better man."

Her hands shook, and she quickly looked away.

"What about your brother Duke?" Kelton asked. "His lifestyle isn't conducive to an ex-con. He might pose a problem for you, entice you to do things for him that could put you back in prison."

I lifted my hands. The cuffs banged against the table as I placed my forearms on top. "I've never worked for Duke before. I'm not about to start now." Duke didn't want me in his business anyway. He'd told me that a time or two.

"I would hate to see you dead before you were twenty," Duke had said.

I hadn't argued with him. I didn't care about money laundering. Selling drugs was an easy business anyway.

"But he is my brother, and we do have a few family issues to work out." Then it dawned on me. Jade's sister and Duke were an item. Maybe that was the girl who had answered the phone. "Jade, how's your sister?" Savannah Kelly was a wild one. She was into drugs but had never gotten them from me. I'd promised Jade in high school that I would never sell to her sister, and I hadn't.

Jade winced. "Sir, can Duke affect Denim's parole?"

My eyes went wide. "Are you worried about me?" Her tone led me to believe she was, and warmth blossomed in my chest.

Jade stiffened as though she hadn't meant to ask that question in front of me.

Kelton scribbled in his binder. "Duke could be a problem for your parole."

"What?" Horror careened through me, and my stomach knotted. "He's got nothing to do with me. He hasn't even visited me in prison."

"If he comes up in your hearing, make sure you express that," Kelton said.

I gritted my teeth. I would seriously squeeze the life out of my brother if my parole was denied because of him. "You know, the FBI seems to think I'll get parole."

Kelton reared back, his jaw tightening. "Come again?"

Jade's green eyes sparked with an emotion I couldn't figure out.

I was hesitant to say anything more. I pointed at Jade. "Is she bound by the same client-attorney law?"

"She is. Otherwise, she wouldn't be here. She works for me and only me. So talk."

"Two agents showed up here about two weeks ago, asking me to help them get dirt on Duke when I got parole."

Jade licked her lips. "Would you?" Her question sounded more like a plea than anything.

If she knew me, she knew I wouldn't. She'd known how tight Duke, Dillon, and I had been as teenagers. But I got the feeling she was dying for me to hand Duke over to the Feds. Suddenly, I was curious if Duke had done something to Jade. If he had, I would kill my brother with my bare hands.

"Who were the agents?" Kelton asked. "Jade, take notes, please."

A hint of excitement washed over her.

"Agent Travers and Agent Brock. They're watching my brother. They'll expunge my record if I help them. My murder charge would disappear."

Kelton scrubbed long fingers over his clean-shaven jaw. "What did you tell them?"

"In so many words, I told them to fuck off."

"You don't want your record cleared?" Shock rode Jade's tone. "Your brother isn't an angel."

*Neither am I.*

Kelton seemed proud of his employee.

Jade had never liked the shit we'd been into as kids—gangs and drugs mainly. Eight years later, her opinion hadn't changed. Then again, gangs and drugs were petty stuff compared to money laundering and guns.

I picked at a cut on my finger. "None of us are angels." *Except for you.* She had been pure and innocent, and I'd never wanted to see the light snuff out of her eyes. Part of me was relieved she still had a spark, and I outright grinned that she seemed to have her shit together.

"What's with the smile?" she asked.

*Nothing and everything.*

Kelton interrupted our little interlude. "If you get out on parole, you need to stay away from your brother. You could put your freedom in jeopardy. Unless you consider the FBI's offer."

"He's my brother." That nagging doubt of whether Duke was responsible for my incarceration was glued to the back of my mind. I wanted to believe Duke hadn't framed me. I wanted to believe our bond was as tightly sealed as it had been when we were kids. "Would you abandon yours?"

The Maxwell brothers were tight—so tight they would die for each other. Dillon bragged constantly about them and talked about his dream that maybe one day Duke, Dillon, and I could develop a bond like them.

Hell, we had been brothers through and through while growing up. We would've died for each other back then. Sadly, our paths had gone in different directions. I believed the three of us wanted the same things—family, wealth, and a life without guns, drugs, and gangs. Dillon was the only one who had done something with himself. He'd opened a women's shelter to help those in need.

Kelton cleared his throat, his nostrils flaring. "We're not here to talk about me. I care about you—my client. As much as Duke is blood, you can't go near him."

"Are you afraid I'll revert to selling drugs?" Not that Duke sold drugs. Or for all I knew, maybe he did.

Kelton smoothed a hand down his red tie. "As your attorney, I'm advising you to consider what kind of future you want. One back here?" He waved his hand around. "Or one out there?" He stabbed a finger at the small window.

"You should take them up on their offer," Jade rushed out. Then she froze, fear resonating on her as she regarded her boss. "I'm sorry. I didn't mean to say that."

"It's all right," Kelton said. Then he fastened his blue gaze on me. "Let's say for argument's sake, you take their offer. You would be taking a criminal off the street. Your record would be cleared, and you would have a future without the murder charge hanging over your head."

I belted out a laugh. "I get that you uphold the law, Kelton. If I were in your shoes, I would tell me to take the offer too. But what kind of life would I have if I put my brother behind bars?" As pissed off and confused as I was with Duke, I wasn't sure I could send him into a hellhole. "Besides, I want my record cleared because I didn't kill Hector Alvarez, not because I gave the Feds someone they're itching to put away."

*But Duke might be responsible for sending you to jail. If he is, then you get what you want, and you put a criminal away.*

Jade squeezed the hell out of her pen. "He's evil. He's responsible for Savannah going to jail."

My jaw came unhinged. "Savannah's in jail?" I guess she wasn't the lady on the phone.

Kelton let out a heavy, frustrated sigh. "Let's get through your parole hearing. Then we'll deal with the FBI situation."

I desperately wanted to hear more about Savannah and more of Jade's melodic voice. I needed to take in all of her—her voice, that fruity scent wafting around the room, and her appearance. Then I could have the images of her embedded in my brain for when I jacked off later that night or maybe when Farley brought me back to my cell.

But Kelton was right. I had to get out first. Any amount of speculation and arguing over whether or not I should narc on Duke was pointless.

One thing was certain—I would do everything in my power to be the professional, stoic inmate at my parole hearing and convince them I was worthy of reentering society.

Because when I was free, Jade and I had some catching up to do.

7

___________

## JADE

Kelton and I left the prison, not saying a word to each other. I was in my own head, coming up with an apology for speaking my mind about Duke. But Denim had my mind completely out of sorts with his damn sexy smile as he undressed me with his eyes. Professionalism had gone out the window. Well, maybe not the entire time. Or maybe I had been professional on the outside, but my stomach had been rattling, and my hands had been trembling. I'd had to squeeze the pen just so my fingers wouldn't shake like a powerful earthquake.

My heels scuffed along the pavement. The clicking and clacking centered me as I kept up a brisk pace with Kelton. He seemed deep in thought. I had a feeling he was waiting for us to get into the car before he unleashed his wrath on me, or maybe he was searching for the right words to fire me.

I inhaled deeply, hoping the crisp fall air would soothe the burning sensation in my throat. But all it did was saturate me with the musty scent of rain that lingered in the air. I glanced up at the sky. Dark, ominous clouds greeted me. The setting was appropriate given how the morning had gone thus far.

I'd gone through every scenario the night before on how to keep my shit together when I saw Denim. *Don't look at him. Don't stare at him. Doodle to keep my hands occupied. Don't fidget. Be professional.* I'd repeated those things before I'd fallen asleep. But saying them and prepping for the day hadn't helped one freaking bit.

The man had commanded the room. Granted, I wasn't digging his prison attire, but I, too, was undressing the gorgeous hunk with my eyes. When he strutted in, I noticed that his angular jaw was unshaven. *Yum.* His blond hair was unkempt and curled at the edges as it grazed his shoulders. *Double yum.* His blue eyes were clear, bright, and glued to me like I was a magnet.

My heart skipped, tripped, and jumped when he smiled at me.

*Damn him.*

That spark we'd had in high school when we had first met outside chemistry lab flared instantly. But what had me squeezing my thighs together was the hunger swimming in his blue depths—sheer, clear, and absolute.

He knew I knew it too. I could feel it in my bones.

*He hasn't been with a woman in six years. What you saw on him was desperation for any woman.*

If we had stayed in that room any longer, Kelton would've fired me instantly. I had been ready to undress myself and show Denim what he'd been missing since high school.

Then again, I was also ready to yell and scream at him for leaving me. I'd gone through some of the stages of grief, but I didn't think I'd ever landed on hope and acceptance. I still had remnants of anger.

Two beeps from Kelton's key fob blared in the parking lot, severing my Denim rollercoaster ride. He was like a powerful drug for me. I thought I had detoxed from him and gotten him out of my system. But I felt like I'd just fallen off the wagon and into the web he'd spun around me all those years ago.

It had been a mistake for me to come with Kelton. My only takeaway was that I still had feelings for Denim, and sadly, that had nothing to do with becoming a paralegal.

*Pathetic.* I could've insisted on staying behind, but that would have only shown Kelton that I wasn't cut out for the job. I could've called in sick, but leaving my boss hanging was more embarrassing and maybe grounds for him to fire me or, at the very least, give me a warning in my employee record. I wasn't my sister. I didn't rebel or stomp my feet when I didn't want to do something. That wasn't me.

Kelton and I got into his car just as the clouds opened up, unleashing a downpour. A hard shiver racked my body. Suddenly, Mom's voice was in my head, and I couldn't stop the memory from surfacing.

*"Jade, dear, take the dog out before dinner," she'd said.*

*"Savannah can do it. I'm doing my homework." I kicked Savannah, who was lounging on the couch with her headphones on, listening to some metal band she loved.*

*Savannah snarled as she drilled her brown eyes at me. "What?"*

*I pulled her headphones off her head. "Take the dog out."*

*She swatted at me. "No. It's your turn."*

*Mom rushed into the living room, wiping her hands on her apron. "Girls." Her motherly tone was hard and commanding. "Jade, I asked you." She pointed to the kitchen. "Boomer is waiting at the door, and it's about to storm. So get to it."*

*I threw my book on the couch before stomping out. It was pointless to argue. Even if Mom ordered Savannah to take out Boomer, she wouldn't. She always disobeyed. At thirteen, she was a force to be reckoned with.*

*I stepped out onto the back porch as Boomer, our two-year-old lab, took off down the steps before I could get his leash on. Normally, we could let him out in the backyard, but our fence had fallen from a summer storm that year.*

*"Boomer," I shouted. "Get back here."*

*I ran after him as rain began to fall—a cold, hard winter rain.*

Kelton snapped his fingers. "Jade."

I blinked the memory away and silently scolded myself. I had no business wigging out in front of my boss, and during work no less. But sometimes it was hard not to relive the past.

"Close your door," he said.

"Oh. I'm sorry." I quickly pulled the door shut until the sound of it closing made me jump.

He turned over the engine. "Are you okay?"

*Not at all.* But he didn't need to know the war raging in my head or the fact that sometimes rain triggered too many demons and night-mares about that fateful night.

I strapped myself in. "I'm good."

Arching a brow, he shifted his Audi into gear. "Liar."

I shouldn't be surprised that a lawyer would see right through me. According to Mallory, good lawyers could read people better than they could read themselves.

"The rain makes me jittery." *And Denim is having a field day in my head.*

"Want to talk about it?"

I set my purse on the floorboard in between my legs. "Not right now if that's okay?"

"Fair enough." He took a left onto a two-lane road. "Nice work in there."

I stifled a gasp. "Really? I spoke out of turn and let my emotions get in the way." Maybe he hadn't heard me say I wanted Denim to throw Duke to the FBI.

Duke belonged in prison, preferably before my sister was released. Otherwise, she would run back to him. I wasn't sure if he would take her back. They had an on-again, off-again relationship. Regardless, I would do everything in my power to keep her away from him so she wouldn't fall into the same deep, dark hole of drugs and stealing again. I knew that was a feat in and of itself. I'd never been able to tame Savannah, and the older she got, the harder it became. I was hoping prison would reform her and make her see that crime didn't pay.

Kelton let out a hearty chuckle. "Maybe a little. But you contributed and asked appropriate questions. You got Denim to open up, and that was helpful. Thank you."

I smiled for the first time in a long time as a warm feeling coursed through me. It felt good to have someone compliment me on my abili-ties, especially since I thought I'd screwed up.

"After seeing Denim, do you think he's innocent?" Kelton asked.

I was beginning to believe that Kelton had brought me along not for a training exercise or because I was his assistant, but rather because of my intimate knowledge of the man. "Yes. I believe without a doubt he's innocent."

"Was it his speech or something else that makes you believe his innocence?"

His speech about how prison life had shaped him had been sincere. He'd put a lot of feeling behind his words. But it wasn't his words. "When Denim lied to me when we were dating, he would roll a shoulder. He didn't do that today." It was possible he could've learned how to lie better, but I didn't think that was something Denim would do. Or maybe he was too focused on undressing me with his eyes instead of lying.

My dad had always said, "Once a liar, always a liar." In addition, I wasn't blinded by Denim's good looks or charm. Or by the fact that I wanted to tear his white T-shirt off his broad chest and run my hands over every dip and valley he had.

"Hmm," Kelton said.

Cars passed, rain fell, and silence mixed with the *swish, swish, swish* of the windshield wipers.

Kelton merged onto the highway five minutes later. "Tell me about Duke Hart."

I cocked my head. "Don't you know him?" I assumed he did given that he and Dillon were friends and Denim was his client.

"Not really. I know of him through Dillon. But even then, Dillon hardly talks about Duke."

Sighing, I folded my hands in my lap. "Duke is the reason my sister is in jail." *Oh, and I want to kill him.*

Kelton sped up but stayed in the far-right lane. "He might've had some influence on her, but her actions were hers alone. I mean, he didn't tell her to rob a convenience store. Right?"

"True." *But let me believe that Duke is at fault.*

"What do your parents think?" he asked.

The windshield wipers were working hard, and traffic was moving, but not very fast.

I picked at a nail.

*Boomer wagged his tail, trotting up to me as the wind whipped the rain sideways.*

*"There you are. Come on." My feet dug into the squishy, wet grass as I practically dragged Boomer into the house by his collar.*

*Once inside, he shook all the water off him, slinging mud and dirt everywhere.*

*Mom scolded him then turned to me. "Get cleaned up."*

"Jade." Kelton tapped on my shoulder. "Did you hear my question?"

I shook off the memory. "I'm sorry. They died in a fire when Savannah was thirteen, and I was fourteen." I'd been known to check out during rainstorms, especially around the time of their deaths, which was coming up next month.

If they were alive, they would be devastated. However, I often thought if they hadn't perished in the fire, Savannah might have been a different person. She'd had a hard time coping with their deaths. So had I, but everyone handled death differently. Savannah acted out. I dove inward. But I was also the older sibling. It had been my responsibility to take care of her.

"I'm so sorry. Did you live with a relative growing up?"

"Our aunt, who's now on a charity mission in Africa. She wasn't ready to take on two teenage girls. My mom's sister was single and still a kid herself. I mainly took care of Savannah, but that was tough. We both changed after our parents died. She rebelled with boys, petty crime, and drugs. I became a hermit, focusing on school." *And Denim.*

"If you would like me to look into your sister's case, I can."

Tears pooled, mainly because I was remembering my parents. "Thank you. But they have her on tape. Plus, she confessed." I didn't have to ask her why she'd turned to robbery. Money had been scarce for both of us, more so with her since she was into drugs and could barely hold down a job.

"I just want you to know that I take care of those who work for me. If there's anything I can do, don't be shy in asking for my help," Kelton said. "You're family now."

More tears threatened to spill. I didn't know what family was anymore. I'd been on my own since my aunt jetted off to Africa three years ago. My dad had a sister in Washington, but I'd only seen her once at Christmas when I was a little girl.

Silence ensued again and stayed with us until we reached the outskirts of Boston.

Kelton tapped his fingers on the steering wheel as he slowed the car to a complete stop. Blue and red lights flashed up ahead.

"Kelton, speaking of my sister, would you mind if I take Friday morning off to go see her? I hate to even ask since I just started, but I haven't heard from her in two weeks. With all the talk about my sister, Duke, and the FBI, I want to check on her." I had to be honest with him. Granted, I could call the jail, but I would rather see Savannah.

"Is she okay?"

I shrugged. "She's been in a few fights. I just want to make sure the bad feeling I have is nothing serious." Despite our differences, she was my sister, and I cared about her. Plus, if I were being honest, I was feeling a bit of guilt in the pit of my stomach over how I'd practically ignored her claims about needing money and the severity of the conse-quences if she didn't get it.

"Of course," he said. "No matter what, family always comes first."

I slumped my shoulders. Maybe my future was looking brighter. I had a good job. I could find a decent place to live, pay my bills, put money away, and maybe I could help Savannah when she was released. I didn't need anything else.

*Liar.*

I wanted a family. But at the moment, I would settle for a good man.

*If Denim gets out, then he's your man.*

Hell no.

8
________

# JADE

I waited in the large, barren room save for cold metal tables and chairs and cameras jutting out from the corners. A clock on the wall provided the only sound with the *tick, tick, tick* of the second hand. I bit my nails, waiting for Savannah, watching for the thick steel door to open. Other than me, a young man stared at the scratched tabletop next to me, an older woman occupied a table in the far corner, and a middle-aged prison guard sat at a desk adjacent to the visitors' entrance.

I hadn't heard from Savannah since her phone call the day of my interview, and I was curious if she'd finally talked to Duke.

The click of the lock made me flinch, and I dropped my fingers to my lap, straightening my spine.

A blond girl who had to be nineteen or twenty breezed through the door first and beelined it over to the older woman. On her heels, a gal as young as the first bounced in, smiling as her red ponytail swung from side to side. The young man rose, beaming at her with love pouring off him.

I sighed, hoping one day a man would look at me that way. But love flapped its wings and flew out the high window in the room when my sister stomped in. Her bruised face was pinched, her brown hair was oily, and bandages covered her hands and arms.

I pressed my lips together, holding back the need to scream and shout despite the fact that my heart was breaking at how her life had turned out.

She slid into the chair across from me, slumped her shoulders, and stared.

"What happened to you?" My voice cracked in several places.

She touched the stitches above her left eyebrow. "This is what happens when you hang up on me."

My eyes nearly popped out. "You're blaming me for your condition?"

"I asked you for help."

I clenched my fists, mostly to get them to stop shaking. I was at a loss for words. But words didn't work on Savannah. Actions didn't either. I tried not to give in to her demands, but sometimes it was easier to give her what she wanted and get her off my back. However, I was trying to turn over a new leaf. I was trying to distance myself from her, although I was taking baby steps. It had helped that she was in prison. Otherwise, she would be beating down my door and getting in my face until I broke down and gave her what she wanted, which was, nine times out of ten, money.

She crossed her arms over her chest. "Why are you here?"

"I hadn't heard from you, and I wanted to make sure you were okay." After seeing Denim's cuts and bruises, I'd thought of Savannah.

She twirled a finger around her face. "Well, am I?"

A violent scream was stuck in my throat. Instead, I clenched my teeth. "Cut the bullshit," I whisper-yelled. "You're not pinning your actions on me. I've done nothing but try to help you since Mom and Dad died. You chose the path you're on." I stabbed a finger at her. "You chose to fall in love with a criminal."

She popped forward. "And you think Denim is a saint? Newsflash, sis. He's as bad as Duke. Oh, wait. He's in jail for murder. Much worse than Duke."

I wasn't about to waste my time rehashing an argument we'd had many times before. "I'm not here to talk about Denim or me. What did you want from Duke? Have you talked to him?"

"You're still in love with Denim. He'll get out of prison one day. Then what will you do?"

*Run as far away as I can.* "Coming here was a mistake. I thought prison would change you. But you're still a bitch."

She sneered as she leaned in. Her green eyes were pinpricks. "You don't know what it's like in here. You know something? Leave! Push me away."

*Don't engage. Get up and walk out.*

I pressed my hands on top of the table, motioning to stand.

"Wait," she said, losing the narcissistic attitude. "Duke isn't accepting my calls. He owes me money. I need it."

"What could you possibly need money for in prison?" If I weren't mistaken, the state gave each inmate a monthly stipend for toiletries and such. "Drugs?" She'd dabbled in coke. "Gambling?" My sister was good at cards. After Dad had taught her how to play poker, she was hooked. She'd played in high school, taking people's money left and right.

She checked on the guard at the door. "I just need it." Then she sized me up, looking at me as if she were really seeing me for the first time. "Since when do you wear expensive clothes?"

I glanced down at my pink silk blouse and gray slacks. "I got a job."

She perked up. "So you have money now?"

I shook my head. "I just started. And don't think for a second I'm loaning you any of my hard-earned cash." I was all for helping her, but not so she could sniff it or gamble it away.

"Then don't bother showing up again."

I closed my eyes briefly, pushing down the need to lash out. "Mom and Dad would be so disappointed and heartbroken to see you like this."

Her eyes narrowed to slits. "Stop throwing Mom and Dad in my face. You've done that repeatedly since the fire."

"You know next month is the anniversary of their deaths."

"Your point is?"

For a stunned second, I held my breath. "Shape up, Savannah. And let's be real. I can't do anything for you while you're in this place."

"You could've gone to Duke for me. He would've helped me."

*Don't scream. Take a breath. She's your sister. She's hurting.*

I puffed out air. "Pfft. If he doesn't want to talk to you, then he's not about to help you. How much do you need?" I wasn't loaning her any money, but I was curious.

*Curiosity killed the cat.*

"Two grand."

I rubbed my temples as a dull throb started. "Gambling?"

She visibly swallowed as her skin turned ashen. "Protection."

I knew nothing about prison, but I couldn't wrap my mind around her answer or the questions I had. But I was certain she wouldn't come clean with me.

She leaned over the table, and strands of her oily brown hair fell forward. "I'm serious, Jade." Fear replaced the derision in her tone. "The only way I will make it out of this shithole alive is to pay for protection. You've got to ask Duke for money or find some. At this point, I don't care how."

"Does someone want you dead?"

"I'm in prison. Everyone wants someone dead."

I often wondered how our lives would've turned out if Mom and Dad were alive. Probably the same way, although the fire had messed up both of us. We'd been lucky that Dad had gotten us out of the house. But then he'd gone back in to save Mom and never made it out.

*"Dad!" I screamed at the top of my lungs as flames engulfed our rundown shack. "Mom!" I ran through the rain and mud, stones poking at my bare feet. But I didn't get far.*

*A fireman lifted me up. "No. No. No. You can't go in there."*

*Tears poured down my cheeks as the hard rain fell from the sky.*

Savannah tapped on the table. "Jay. Why are you crying?"

I wiped a tear away and sniffled. "How far does two grand get you?"

She lifted a shoulder. "Four months." A lone tear cascaded down her cheek. "Will you help me?" Her plea was heartbreaking.

She'd begged before, and the end result was that she came back for more. *You're in a no-win situation if you give in to her. You'll throw your hard-earned money at your sister, leaving you with nothing once again.*

I should go to see Duke. I should make her his problem. After all, the day of my interview, Savannah had told me Duke owed her money.

Despite the cuts on her face, I wasn't about to fall under her spell quite so easily. Fights happened in prison. Denim was evidence of that. I had to be certain she really needed the money for protection. But I didn't know how to be sure of that.

Yet if I didn't give her money and something happened to her, I would feel like shit. I would blame myself.

A scream blared in my head.

She sighed. "Will you help me?"

"I can give you five hundred dollars when I get paid in two weeks." I'd already used my first check to pay bills.

"That's too long. I need it sooner rather than later." She blinked, and more tears fell.

"Savannah, I can't just jump when you bark. I don't have a sugar daddy either. Life on the outside isn't a bed of roses for me." Not that I wanted to trade places with her. "Don't you dare fire back with 'prison is worse.' I can only imagine. You're going to have to protect yourself until I can figure something out. After all, you're a fighter."

She laughed maniacally. "I'm a bottom-feeder in this godforsaken hellhole."

*You should've thought about that before you robbed a store.* The comment was on the tip of my tongue. But saying that would only get us into a screaming match, and I was tired. I also needed to get my butt to work.

"I can't promise you anything, but give me a week. That's the best I can do." *Maybe I should call Duke once and for all.*

I said my goodbyes to Savannah then hurried out of the prison and into my beat-up car. I'd just popped my head back against the headrest when my phone rang.

"Are you on your way back?" Mallory asked.

"Yeah. Is everything okay?"

"Denim got parole. It's so unusual for the parole board to make a decision on the day of the hearing. He walked in, sat down, answered some questions, and boom. No deliberation or anything."

*Shit.*

I'd thought I had months to prepare my psyche and my heart. "Please tell me he's not sitting in our office."

I couldn't deal with Savannah's problems and Denim.

"He'll be out by early next week."

I growled. "I'm screwed." I had shared with Mallory how I'd felt after seeing Denim—confused, elated, angry, frustrated, horny, and pretty much every emotion possible.

The only good that could come from Denim inserting himself back into my life was a hot night of sex. But even that would end in heartache. Because I knew one kiss, one ride on the Denim train, and one night of unbridled passion would bring me to my knees and have me begging for more.

**9**

---

# DENIM

I had been singing "Hallelujah" in my head since I heard the parole board grant me freedom.

*Fucking freedom.*

I couldn't wait to feel the sun on my face for longer than an hour at a time. I couldn't wait to drink a beer, fuck a good woman—as in Jade —put my feet up, and watch a football game in peace. Above all else, I couldn't wait to find the person who'd set me up.

For the last four days, I'd been on a high like no other. I'd never believed the day would come when I would walk out of prison.

Stew and another guard escorted me out, and the closer I got to the gate, the more my heart rammed against my rib cage.

*Boom. Boom. Boom.*

It was the best feeling ever, the best sound in my ears ever.

I kept my head forward, not daring to give the place one last look.

The sun was high in the sky, colorful leaves rustled along the pavement, and a brisk wind slapped me in the face. *Best slap ever.*

I inhaled the fresh-cut grass, probably from the lawn on the other side of the road. I took in another breath, and my legs ate up the distance to freedom.

The gates opened up as the guards kept pace with me. I laughed. It wasn't as if I would run back to the rat-infested building or do anything to screw up my parole before I even left the premises.

Dillon leaned against the passenger door of his shiny, expensive blue car. My brother had done well for himself, the legitimate way no less. I made a mental note to pick his brain. As the owner of a women's shelter, he knew the ins and outs of running a business.

He smiled as his brown hair whipped around in the wind. I loved seeing him, but I would rather see Jade's long inky-black hair blowing in the wind as she waited for me. Now that would blow my mind. *Hey, a man can dream.*

Twenty more feet, and I was free from the monotonous routine I'd lived with for six years—free from guards on my ass, dark holes, and violence. And the list went on. Above everything else, I wouldn't have someone barking orders of when to eat, take a shit, or when to sit. I wouldn't have Costa breathing down my neck. He was still in solitary.

*Fuck you, Costa.*

My pulse sang a happy tune, and with each step I took, ten pounds of weight dropped off my shoulders.

Before I crossed through the gate, Stew gripped my shoulder. "I wish you the best, Hart."

I pivoted on my heel and shook his hand. "Thanks for having my back in there."

"Go," he said. "Enjoy your first day of freedom."

He didn't have to tell me twice. I respected Stew and appreciated his help, but frankly, I didn't want to see him again. If I did, that meant I would be back in a four-by-four cell. *No, thank you.*

The gates slid closed behind me as I waltzed up to my brother with a smile I doubted I could get rid of anytime soon. "I'm free!" I shouted at the top of my lungs.

Dillon laughed. "I bet it feels fucking wonderful."

I couldn't even put into words how I felt. Tears stung my eyes, and as shocking as that was, I didn't even give two fucks if I bawled like a baby. I threw myself at my brother and hugged him hard. "You have no idea." I couldn't remember the last time I'd cried, but I let the tears flow.

Once we pulled apart, he slapped me on the shoulder. His eyes were brimming with tears too. "Come on, let's get a beer."

A beer, a good fuck, and a good plate of spaghetti… or rather a burger—a good, juicy burger.

Adrenaline coursed through me like a live wire. I wanted to do so much. Hell, the way I felt, I could run down the road and back to Boston. I just wanted the wind on my face and to see civilization again. I wanted to see people, women, children, and men who weren't out to kill me.

I slid into the passenger seat. The new-car scent wafted over me. *God help me.* I felt as though I were a newborn. I inhaled deeply, relishing the aroma of leather. It was a stark contrast to the disgusting smells of piss, shit, and bad breath I'd lived with.

Dillon climbed in. "You okay?"

"Never fucking better. I like your ride." I couldn't remember the last time I'd driven a car. I had my license but had never had a need for a car in Boston with the subway.

Dillon lightly slapped me on the arm. "I'm glad you're out. We have a lot of catching up to do."

"Let's pay Duke a visit." As much as I didn't want to ruin the high I was on, I wanted answers.

Dillon adjusted the air temp then started the engine. "Kelton warned you not to see our brother."

"I know." But Duke had been on my mind since the Feds had shown up. I figured it was better to rip off the Band-Aid, so to speak.

"Let's talk to Kelton first," Dillon said. "I'm sure he knows it will be impossible to keep you from seeing him."

"Can we stop by his office? I want to thank him."

Dillon navigated onto the road, and before long, the prison became a dot in the rearview mirror. I tossed a quick glance over my shoulder and stuck out my middle finger.

Dillon smirked. "You sure you want to thank Kelton, or do you really want to see Jade?"

"Does it matter? I want—no, need—to bask in soft skin, long legs, and plump lips." Not that Jade would jump my bones the minute I saw her. Yet just seeing her would make my day even better.

My brother shifted his attention back and forth from the road to me. "You look better out of that prison uniform."

I rubbed my hand along the soft fabric of my shirt. "Feels good too." Hell, my feet were tingly and happy in the army boots instead of white canvas shoes.

"I have a room ready for you at my place," Dillon said. "Grace can't wait to see you either."

I clutched my chest. "How is our baby sister?"

"Good. She helps me at the shelter."

"What are you not telling me?" I asked.

"Grace has a lot of healing to do, man. That's all."

I didn't doubt that. It would be hard for anyone to overcome the horror of being a sex-trafficking victim. But now that I was out, I hoped I could spend time with her.

"Did you find out why your parole was expedited?" Dillon asked. "I tried to get ahold of Kelton, but he's been in court."

"I haven't. I need to tell you something, though." At the parole hearing, I couldn't talk to Dillon except to say hi. "The Feds want me to help them take down our brother." I knew that anything we talked about wouldn't leave the car. Dillon wasn't the type to go running to Duke or anyone else.

A muscle jumped along his unshaven jaw. "What was your response?"

"I told them to take a hike. But here's the kicker. They believe Duke was at Alvarez's apartment the night he was murdered." I focused on my brother, eager to see how he would react.

Not much shocked Dillon or angered him unless our belligerent old man was beating one of us senseless. Dillon's knuckles instantly turned snow white as he gripped the steering wheel. "What the fuck?"

"I don't believe them. Do you?" A tiny part of me did, which was that fucking doubt in the dark recesses of my brain.

"Not sure. The Feds might say anything to get you to do what they want."

"My thoughts exactly."

The highway was teeming with traffic as we headed into Boston. Despite how anxious I was to get answers from Duke, my pulse thrashed around at seeing cars and people, women in particular.

My dick jerked at the thought of sex. I only wanted one woman, though. One with black hair and sparkling emerald eyes. Yet I wasn't sure I could pussyfoot around Jade and wait for her to come to me. Given how I'd dumped her, I doubted she would make the first move. I had to be the one to beg and grovel.

Regardless of my need for sex, seeing the cityscape in the distance and the fall leaves fluttering to the ground along the highway made my stomach giddy.

I couldn't wait to walk the streets of Boston and smell the aroma of Italian food, or any food other than the slop I'd eaten in prison. My mouth watered at the thought of a plate of spaghetti and meatballs the size of my fists, and I had big fists.

My brother's phone rang, and a moment later, Kelton's voice was blaring through the speakers. "Well?"

"He's out," Dillon practically snapped at his best bud.

"Whoa! What's got into you?" Kelton asked.

"Duke," I said.

"Speaking of your brother," Kelton started.

Dillon and I exchanged a surprised look.

"It seems the FBI was instrumental in your speedy release, Denim. The bad news is they're acting as your parole officers for now. You'll be checking in with them rather than a court-appointed one."

I sucked in a sharp breath. "You've got to be kidding. That means they'll do everything they can to fuck with me until I give in and narc on Duke." They would probably threaten to send me back to prison if I didn't do what they wanted. After all, if they'd convinced the parole board to let me out, then they could sure as fuck come up with an excuse to throw me back in.

Dillon's face was turning a dark shade of red. "But wouldn't Denim have gotten parole anyway? He checked all the boxes for an early release."

A female voice interrupted Kelton. "Sir, here's the file you wanted."

*Jade. Sweet, sweet Jade.* Her voice had always taken me to a special place where the world was perfect and kind, and violence didn't exist.

The line was quiet for a beat until Kelton cleared his throat. "If Denim hadn't gotten into a fight right before his hearing, then sure. But the board was ready to deny him parole."

I ran a finger over my eye where Costa had punched me. By the time of my parole hearing, I'd had the stitches removed. My appearance had barely shown signs of a fight. "I told them I was attacked." I hadn't gotten disciplined, but the warden had still been required to make a note in my record. "I told them they could check with the warden."

"You're out," Kelton said. "Do everything in your power to stay out. As much as I like billable hours, I care about my clients."

"Can the Feds send me back to prison?"

"As long as you don't violate your parole, you'll be good."

Dillon's knuckles were still white as he clenched the steering wheel. "But the Feds will fuck with Denim, though. Won't they?"

"They'll throw down some threats." Kelton's tone was even as though he'd told clients that very statement a million times. "If they do, I want to know about it. For now, one of the agents will be in touch. Whatever you do, please don't tell Duke about the Feds. They'll slap you for intervening in an ongoing investigation. That, my friend, will get you arrested."

*Fuuuck!*

"So Denim is clear to see Duke?" Dillon asked.

Kelton sighed. "I don't think there's any way around not seeing him."

"I forgot to tell you something during our parole-prep meeting," I piped in. Jade had jumbled my mind that day. "The Feds think Duke was at Alvarez's apartment the night of his murder."

"It could be a ploy to get you to do their dirty work." Kelton's voice boomed in the car. "If you talk to your brother, do not—I repeat, do not—bring up Alvarez and your suspicions. You could cause a chain reaction where both of you could end up in cuffs. Heed my advice. For now, enjoy your first day of freedom, Denim. We'll be in touch." Then the line went dead.

I stared out the passenger window, seething. The happiness I had felt when I'd walked out of the prison gates evaporated. I wasn't even in Boston yet, nor had I had my first beer, and my world had gone to shit. I could get onboard with checking in with a parole officer, but not the FBI.

We rode in silence, not saying a word to one another.

I didn't want to start on some self-pity trip, but it was hard not to feel sorry for myself. Someone had set me up. I'd spent my prime years in prison for a murder I didn't commit, and I'd learned Duke could be involved in the murder, and now I had to answer to the Feds.

"I want to throttle Duke." Dillon's deep tone zapped my pity party.

"Can we talk about something else?" I was going to heed Kelton's advice and enjoy my first day of freedom. Duke could wait. The Feds could wait.

Dillon rested his arm on the console, relaxing back in his seat. "Maggie and I finally set a date for our wedding."

"That's great, bro." I hoped I sounded happy and excited. Dillon deserved nothing but me showing him love and support. Yet my stomach was still knotted so tightly, I suspected it would take more than happy words to loosen it.

"I was waiting for you to get parole before I asked. Would you be my best man?"

I slapped a hand over my heart. "For real? You're not asking Kelton or Kross?" Dillon was tight with two of the Maxwell triplets.

"You're my brother, man."

Emotions rushed through me, causing tears to spring forth again. *What the heck is wrong with me?* I hadn't cried since I was a little boy, and in a matter of an hour, I'd had the urge to cry twice.

"I would be honored. Can I bring a date?" I could feel my lips pulling into a smile as I thought of the one person I would ask.

"Of course you can bring Jade."

I chuckled. "How do you know my date would be Jade?"

He gave me a sidelong glance. "Really, man. You're still in love with her. You always have been. I get why you broke up with her. I have to say I don't blame you either. She didn't need to be part of your dark world." Dillon knew me better than I knew myself sometimes.

"I don't know if she wants anything to do with me. Considering I'm about to report to the FBI, I don't know if I want her caught up in the mess that's about to unfold." My problem was that I wasn't sure I could stay away from her. Since seeing her, I hadn't been able to get her out of my mind.

"I'm sure you'll figure it out. Just don't fuck with her heart. She's a good person."

If Jade took me back, it wouldn't be for a tryst or a one-night stand. I'd had years to ruminate on what I wanted when I got out, and I wasn't getting any younger. If anyone would break hearts, it would be her severing mine into a trillion pieces.

I wanted to change the subject. "When's the wedding?"

"The day after Christmas," Dillon said. "Kelton is officiating the ceremony, and his older brother, Kade, offered to host the wedding ceremony and reception at his new mansion."

"You mean in five or six weeks?"

He sported a big grin, basking in happiness. "It's a small wedding. Maggie and I don't want a big blowout."

"Is Duke invited?" I didn't care one way or the other. It was Dillon's wedding not mine.

He lifted a shoulder. "I'd planned on asking him to be part of the wedding party. In light of the Feds, I'm hesitant now."

On that note, I wondered if Duke and I would be around to see Dillon get married. Hell, we could both be in prison together if things got out of hand.

I rested an elbow on the console. "What could go wrong?"

"When it comes to the Hart family, a million things." Dillon sounded as sure as the cars speeding by us.

He wasn't kidding. Our dysfunctional family could put a damper on anything. But I wasn't about to ask who else in our family was invited. Surely, not our old man. I didn't think Dillon would invite him.

"Can you drop me off where Jade works?" All the talk about Jade had me itching to see her. I also had a desperate desire to be around someone who was kind and caring. Plus, I could use her advice. She'd always been one to give it to me straight, and in addition to Dillon, Jade had believed in me at one time. As much as I wanted to fuck her until my brain became mush and my dick went limp, I wanted to talk to her and absorb her pretty looks and ball-busting smile.

"You can't go up to her office. You need an appointment. Security is tight in that building."

"Then I'll wait in the lobby or have security connect me with her." I would probably do the former. That way, she couldn't easily dismiss me over the phone. Besides, it was well after lunch, and quitting time was only a couple of hours away. I had nothing else to do except get a beer with Dillon, but seeing Jade was far better than alcohol.

As Dillon slowed to exit into downtown Boston, I promised myself I would be all those adjectives I'd bragged about at my parole hearing —responsible, confident, a law-abiding citizen, and an overall good person. I wouldn't ever return to prison. If my fate said otherwise, I would kill myself before I stepped foot in a place like that again.

My cell phone rang just as I was coming out of Kelton's office. The familiar "No Caller ID" lit up the screen.

I briefly closed my eyes, debating whether to answer Savannah's call or not. It hadn't been quite a week yet, and I wasn't due to get paid until Friday. I hadn't had time to find any other methods of borrowing two grand either. The most I could give her would be the five hundred dollars I'd promised her.

I slid into my chair just as my phone stopped ringing.

Mallory peeked around from her cubicle, an act that was becoming quite the norm. Not that I minded, although sometimes I wanted to be left alone to get work done. "Your phone rang while you were in with Kelton too."

I blew out a breath. "It's Savannah."

Mallory came around the short fabric-covered wall. "We haven't talked about your visit. Is she okay?"

I didn't want to burden her with my problems. Mallory had been through hell with me, and she deserved a break. But I knew my BFF, and she wasn't going to leave until I gave her something.

"I'll tell you later." I didn't want to go into detail. There were too many ears around us. "On another note, Kelton was just talking to

Denim." My stomach dipped again, just like it had when I'd heard Denim's husky tone through the speakerphone.

She crossed her arms over her black sweater dress, her blue eyes narrowing. "No one's around."

That was true. We were close to quitting time, and some of the other paralegals had closed up for the evening.

I sighed. "Savannah was pretty beat up when I saw her."

Mallory pushed out her small shoulders. "I'm sorry. But doesn't that happen? You said yourself Denim was bruised from a fight."

For the first time, I felt uncomfortable talking to Mallory about Savannah. I didn't want to be scolded or have her tell me that Savannah made her bed, or that it was time for me to back away. Savannah was family, and family came first. I'd agreed with Kelton when he'd told me that very thing, and my belief hadn't changed.

"Put yourself in her shoes or mine, Mal. Let's say your sister, Cara, was in prison or shacked up with a man like Duke. What would you do?" I knew Mallory, and she would be devastated if Cara did anything like Savannah had.

"Fair point," she said. "I'm only trying to protect you."

"I know. I love you for that."

"Is that why she's calling, though? Surely you can't fight her battles for her."

I moved a notebook around on my desk. "She wants money for protection."

For a moment, I'd almost called Duke. But I would rather pull out my teeth than ask him for money.

Mallory lowered her arms and pressed her hands on my desk. "Maybe you should find out if what she's telling you is true before you give her money you busted your butt for. Please."

"How? It's not like I know someone inside. I could talk to the warden, but he would probably give me some scripted answer about how he wouldn't let anything happen to any one of the inmates." Or he would tell me that everyone in prison was scared.

"Ask Kelton for advice, then. He said he would help you. Maybe he can pay a visit with you to the prison. Lawyers have a way of getting through to people."

Savannah was my problem, not Kelton's, and despite his offer to help, I couldn't bring him into my mess. I didn't want him to think I couldn't handle my own business.

But Mallory was right. Before I went into full panic mode, I somehow had to confirm if Savannah was in danger.

I massaged my temples. "I have to get something done for Kelton before I leave."

She placed her hand on my shoulder. "Why don't we grab a drink after work?"

The idea of a drink made me wet my lips. I could taste the tequila on my tongue. "I'm not sure if that's a good idea." Between the Savannah situation and knowing Denim was out of prison, my pulse was in overdrive. "I might drink until I pass out."

"I won't let that happen," Mallory said.

I pressed the button on my keyboard to wake my computer when my phone rang again. Savannah was relentless when she wanted something. "I should take it."

Mallory stabbed her finger toward her desk. "I'll be right there if you need me."

I waited for Mallory to leave, shook off the nerves, and answered.

"Jade." Savannah's voice was frantic. "Did you get the money?"

"I told you a week. I don't get paid until Friday."

She growled. "Call Duke. Please!"

"Did you get into another fight?"

"No, but I'm running out of time."

"Savannah," I whispered. "Are you being honest with me?"

"Are you kidding me?" She was practically shouting.

I cupped my hand over my phone. "Fights happen in prison. Surely the warden wouldn't let anyone die."

She let out an evil laugh. "Why don't you spend time in prison, then."

I gripped the phone so hard, I swore I would crush it. "You've never given me a reason to trust you."

"Why the change of heart? Have you been talking to Mallory?"

She was impossible.

"I'm doing the best I can."

My sister released a long breath. "Are you going to help me or not?" The fear I'd seen on her face came through in every word. Her moodiness was maddening.

If I didn't help and something happened to her, I wouldn't be able to live with myself. If I did help her, and she was blowing smoke up my butt like she'd done ninety-nine percent of the time, I would go nuts. Either way, I was screwed.

"There's nothing I can do until I get paid." I was done worrying about her. I was done tossing and turning in my pathetic dump of an apartment, wondering how to get her two grand. I wasn't jumping through hoops to ask anyone for help. "You're just going to have to take care of yourself until then. I have to get back to work. We'll be in touch." I ended the call before she made me feel even worse than I already did. With a shaky hand, I set my phone down.

Kelton came out of his office with his briefcase in one hand and his phone in the other. "Jade, I'll see you in the morning. Please make sure Mr. Cahill's file is on my desk and ready for tomorrow."

I didn't meet his gaze. "Yes, sir."

He loomed over me. "Is everything okay?"

I blinked, hoping my eyes were dry and my makeup was intact. Then I lifted my head. "Yes."

He studied me, his blue eyes penetrating me as though I were a witness on the stand in a high-profile criminal case.

I sat up straighter. "I'm fine."

His deadpan expression was unnerving. "Very well. Call me if something comes up." He started to walk away.

"Kelton," I called. "Thank you."

"For?"

"Hiring me." I still had a ton to learn, but he'd been open, nice, and patient with me so far.

He angled his head. "No need to thank me. Just keep up the good work."

I puffed out my chest as a smile broke free. "I will. I promise, I'm fine." I needed to reassure him, or maybe I needed to reassure myself.

He inclined his head. "I'll see you in the morning."

As I stabbed a key on my computer, I made a promise. I wouldn't take Savannah's calls while I was at work from then on. My concentration, efforts, and energy needed to be on my job during the workday.

I dove into Mr. Cahill's file, and within the hour, I had everything done. After I deposited the file in Kelton's office, I closed down my computer and tidied up my desk.

Mallory came over. "I need to take a rain check. I just found out I have to type up a deposition for my boss before he leaves tonight." She frowned. "Sorry."

"No worries." I could use some alone time. In fact, I probably had time to check out a new apartment building. When I'd called the apartment manager the other day, she'd told me the office didn't close until six. That gave me an hour. "I'll see you in the morning."

She tucked her auburn hair behind her ear and darted off.

Five minutes later, I was in a packed elevator, smashed up against a tall man who smelled like suntan lotion.

"Sorry," he said in my ear, his hot breath breezing over my neck.

I shivered. "No problem." I wanted to give the guy pressed up against my back a passing glance, but I was sandwiched between him and a woman who had a backpack full of bricks pressing against my boobs. That time of day, it was hard not to rub arms with people. Everyone seemed to leave at the exact same moment.

Finally, the elevator doors opened to the lobby. People hurried out as though the elevator were filled with spiders. I managed to move out of the way of one gal who was in a rush, holding the guy behind me hostage in a way.

Once we were finally out, I was able to get a look at him. He was tall, wore a nice tailored suit, and stood about six feet tall. His thick brown hair was parted on the side, and the hint of a five o'clock shadow graced his round jaw. When he smiled at me, he had one tooth that overlapped the other.

We walked side by side toward the exit. "Everyone is anxious to go home," he said, his voice deep and smooth. "By the way, I'm Todd Bennett. I see you work for Davenport."

I curled a lock of my black hair around my ear. "I'm Jade Kelly. What about you? Where do you work?" He'd been in the elevator when I got in, which meant he worked on a floor above me.

"I work for Carter and Associates. It's a financial firm on the twentieth." His voice was deep and smooth.

Dark-haired men weren't my first choice, but looks weren't everything. I liked a man who had a great personality, was funny, confident, and didn't play games. The few men I'd dated over the years had one or two of those qualities, but none of them had passed with flying colors, although I was probably reaching for straws. Denim had never been perfect. Maybe I was being picky, but I didn't want to just settle.

Todd and I followed the hordes of people toward the exit.

"Would it be presumptuous to ask if you would like to get a coffee sometime?" he asked.

"Not at all, but time is usually not my friend with late hours at work."

Todd loosened his tie. "Cool. I tend to work long hours too. Can I call you tomorrow?"

I didn't see why not. He had a disarming smile and seemed sweet. Coffee didn't mean anything, and I could use a new friend, especially one who was a distraction from the man who seemed to take up a large part of my brain. "Sure."

He slid out of traffic and into an open area of the lobby. "I'll call you now. That way, you have my number."

I followed him, rattling off my number. When my phone rang, I hit the accept button then proceeded to plug his name into my phone.

He nudged me. "Some guy is staring at us. Do you know him?"

I followed his line of sight, but my brain didn't connect yet. "Guy?" When my mind finally kicked into gear, I faltered back a step.

Denim was sitting on one of the five benches against the windows, staring intently in my direction with a creased brow. If I knew him, he was wanting to kick Todd to the curb. I would like to see him try. It was none of his business who I talked to or went out with.

I swallowed as my heart went pitter-patter. "I do."

"I don't get in the middle of relationships," Todd was quick to say.

I let out a nervous laugh. "He's actually a client of ours." That wasn't a lie.

Todd raised a dark eyebrow. "Only a client?"

I couldn't blame him for being wary. Denim was exuding a jealous, hardcore vibe, which didn't surprise me. Denim had always hated when guys looked my way or flirted with me, but we weren't in high school anymore, and I wasn't his.

"I promise. Only a client." No way was I walking into Denim's arms or starting up a relationship with him again only to have my heart stomped on.

"Good," Todd said. "We'll talk tomorrow, then."

I barely registered Todd leaving or felt my legs moving toward the ex-con, the man who had my body warming and my panties wet. I should've ignored him and left, but somehow my body wasn't in sync with my brain.

Denim stared at me, his blue eyes drenched in hunger so potent, I was afraid he would leap off the bench and attack me.

I shivered, secretly hoping he would do just that.

He smirked, watching every step I took, raking his gaze up and down my body.

Another shiver zipped through me. I mentally slapped myself, hoping to shake off memories of him naked. But the closer I got, nothing was working. So I homed in on the sound of my high heels clicking on the tiled floor, hoping to distract myself or slow my thrashing pulse. But after a second of locking eyes with Denim, I was screwed.

He was starving and not for food.

I settled ten feet from him, not daring to get close. The man was a hugger, and one hug from him would undo me. Then the heartache and hurt I'd felt for years after our breakup would vanish, and I would be a pile of mush in his arms.

He wiped his large hands on his stressed jeans as he pushed to his full six-foot height. "Beautiful." His voice was raspy and sweet.

*Damn him.*

I gripped the strap of my purse for dear life. Otherwise, I might run my hand through his blond locks or my fingers over his thick lips.

*Oh my!* Just looking at his lips was prompting memories of him kissing my body from head to toe.

"What are you doing here?" I was surprised my voice didn't fail me.

"I need some advice."

My lips parted. "From me? I'm not your lawyer."

His smile paralyzed me. "I don't need legal advice. I just need a friend. You always gave it to me straight."

*And you broke my heart.*

A war raged in my head over whether to give in or tell him to leave. My resolve always shattered when it came to Denim. But I couldn't let him play with my feelings, even though he sounded sincere. I'd locked them up tight long ago.

*What am I saying?* It was too late. My heart was beating so hard and had been the moment he'd ambled into that visitors' room at the prison. Still, I wanted to believe I was becoming a stronger person and not allowing people like Denim and Savannah to pull my strings as if I were a puppet.

I folded my lips between my teeth. "I have somewhere to be." *Liar.*

His gaze traced my face. His eyelids were heavy, and his breathing was not quite steady. "Should I make an appointment, then?"

A laugh broke free. "Who are you?" When Denim wanted something, he would take first then ask later.

He chuckled, a sound that took me back to the past and the good times we'd shared. "I'm sorry. Maybe another time." He gave me one last long look then swaggered out.

I stood there, astonished, watching him fade into the crowd.

**11**

———

# DENIM

I had to walk away. Otherwise, I would've pulled Jade in for a long and slow kiss. As much as I was desperate to taste her, I didn't want to make the first move. I had no right to. I had no right to think she would walk back into my arms. I didn't deserve her either.

She was good. I was bad.

She was pure. I was anything but.

We could never be. Yet there I was. I'd almost fallen to my knees and begged her to talk to me, to stay so I could get lost in her stunning green eyes. I wanted to run my hands through her long black hair and run my lips over every inch of her.

I was starving for her to tell me she would give me another chance. I was hungry for her to say she forgave me, especially after seeing that she'd grown and matured into a beautiful woman. She had been gorgeous in high school, but now she seemed to have a glow about her, one she hadn't had in high school.

I scanned up and down the street, taking in the city air, which was laden with a mixture of diesel exhaust and a hint of cooking oil from the fast-food burger joint on the corner. My stomach growled, but my taste buds wanted Italian. I plowed through the group of hurried businesspeople and found an out-of-the-way spot against Jade's building to get my bearings.

Secretly, I was hoping she would chase me. A laugh broke out in my head. I'd been the one to chase her in high school. Now the tables were turned.

Then again, if she was dating that dude she'd been talking to, I had no chance. I'd wanted to tell him to take a hike, but I wasn't the type to steal another man's girl, although I wasn't sure how long I could stay away from Jade. I'd always been good at walking away and not looking back. But after seeing her, my self-control was teetering on the edge.

Horns honked, people talked on their cell phones, and a delivery truck beeped as the driver backed up into an alley across the street.

I gave the entrance to Jade's office building one last glance. When I didn't see her in the group who'd exited, I sighed heavily.

*She doesn't want anything to do with you. Maybe it was for the best.*

I spotted an Irish pub a block up. It wasn't Italian, but they probably had good beer. I was about to kick my legs into gear when a man leaning against an electronics store caught my attention. The short guy was watching me. My radar went up, as did the hairs on the back of my neck. Costa's words blared in my head. "Tito Alvarez wants you dead."

Or maybe the Feds were following me. But the dude staring at me didn't scream federal agent. He was casually dressed in jeans, a leather jacket, and a red ball cap. I couldn't quite make out his features. The bill of the cap shadowed his face, and with dusk setting in, the lighting wasn't great.

My mind raced to figure out how anyone other than Dillon knew where I was. Maybe we'd had a tail when we left the prison.

Gulping in air, I stiffened. *What if Tito is watching Jade?* He knew I had a hard-on for her. He probably knew I was out too and that she would be my first stop.

Well, there was only one way to find out if the ball cap guy was on my tail. I started walking, keeping my head down as I dodged people. On the next block, I stopped at a men's store and checked out the mannequins, hoping I could see behind me from the reflection in the window.

Before I could orient my vision, someone grabbed my arm. I fisted my hand, ready to attack when warm breath tickled my ear. "Shopping for men's suits? You would look good in one," Jade said excitedly.

Her touch was electric, sending charges of heat straight to my groin, but that quickly fizzled out. If I was being followed, I needed to get her off the streets, or at least away from me. I was an idiot for showing up at her place of employment. I wanted to scratch out my eyes. I'd always kept my distance from her because of my enemies. Yet I'd just fucked up.

"Why are you tense?" she asked innocently.

*Fuck.* I didn't want to frighten her. I spun on my heel and plastered on a fake smile. "I'm not. I'm surprised." I feverishly searched for the man with the red ball cap.

She tapped my face. "What's wrong?"

Coming up empty, I rounded my attention back to her. "Nothing." My tone was flat and didn't sound like the Denim who had been sweet and kind to her several minutes ago.

She jerked her head in all directions, her black hair flying around her pretty face. "Who are you looking for?"

*Smart girl.*

I strapped on my charm. "No one. Want to get a drink?" We were too exposed.

She pursed her plump lips. "You're not fooling me, Denim Hart. Something is wrong."

I'd never lied to her, and I wasn't about to start. "I think someone is following me."

"It's probably the FBI agents," she said flippantly. "Kelton told you they would be in touch. Or maybe they're watching you to see if you pay a visit to Duke."

"FBI or not, I would feel better if we weren't standing here like sitting ducks."

"There's a nice coffee shop a block that way." She pointed toward the Irish pub I'd spotted earlier.

I grasped her arm. "Come on." With mechanical precision, I scoured the stores, alcoves of buildings, and people up and down both sides of the street, but I didn't find the perp. I turned back to Jade and blinked. Then a loud boom rang out before the window of the men's store shattered.

Flying behind a parked car, I pulled Jade down with me. Screams peppered the air. Tires screeched. Jade's eyes were nearly popping out of her skull. Maybe now she would believe me.

A gray-haired lady froze against the window of a shop next to the men's store. She was fixated on something across the street.

"Stay down," I said to Jade.

"Where are you going?" she asked horrified.

If I didn't get that lady to cover, she might get shot. I briefly closed my eyes and counted to three. On three, I rushed over to the woman, staying low to the ground. When I did, another shot blasted. I grabbed the lady just as more glass shattered somewhere nearby.

The woman screamed in my ear.

Jade waved her hand at me. "Denim, get down!"

Sirens blared in the distance.

Once I got the lady next to Jade, I stood to my full height. If that day was the day I died, then so be it. At least I could go to my grave knowing I'd saved a life. By the time I zeroed in on the shooter, he was running, pushing people to the ground as he distanced himself from the scene.

I was tempted to chase him, but Jade's voice stopped me. "Don't you dare run after him," she said as though she were in my head. She knew me well.

I heeded her advice. I really didn't want to die on my first day out of prison. I also didn't want to leave her alone in case the shooter had a partner lurking close by. I was certain the shooter was after me, which meant I needed to get the fuck out of there more than ever.

I held out my hand to Jade. "Come on."

She surveyed the area as she took my hand. "Thank God no one is hurt."

I double-checked to make sure before we left.

"Thank you," the gray-haired lady said. "I was in shock and couldn't move."

"No problem. I'm just glad you're okay," I responded.

The cop cars were trying to muscle their way through the stop-and-go traffic.

"We should get out of here," I said in Jade's ear. "It's not a good idea for me to wait for the cops." Despite wanting to be a model citizen and do the right thing, I didn't want to hang around for the cops. They would have too many questions, and if they ran my name, they wouldn't hesitate to throw me in a cell until they got answers. That wasn't the place I wanted to be on my first day out of prison. Besides, I hadn't done anything wrong.

More importantly, I had to get Jade somewhere safe. Then I had to walk away and never look back—a repeat of high school. It would gut me to do that to her again, but her safety came first.

"Let's go," she said. "I'm sure the police will have enough witnesses to tell them what happened. You don't need the attention."

No one knew who the shooter was targeting, so the cops wouldn't get much.

Five minutes later, we entered a coffee shop. The aroma of coffee hit me like a Mack truck. The trill of a coffee grinder competed with the buzz of voices from the chatting patrons scattered around at tables.

I ushered Jade to one of four booths along the window that looked out at the busy street. We probably should've grabbed a table in a dark corner, but they were all taken.

Jade slid into the black leather seat as I sat across from her.

A waitress bounced over. She had bright brown eyes and hair to match. Giving us a big smile, she set down a one-page laminated menu and two waters. "I'll be back to take your order."

The place was more like a diner than a coffee shop, not that I cared. I just wanted to be off the streets.

Jade reached for the water. "I'm thirsty."

I did the same. I needed something harder than water, but the cool liquid quenched the dryness in my throat.

After we drained half our glasses, the waitress returned. "What would you like?"

"A soy latte," Jade said as though she had the menu memorized.

That seemed like a fancy drink to me. In prison, our choices had been coffee made from acid and grinds.

I skimmed the menu. *Definitely no Italian.* I found mostly sandwiches and sweets plus a list of different coffee drinks.

"I'll take a caramel latte." I'd never had a latte, but I loved caramel.

The waitress collected the menus and moved on to her next table.

Jade gathered her black hair and draped it over one shoulder. Her cheeks were rosy, but she didn't have a scratch on her. *Thank God.* I would die if she had gotten hurt.

I took a moment to scan every head in the restaurant even though the shooter had darted in the other direction. "We should be safe for the moment." With the cops on the scene, I didn't think the shooter would show his face, and we were far enough away that I wasn't worried about anyone finding us.

Jade drank more water. "We know now he wasn't the FBI."

I shoved my hands through my hair. "I'm sorry. I shouldn't have shown up at your work."

Her nose twitched as she pinned me with her sultry green eyes. "You're not pulling that shit on me again. You're not shutting me out."

I reached over and grasped her cold, soft fingers. "You're not safe."

Her cheeks reddened. "You don't know for sure if he was shooting at you."

I was more than certain that man had been trying to kill me. When I'd popped up to help the old lady, he'd fired again. "The dude who busted me up in prison said there's a contract out on my head."

She gasped. "Who? Why?"

"Tito Alvarez, my old boss's brother. I suspect he doesn't want me to see the light of day."

A crease formed in between her dark eyebrows, a sign I knew well. That meant she had a thousand thoughts going through her head. "Why wait six years?"

That was the million-dollar question. "I haven't figured that out yet."

"Do you know for sure it's Tito Alvarez?" She twirled locks of her hair around her finger, and suddenly getting shot at took a back seat. I wanted to play with her hair like I'd done many times when we were lying on the grass at the local park, talking about nothing and everything.

I shrugged. "I'm not sure what I know except I didn't kill Hector."

She held her head high. "I know."

I reared back. "Did Kelton find something to confirm I didn't?"

She leaned in, batting her lashes. "No, but I know you. You've done a ton of bad shit, but murder isn't one of them."

My heart slammed into my ribs. If I wanted anyone to believe me, it was her.

Jade's gaze drifted from me to the window. "What if the person who killed your boss wants you dead so you don't find out the truth?"

"Tito wouldn't off his own kin. The two were tight." Although Hector had been known to take Tito down a notch in front of everyone, which hadn't sat well with Tito. No matter how pissed off Tito had been at Hector, they were blood.

"Costa specifically said Tito put a hit out on me."

She captured a nail in between her teeth. Suddenly, I wanted to be that nail. "What if the person trying to kill you wants you to believe it's Tito?"

Suddenly, Duke came to mind, and I ground my back teeth together.

The waitress returned, setting the mugs down as a blender whirred behind the counter.

Jade lifted her cup to her lips. "Your mind is going round and round."

The minute the strong espresso hit my tongue, a world of wow exploded in my mouth. The latte was rich, smooth, sweet, and was gold compared to the shit I'd had in prison. "I have so many things I want to do, but with the Feds wanting to shove me into a no-win situation—and now someone trying to kill me—I'm almost worse off now than before I went in." Well, that wasn't exactly true. I was free, and I was sitting across from a woman who held my heart in the palm of her hand. Those two things trumped the shit storm brewing around me.

She kept her mug close to her lips. "Kelton will help you find who the real killer is."

Kelton, killers, and prison skipped town as my mind took a long hike back in time.

*"God, Jay," I said through a pained breath. "You're killing me with those lips."*

*She giggled as she continued to suck my cock in a janitor's closet, dragging her nails over my balls.*

*I groaned loudly.*

*She batted her long lashes up at me. "Shh. Someone will hear us."*

*Like I gave a fuck. The students in the hall could watch for all I cared.*

*Then she took me deeper, until my eyes rolled back in my head.*

*I banged my fist on the wall I was leaning against and thrust my hips out. "Suck harder," I growled.*

She waved a hand in front of me. "Denim, where did you go?"

I sighed, relieved she couldn't see the bulge in my jeans. Hell, if she hadn't distracted me, I might've lost my load like a pubescent teenager.

"So, are you dating?" I asked.

Her cheeks flushed through the light amount of makeup she was wearing. "No one at the moment."

Maybe that guy in the lobby was someone she worked with.

*Thank you, universe.*

"What about you? Any dates in prison?" She stiffened as though she'd been thinking about those two questions but hadn't meant to ask them out loud.

I let out a belly laugh. "Would you be disappointed if I said yes?" I had hooked up with a nurse a time or two.

Her face blossomed red. "Why would I care?"

I raised an eyebrow. "You followed me, got shot at, and you're sitting here. So I would say you do."

She snarled, her nose twitching.

I couldn't help but smile. "You hate that I'm right."

She stuck out her tongue.

I adjusted my dick.

She was making it difficult for me not to leap over the table and take her in the booth. But the playfulness between us vanished when her phone rang.

Sighing, she dove into her purse and plucked out her phone. "Hello." The spark she'd had in her eyes a moment ago darkened. "Where? Of course. I'm on my way." Her hand shook as she lowered the phone. "I gotta go. Savannah was medevacked to Mass General."

*Holy shit!* She didn't have to tell me why. I knew all too well what happened in prison when men were sent to a civilian hospital.

**12**

---

## JADE

I paced a small area near the crowded waiting room. "Stupid me. Stupid, stupid, stupid," I mumbled to myself as I bit my nails.

After two hours of the *whoosh* of the sliding doors opening and closing, a baby wailing, a man moaning as he held his leg, and my pulse pounding in my ears, I wanted to scream.

I had some patience, but not when Savannah's life was hanging in the balance. My stomach was knotted, my head hurt, and I wanted to kick myself over and over again until I was black and blue.

Savannah had been telling the truth. I didn't know all the details, but what I'd learned so far was that she'd been severely beaten and was barely breathing. They'd rushed her into surgery, and she was still there.

*Why didn't I believe her? Why didn't I help her?*

I wiped a tear away, clutching my chest, willing my heart to stop hurting and racing. I felt as though I'd been crushed by a compactor that flattened cars. But nothing would take away the pain gripping me until I knew Savannah was okay. Even then I wasn't sure I would get past the guilt, which was more maddening than the pain.

With my attention on the shiny floor, I pivoted on my heel and resumed counting my steps, ten steps in one direction and ten in the other. Whenever I freaked out, I counted—sometimes to twenty and sometimes to fifty—but that day, ten was the magical number that kept me from screaming at the top of my lungs.

When I reached nine, I plowed into a rock-solid body that felt like a brick wall. My nose hit Denim's chest before he wrapped his fingers around my wrists. The clean, soapy scent of his button-up shirt invaded my nostrils, and I wanted to bury my nose deeper into him. Maybe I could snuggle into him just for a moment.

"You need to relax," he said in a raspy tone that I had missed terribly.

Regardless, what I needed was his muscled arms around me. I needed him to tell me everything was going to be okay. But Denim had never been one to lie or tell me what I wanted to hear. It didn't matter what he said, though. He couldn't break through the guilt that had me wanting to puke my guts out.

I shrugged out of his hold and resumed my ten steps down toward the emergency exit doors and ten steps back.

On my return, he tugged me to him and tipped up my chin with the knuckle of his forefinger. "I'm here for you."

My bottom lip trembled. He didn't know how much that statement meant to me or how grateful I was that he was there with me. "Why?"

He'd been a saint, holding my hand on the taxi ride from the coffee shop to the hospital. We hadn't spoken in the taxi, and we hadn't needed to. The light gentle circles he'd traced on my palm kept my madness at bay.

He dragged his calloused fingers up my cheek and tucked my hair behind my ear. "Because you need a friend, love."

*Love.* His pet name for me was new. In high school, he'd called me baby or baby doll. I shouldn't complain, but I wasn't a fan of the pet name. The word "love" evoked too much heartache for me. Yet what had me looking away was the pity in his eyes.

I didn't know what I hated more, the word "love" or his pity.

Nevertheless, I was ready to bawl my eyes out, and not only for Savannah, but for the memory of Denim walking away.

My pulse beat a furious rhythm in my ears. *Pound. Boom. Pound.*

He guided my face back to look at him. "Hey."

A tear slid down my cheek. "Don't, Denim."

Cocking his head, he slid his hand around my waist until his palm was seated on my lower back. The heat of his hand penetrated through my clothes, and a string of tingles zipped down my body from my head to my toes.

He hauled me to him until our chests mashed together. "Don't what?"

I shrugged. I didn't know how to answer him or if I wanted to open a door that had been closed for years.

His sexy looks, gentle touches, and caring personality were making it extremely difficult to keep that door shut tight. Plus, his growing erection was pressing into me and creating heat so strong that it dampened my panties.

*Damn him.*

For so long, I'd wanted him in my life. I had wanted to feel him against me, feel his breath tickle my ear, and take in his manly scent, which had been a mixture of sandalwood and cherries. I smiled at the latter. He'd always washed his hair with his sister's fruity shampoo.

His lips grazed my ear. "You should smile more, Jade. You're beautiful, especially when you blush."

I was more than blushing. Goose bumps popped up along my arms as butterflies fluttered in my stomach. God, I hadn't had this light-headed feeling in forever.

*Don't get lost in his charm. You know what happens.*

My heart couldn't afford to get drunk on his words. Besides, I was there for Savannah not to fall back in love. I took one step back.

His hand caught mine. "Please." That one word held an ocean of need.

I inched back another step. "I need to sit down." *Or run as far away as I can.*

He let me go, dejection washing over him.

I mentally shook off the urge to throw myself at him as I found an empty seat in the back of the room. Sitting, I captured a nail in my mouth.

Denim followed, folding his hot and muscled body into the chair next to me. When his leg brushed mine, heat surged up my thigh and settled in the exact spot that was throbbing furiously.

Clenching my legs together, I scanned the room for nothing more than to distract my brain from fantasizing about a quick tryst with him in a closet somewhere in the hospital, much like we had done a few times in high school.

He leaned in. "Remember the janitor's closet?"

My jaw nearly hit my lap. "Oh my God. What made you think of that?"

He chuckled loud and free. "I've been replaying that day over and over since I saw you in prison. And if I'm correct, you were thinking about it too. Weren't you?"

*Hell yeah. I'm thinking about how I gave you the best blow jobs ever and how we couldn't get enough of each other.*

"No." My voice cracked.

His grin was evil and wicked. "Right. Your cheeks are so red, Jade. You want me as bad as I want you."

My gaze dropped to his groin, but he had his hands in his lap. I would bet a million dollars those hands were covering the bulge in his jeans.

He laughed again.

The crying baby was off the charts, so the mom popped out of her chair, coddling her child.

The crying sound was what I'd needed to switch gears. "Do inmates pay for protection?" I whispered.

Denim lost his smirk. "Can't we talk about the janitor's closet?"

I understood that he was as horny as a dog in heat. Heck, it was his first day out. Then I sucked in a sharp breath. "That advice you said you wanted—does it have anything to do with getting laid?"

He arched a brow while one corner of his lips turned upward. "Are you hoping that's why I showed up to see you?"

A delicious shiver racked my body. *Yes.* "No."

"Liar."

I sighed and looked away. Otherwise, I would jump on his lap or find a closet. "Tell me about prison life." Sex with Denim was a great distraction, but talking about it wasn't for prying ears.

He gently pulled my hand from my mouth. "You still bite your nails."

I pushed out a shoulder. "Don't change the subject." Now I sounded like Mallory.

Draping an arm around the back of my chair, he leaned in. "I'd rather talk about sex."

I crossed one leg over the other and squirmed in my seat.

"I'm getting to you," he whispered, sniffing my hair. "You still smell like the beach. Mmm. I could—"

I pushed him away or tried to.

He didn't move, licking his lips as he studied me. No doubt he was thinking of me and him having sex. *Oh my.*

*Stop torturing yourself, Jade.*

I cleared my throat, trying to remember what I'd asked him and came up empty. "It's my fault Savannah is fighting for her life."

He stiffened. "Why do you always blame yourself when it comes to her? You did that in high school. It drove me insane then, and it still does." His husky tone turned flat. "Your sister is her own person. You can't change her."

I stuck out my chin. "She wanted money for protection. I didn't know whether to believe her. She begged me to ask Duke."

"You didn't."

"If you haven't noticed, I'm not a Duke fan."

He dragged a hand along his stubbled jaw. "Anyone inside has to watch their back. It's not that much different in prison than on the streets. Gangs, power plays, and enemies exist inside. It's worse, though. Out here"—he waved a hand at the window behind us—"you can run and hide. Inside, you have nowhere to run except behind a person you trust to have your back."

*Well, crap.* "Did you need protection?"

"I wouldn't say protection, but in the event I did, I bartered with a gang leader."

Savannah hadn't been lying to me.

*You can't beat yourself up. You don't know anything about prison. And let's not forget that it's hard to trust someone who has repeatedly lied to you.*

The one time I chose not to believe her, and now she was fighting to breathe.

Denim twirled my hair around his finger. "Are you in there?"

I inhaled a quiet breath. "So if it's not sex you want, then how can I help you?"

He nipped at my ear. "Sex is always on the table."

I huffed. "Let's be serious."

He moved back until two inches were between us. "I am serious." His playful tone vanished as he pouted. "But I get it." He sighed.

The double doors into the hub of the emergency room opened, and a petite nurse came out. "Jade Kelly?" She scanned the room.

I vaulted off the chair, over Denim, and ran up to the nurse. "I'm Jade."

"Your sister made it through surgery but isn't out of the woods yet," the cute brunette nurse said. "The doctor will fill you in. Follow me."

I rushed up to Denim, threw my arms around him, and kissed him on the cheek. "Thank you."

He stiffened as though he hadn't been expecting my affection, or maybe he didn't want me to feel his semi-erection. "No problem."

I broke away to find an unsettled look in his blue depths. It was the same expression he'd had the day he broke up with me. As soon as I walked away, I had the feeling that I would never see him again, and my stomach hurt at the notion. But I couldn't let my heart feel for him. I couldn't let him destroy me like he had in high school.

I would like to believe I was stronger now. Yet no matter how strong I was when it came to Denim Hart, he knew how to spin his seductive and charming web around me.

## 13

### DENIM

I watched her walk away with the nurse, and as soon as the double doors closed, I felt as though she'd just ripped out my heart. I couldn't pinpoint the exact reason why. Maybe because she was over me as evidenced by the peck on the cheek.

The day was ending on a fucked-up note. I'd lost the high I'd been on when I left prison. I'd lost that euphoric sensation of feeling as free as a bird.

Now I felt trapped, lost, and confused. Plus, I was about to blow a gasket if I didn't get answers or get laid. I knew the latter wasn't happening anytime soon because the only woman I wanted was Jade.

Threading my fingers through my hair, I turned, absently scanning the room as I considered my next move. I could head to Dillon's or finally try to get answers from Duke. Maybe I could at least find out why he hadn't paid me a visit while I'd been inside.

My brain hadn't processed either option when I spied a man sitting in the far corner of the waiting room, sporting a red ball cap that looked similar to the one the shooter had been wearing.

My eyebrows came together. Surely the dude wasn't stupid enough to follow us to the hospital. Then every muscle in me tightened.

*Jade.* I couldn't leave her alone. Another dark and twisted thought slammed into me. *What if Tito had something to do with Savannah's attack? What if Tito was going after my family and friends?*

I needed to warn Dillon, although he could take care of himself. Still, he owned a shelter for battered women. If I knew Tito, he wouldn't think twice about hurting a lady, or anyone, for that matter.

The bill of the man's cap shielded his features as he read on his phone. I took one step, my mind racing like a horse in the Kentucky Derby. *What if he has a partner with him?*

I gave the room a once-over from where I stood, that time in more detail. Two hallways jutted off in front of the information desk to my right, leading to exits. To my left was the main entrance, and directly in front of me were sick patients looking pale. Some wore masks, others dozed, and others read on tablets.

A large woman stood up, blocking my view of the man.

Then two things happened at once. The paramedics rushed in from a side entrance as the crying baby wailed for the fiftieth time.

"Get out of the way," a lady paramedic shouted.

It took me a second to realize she was talking to me. I backed up against a wall as a bloody man on a stretcher mumbled cuss words.

Hospital personnel rushed out through the double doors where Jade had disappeared.

A blond nurse spoke to the paramedics. "Maintenance is working on the door to the other entrance. It should be fixed within the hour."

"The bullet didn't go all the way through," the male paramedic said, his voice fading as they wheeled the patient into the epicenter of the emergency wing.

A slew of memories flashed before me.

*The night was sticky and humid. The sweat slid down my temples as I hoofed it two blocks to Hector Alvarez's apartment. I was late, and the fucker was about to cut off my head. Hector hated when anyone was late. As I drew closer, I saw blue and red lights lighting up the rundown neighborhood. I stopped in my tracks, watching the paramedics wheel someone into their rig from Hector's building.*

*I slipped into the shadows as cops and neighbors filled the street. I pulled out my phone and called Hector.*

*"Can't talk, Hart."*

*"What the fuck is happening?"*

*"Tanya is dead. They killed my girl,"* he growled through the phone. *"I'm going to kill them."*

A lady screamed, severing my nightmare.

The large woman who'd been sitting next to the man in the ball cap doubled over, holding her stomach. One of the nurses who'd come out to meet the gunshot victim hurried to help the large woman.

I checked on the man in the ball cap, but he was gone.

*What the fuck?*

I frantically searched every chair and face, but there was no dude in a red ball cap. I scanned the two hallways. *Nothing.* Wondering if he'd gone to the bathroom, I hoofed it in that direction. If he was the shooter, then I wanted to confirm that it was Tito who wanted me dead.

Something Jade had said stuck with me. "What if the person trying to kill you wants you to believe it's Tito?"

If this dude wasn't working for Tito, then I wanted to know who he worked for. Plus, the old adage of "keep your friends close and your enemies closer" had never been more real. If I knew where the ball cap guy was, then I could at least protect Jade.

*Fuck.* He couldn't have followed her. The double doors were locked, or at least the nurse had used a keycard to get them to open.

After checking the restroom and finding it empty, I stopped at the information desk. "Did you happen to see a man with a red ball cap walk by?" I asked the young lady.

She lifted her gaze from a stack of papers. "Sorry, I haven't."

I'd had my back to the main entrance when the paramedics brought in their victim. The ball cap dude must've left.

Clenching my fist, I charged outside like a linebacker ready to tackle my opponent.

A van screeched to a halt under the portico. I slid out of the way in the event someone inside needed emergency medical attention. Two men in bulletproof vests flew out of the back of the van and charged right at me. I wasn't sure who these two yahoos were. Bulletproof vests made me think they were cops, but gangsters were known to wear them too.

Regardless, I wasn't in the mood to get tossed into the back of the van. I also wasn't ready to get axed by Tito or whoever was trying to kill me, although maybe I could reason with my perp or at least draw the attention away from Jade. The farther away from the hospital I got, the less danger Jade would be in.

My reflexes finally kicked in, and I spun around and sprinted through the parking lot.

Heavy footsteps pounded behind me.

Just as I reached the street, the van braked, blocking me.

One of the men chasing me tackled me to the ground. "Move, and I'll hurt you."

"Fuck you," I spat.

He pressed my face into the pavement and, with his free hand, wrenched my arm behind me. Next thing I knew, he was slapping cold metal cuffs on me.

*Motherfucker.*

He dragged me upright. "Get up."

I squirmed as I managed to stand, then I rammed my shoulder into him.

Baldy gripped my arm as he ushered me to the back of the van. "Get in." He shoved his hand into my shoulder and pushed.

I stumbled forward as I climbed in, landing face first on the floor.

A deep, irritating laugh scraped the inside of my skull. "Get him up," Travers ordered one of his men.

Baldy growled something under his breath, and for the second time in a matter of minutes, he yanked me up again. That time he was more forceful, almost jerking my arm out of my socket. Then he shoved me down into a sitting position as though I were a bratty child. "There."

My butt hit the floor hard, and a pointy object jammed into my tailbone. I spat at him.

He was about to dive at me when Travers kicked out his leg, holding up his shiny loafer. "Easy, Frost. We need him."

Travers wasn't getting shit out of me.

"You know I could hold you for fourteen days under a terrorism threat," Travers said.

If my hands weren't cuffed behind me, I would've thrown him the middle finger. "You could, but my lawyer would have me out in a day or two." Still, I didn't want to spend another minute in a jail cell.

Once the doors closed, total darkness blanketed the small space, and the blood rushed to my head.

*Breathe, man.*

I inhaled and exhaled, thinking of anything but the small space. I was a second away from freaking the fuck out. I swallowed thickly as that suffocating feeling I'd always felt in the hole gripped me like a vise. Beads of sweat popped up on my forehead and temples. Nausea sat heavy in my stomach. My mouth was dry, and if I didn't get any light soon or get the fuck out of the van, I would puke then pass out.

Travers shined a light at me. "What's wrong? Afraid we're transporting you back to your warm bunk in prison?"

My breathing was shallow, and if I had any saliva, I would've spat in his face.

"He looks pale," Frost said.

I shivered as more sweat blanketed my neck.

"Maybe we should take him back to the hospital," the other agent said.

Travers lowered the flashlight, leaning forward with his elbows on his knees. "Nah, Oscar. He's putting on a show."

It was on the tip of my tongue to tell him to go fuck himself. Just then, the van swerved, knocking me to one side. Nausea sloshed inside my stomach. In the hole, I didn't have the motion with the darkness. The two together were seriously making me want to claw my way out of the moving van.

Oscar scrutinized me as though he were a doctor. "Boss, I think he's going to black out."

Travers laughed. I despised the sound since it reminded me of my old man, but with the predicament I was in, I would trade my old man for these fuckers. I could fight my father and not run the risk of sleeping in my bunk back in prison.

I sucked in the musty air and swallowed the acid lingering in my throat. "Why the cloak-and-gun snag?"

The butts of their guns peeked out from their hips on all three of them.

"You ran," Travers said. "Didn't your attorney tell you we would be in touch?"

"Not at eight at night," I fired back. "What do you want?" I knew what he wanted, but I asked anyway. "I'm not helping you take down my brother."

A smug grin emerged on Travers. "You will."

I attempted to shake the hair from my eyes but failed. "Just because you're my parole officer, it doesn't mean squat."

Travers's green gaze bore a hole through me. "You see, that's where you're wrong. I got you out. I can throw you back in. I have the power to fudge records and do just about anything to make your life hell."

I smirked as I recalled my conversation with Kelton.

*"They'll throw down some threats,"* he'd said.

"Something funny?" Travers asked.

"Look, man. First, if you don't want me to puke on your shiny loafers, I suggest you take off the cuffs." I wasn't lying.

He studied me for a brief moment then tipped his head at Frost.

Once free, I rubbed my wrists then combed my fingers through my sweaty hair. "Second, you're smoking dope if you think my brother will tell me anything. He hasn't visited me in six years. Besides, Duke is shrewd, cunning, and untrusting."

"Even with his own blood?" Oscar asked.

"When you come from a dysfunctional family, trust has to be earned." Duke had trusted me once, but that was a long time ago.

Travers leaned back, setting the flashlight on his lap. "We suspect the man shooting at you today is one of Duke's men."

I schooled my features, trying to read Travers and figure out if he was telling the truth. But behind Travers's condescending attitude and grin, he was a hard man to read.

If he wasn't pulling my chain, one humongous question stabbed me. When had I pissed off Duke so badly that he would want me dead? Not only that, why would my brother wait until I was out of prison to kill me?

"No comeback?" Travers asked.

The van took a sharp corner as though someone were chasing us. All of us listed to one side.

Then the van began to slow. A solid wall shielded us from the driver, and the back was devoid of windows. So I couldn't tell if we were at a red light or our destination, wherever that might be.

I straightened and crossed my arms over my chest. "You want me to believe that my brother was at Alvarez's apartment the night he was murdered and that he now has men trying to kill me?"

Saying both of those statements out loud made me shiver for some reason, probably because of the question Jade had posed. *"What if the person who killed your boss wants you dead so you don't find out the truth?"*

Duke knew I would go to great lengths to find anything. I'd searched for over a year for our mother, who had taken off when we were boys. I hadn't been successful, but I had put my heart and soul into scouring the streets, asking neighbors, my mom's friends, and even my aunt who had been close to my mom. One of the only reasons I'd stopped was because of something my aunt had said.

"You won't find her if she doesn't want to be found." My aunt knew her sister well. No one could find Mom, not even the cops. They hadn't even found anything in their database of a woman fitting Mom's name or description.

I couldn't blame my mom for ditching my old man. However, I did blame her for leaving her kids with the monster she'd married. I wasn't sure how I would react if I ever saw her again, but at the moment, my mom wasn't my problem. Duke was.

Travers sighed. "Look, Hart. I know I can be a dick. But what we're facing is some serious shit. The paramedics rushed a gunshot victim into the hospital not fifteen minutes ago. That man was in a shootout earlier with a lethal gang in Dorchester. Almost ten or more victims in gang shootings are rushed to the hospitals all over the city just about every night. This shit has to stop."

"Do you know for sure Duke is responsible?" I asked.

"We know he's working with the leaders of several gangs in the city. They just had a big powwow the day before Agent Brock and I met you in prison." He pulled his phone out of his jacket pocket, tapped on the screen twice, then handed me the phone.

The picture in front of me was none other than my brother with two men I didn't recognize. "I don't see anything wrong here."

"The man on your brother's right is Brian McCauley," Frost said. "He runs the gang out of Dorchester. The man on Duke's left is McCauley's lieutenant."

The picture still didn't tell me Duke was selling guns. He could very well be laundering money for them. "Is Tito Alvarez in the mix here?" Travers had mentioned gang leaders in Boston. To my knowledge, Tito had taken over his brother's spot as leader of the Southside Creepers.

"Not that we know of," Travers said. "The Creepers are small potatoes."

"Don't tell that to Tito," I muttered. The man had an ego bigger than the universe, and if anyone wanted power and riches, it was Tito.

"Our offer still stands," Travers said. "Get us something we can use, and your record will be expunged."

My record could be cleared if I found out who murdered Hector. "I want that in writing, and send it over to my lawyer, Kelton Maxwell." I wasn't doing anything until I knew for certain the FBI wasn't jerking my chain. Even then I wasn't sure I would give them anything on my brother.

The van came to a stop.

Travers laughed. "Smart man." Then he cemented his jaw. "I'll get you our offer on paper, but Hart, if you fuck with me, your ass will be back in prison so fucking fast, you won't know what year it is. Are we clear?"

I would rather kill myself than spend more time with true murderers. But I wouldn't let him see me sweat over that. Besides, I wasn't doing a damn thing for him until he came through.

"Crystal," I said.

"Good." Travers sat back. "Maybe after all this is done, you can marry that girl you were drooling over in the hospital."

My eyebrows flew to my hairline. "You had a man watching me inside. He wouldn't happen to be wearing a red ball cap?"

Travers deadpanned. "A woman." He flashed the light in my eyes. "You look disappointed."

Confused was more like it, and suddenly I felt the need to get back to the hospital to make sure Jade was okay. "I need to check on my girl."

"She's fine," Travers said. "Our agent is watching."

I wasn't sure I was comfortable with the Feds keeping an eye on Jade. But maybe the dude in the red ball cap spotted the female agent, and that was the reason he'd bolted.

"Can I go then?" My nausea was still front and center.

He nodded. "Remember, Hart. You're mine, and I can make you wish you were back inside rather than being a free man." The seriousness in his tone kick-started the nausea that had waned.

Suddenly, I was wishing I was back in my bunk because I had a feeling that what lay ahead was not going to be sunshine and roses.

## 14

## JADE

I chewed on not one nail, but all of them on my left hand, as I stared at Savannah through blurry, tear-filled eyes. She was in ICU, fighting for her life. I hadn't talked to the doctor yet, but I didn't need to.

Her face was bloodied, bruised, and swollen. Her head was wrapped in a bandage, and another bandage was wound around her neck. Her hands had cuts on them. She wasn't moving, and if it weren't for the breathing machine, she wouldn't be alive.

I pressed a hand to my chest, trying to get my heart to slow its pace. "God, if you're listening, please hear me. Please watch over Savannah. I know she has a lot of sins to repent, but she didn't deserve to be beaten to a pulp."

I blew out a breath, rubbing the back of my neck as I began pacing behind the curtained room. *One step up, one step back. Repeat.*

Despite our differences, Savannah couldn't die. She was my baby sister. As much as I wanted to shake some sense into her, I couldn't bear to see her like this.

The swooshing sound of the breathing machine hurt my ears and stabbed my heart. I squeezed my eyes shut, and tears spilled out as my body began to shake.

Thank God my parents weren't there to see Savannah. Mom would collapse if she saw her baby girl in such a state. Dad would too, but he wouldn't show his emotions. He had always been the strong one in the family.

I half-smiled, hoping that Savannah took after him now and that she would have the spunk and fight to survive.

It was a good thing the roles weren't reversed. I was so much like my mother, wearing my emotions on my sleeve just like she had. If I'd walked in Savannah's shoes, I would've been dead a long time ago.

I paced three steps instead of one, and then four in the other direction, counting to myself while clenching my fists, biting my nails, crying, and feeling so fucking helpless. *How could something like this happen?* I wasn't naive enough to believe that prisons were the best place to live. *But for Pete's sake, where were the guards, the warden, or anyone when this happened?*

The first chance I had, I would pay the warden a visit. That much was certain. I wanted answers. I wanted justice. And I wanted vengeance. I wanted to strangle the woman who had done this to Savannah.

*Who am I kidding?* I wasn't a fighter. I couldn't throw a punch and never had. Yet as I continued to pace and freak out, guilt sat heavy in my stomach, burning like the inferno I'd witnessed that fateful night. Acid shot to my throat, and I swallowed down that latte I'd had earlier.

I should've gone to Duke. If I had, Savannah wouldn't be hanging on by a thread. If I'd borrowed money from Mallory, Savannah wouldn't be there.

*Stop torturing yourself.*

I shuddered as Denim's words flickered like a bright light in a dark room. *"Your sister is her own person. You can't change her."*

But I could've helped her. I could've pushed harder to get her the money she needed like I had so many times in the past. I should've swallowed my hatred and reached out to Duke.

*Argh! Duke!*

My body shook like a magnitude ten earthquake. His name always conjured up images of me driving a stake through his heart. Maybe I should hunt him down. I knew where he lived, thanks to Savannah.

Despite the searing pangs of guilt in my gut, I knew Savannah couldn't go back to prison, at least not the one she was in. She wouldn't live an hour if she returned.

*"If she makes it,"* a voice in my head said.

*Stop thinking the worst, Jade.*

More tears fell.

A man wearing a yellow bandana around his head, blue scrubs, and a concerned expression walked in. "I'm Dr. Long. You must be Jade?"

Nodding, I came to an abrupt halt, blinking away tears and looking at him as though he were her savior. I prayed he was.

His dark eyes held sadness. "Your sister has a long road ahead of her. Her head injury is quite severe. The slit on her throat was deep, but a little deeper, and she wouldn't have made it to the hospital. We were able to repair and stitch her up. I wish I had better news for you."

I sobbed. "Will she wake up?"

"I'm not sure. Do you have anyone you can call? Family?"

Tears streamed down my face like a waterfall. "Our parents are dead." I dashed away tears. "No one else is in town."

"The next few hours are critical. You should get some rest. She's in good hands here."

I bit a nail. "Can I stay?" I didn't want to go home to my depressing apartment. I wouldn't be able to sleep anyway.

The doctor bowed his head. "I'll let the security guard and the nurses know."

I'd forgotten a guard had been posted outside to watch her. That should have made me feel better, but it didn't. *Where were those guards in the prison when Savannah was getting decimated?*

I pulled out my phone. I needed to call Mallory and fill her in.

Dr. Long regarded me. "You will need to make your call outside. ICU policy."

If I were going to be there all night, I needed caffeine anyway, or maybe a bottle of alcohol. "I'll be back."

As I left, the tightness in my chest became so constricting that I almost couldn't breathe. Once I was near the elevator, I called Mallory.

She answered on the first ring. "Hey. I'm still at work, and my eyes are seeing double."

I sobbed like a baby, holding my stomach.

"What's wrong?" she asked. "Please tell me this has nothing to do with Denim."

"Savannah is in a coma. She was beaten so badly, the doctor didn't give me high hopes she'll make it. It's all my fault. I should've gotten her the money. I should've done something."

"Where are you? I'm coming." She sounded frantic.

"You can't. Only family is allowed in ICU. I should've helped her, Mal. I should've found the money."

"I don't give a shit. What hospital?"

"Mass General," I said as a female voice blared through the intercom.

"Code blue! Code blue!"

Nurses and doctors spilled into the hall from other rooms and ran into the ICU.

I hung up as the floor tilted on its axis. I ran behind the medical staff with a sick feeling gripping my chest.

*Please. Please. Please don't let them go into Savannah's room.*

But when a nurse rolled a crash cart into Savannah's room, waving the female guard out of the way, I swayed as I came to an abrupt halt.

The female guard rushed up to me. "Miss." Her strong hands caught me before I fell. "You need to sit." She guided me to a desk chair on wheels. She might as well put me on a stretcher because I couldn't get air in my lungs.

I had to see Savannah. "My sister." I pushed past the guard, stumbling up to the curtained room.

She padded right behind me. "You shouldn't go in there."

Too late. I had to see Savannah.

Dr. Long had the paddles pressed to Savannah's chest. "Again."

The brunette nurse who had escorted me into the ICU turned a knob on a machine.

Savannah's body jerked.

Dr. Long looked at his watch then at a monitor. All it was showing was a flat line.

*No! No!*

Dr. Long said something, but I only heard a jumble of words.

Part of the medical team began to leave while one nurse removed the tube from Savannah's mouth. Another nurse unhooked her IV.

"I'm so sorry," the guard behind me said.

Dr. Long came out with sorrow pouring off him. "I'm sorry, Ms. Kelly."

I shook my head vigorously. "No. She's not dead."

Dr. Long removed his gloves. "Her injuries were too severe."

"Please. You have to try again," I pleaded, my voice trembling and cracking.

"Is there anyone we can call for you?" Dr. Long asked.

Anyone I'd ever loved was gone except maybe Denim. But he had probably left.

"I would like to spend time with my sister."

Dr. Long pulled off his cap. "Take as much time as you need."

I ambled up to Savannah, my body trembling, tears rushing out. I cried like a baby as I grasped her warm hand. "I'm sorry," I whispered. "I should've helped you." I shuddered. "I wish our lives had been different. I wish Mom and Dad didn't die in the fire." I rubbed the back of her bruised hand. "I love you, Savannah." I leaned over and kissed her on the cheek. "Fly with the angels, baby sister. One day, we'll meet again. When you see Mom and Dad, say hi for me."

I kissed her again before I ran out of the room like a madwoman who was running out of a mental hospital. I had no idea what to do next. But I knew one thing—someone would pay for her death.

**15**

———

# DENIM

I craned my neck up at the twenty-story high-rise as I approached Duke's penthouse. He lived in an area of Boston where the streets were spotless and high-end shops were nestled below expensive apartment buildings.

A light wind pushed a paper wrapper around as the lights in shops began to dim.

Travers had dropped me off two blocks away, not that I was on the clock yet. I suspected the offer in writing would take some time.

I could return to the hospital to wait for Jade, but she might be there all night. And since Travers had an agent watching her, I felt a little at ease. Since I didn't have a phone, I couldn't call her, and I didn't even know her number anyway.

Besides, after talking to Travers and thinking about the shit he'd put in my head, it was time to see Duke. I pulled on the handle of the glass door to Duke's building and found it locked.

The bellman rose from his desk and smoothed a hand down his red jacket. He took his sweet-ass time unlocking the door. "May I help you?"

"I'm here to see Duke Hart."

The sharp-dressed bellman glanced at his Rolex. "It's late, and Mr. Hart isn't expecting any visitors."

I laughed. It wasn't even ten p.m. Surely Duke wasn't an old man and in bed already.

"Let him know his brother wants to see him." I wasn't leaving. Hell, I would park my ass outside if I had to, or I would bug the crap out of the bellman.

*Careful, man. He'll call the cops.*

But I didn't give a fuck. Even if he did, I had Travers to get me out of trouble.

"I'll let him know you were here." The bellman started to lock the door.

I stuck my booted foot in between the doors. "Not so fast."

He lifted his head of thick gray hair. "Remove your foot, or I'll call the police."

If I had a cell phone, I would call them myself, or rather, I would call Travers. "Then you won't mind if I wait inside while you call the cops."

He cocked his head and looked at me as if I were mentally unstable.

I really didn't want trouble. I looked at the name engraved on the bellman's name tag. "Do you have family, Harris?"

He let out a long, low sigh and opened the door. "If he doesn't want to see you, then you walk out without causing a commotion."

I raised my hands. "Deal. But I'll talk to my brother."

He made quick work of getting Duke on the phone.

I breezed past the mailboxes and ponied up to the circular desk in the spacious lobby. "Use the speaker."

"What is it, Harris?" Duke's baritone voice came through loud and clear.

"Hey, brother," I said before Harris could respond.

Duke growled. "Denim."

*Fucker.*

"Let him up, Harris," Duke said, albeit reluctantly.

*Good move.*

Five minutes later, I was walking out of the elevator and into Duke's ritzy penthouse, which had a killer skyline view of Boston. I whistled. "You've done well for yourself, big brother, while I was rotting away without so much as a visit from you."

Duke stood at parade rest in between two pillars that looked like something out of the Greek era.

I raised my eyebrows. "No comeback?"

He folded his arms over his bare chest as though he dared me to get by him.

I didn't know if I would beat him in a fight or not, but I was willing to try. Years of pent-up anger boiled to the surface, causing heat to sear my cheeks. I opened my arms. "No hug for your baby brother?"

His sandy-brown hair was rumpled as though he had been sleeping or maybe rolling around in bed with some hot chick. He studied me for a second then padded across the expansive open floor plan to a bar tucked into the corner near an ornate fireplace framed in stone.

The more I looked around, the more anger swirled like a pile of hot ashes in my gut. My own blood didn't give two shits about me, but he'd put all his energy into building his life.

"This is a new place," I said almost to myself.

Pristine stainless appliances shone beneath the recessed lighting in the gourmet kitchen. Before I went to prison, Duke had lived in a modest apartment in the south end of Boston. However, I did remember Dillon telling me Duke's new place was snazzy.

"Do you even use the kitchen?" I asked. Duke was a terrible cook. He'd tried to fix dinner for Dillon, Grace, and me several times growing up, but he'd burnt everything he made.

He poured amber liquid into two short glasses. "Want a drink?"

I skirted the buttery leather couch flanked by two wide leather chairs and ambled up to the fireplace. A geometric painting of reds, greens, and blues decorated the wall. "Since when are you into art?"

"Since when do you make deals with the Feds?"

My blood turned to ice as I spun around. "Come again?"

He handed me my drink. "You heard me."

I took the crystal glass and commandeered one of the two chairs.

Duke took the other and sipped his amber liquid, glaring at me.

But I wasn't about to back down. I took a swig of my drink, and the expensive bourbon exploded on my tongue. I would probably be drunk in a matter of minutes since I still hadn't eaten anything, not to mention I'd gone six years without a drop of alcohol in my body.

"What's true is I'm out on good behavior." My mind swirled like a major hurricane, trying to figure out how he knew. The only one who knew other than Kelton, Jade, Dillon, and me was Stew, the prison guard, unless word had spread that I'd talked to the Feds. Of course, that wouldn't surprise me since prison was like high school. Rumors spread like wildfire. Regardless, it was clear Duke had an inside man.

Suddenly, Jade's words flashed before me. "What if the person trying to kill you wants you to believe it's Tito?"

*Fuck me sideways.*

What if Duke hired Costa to kill me?

I had to ask. "Did you put a contract on my head?" If he said yes, I was throwing my drink at him.

He eyed me over the rim of his glass. "Now why would I do that?"

I shrugged. "You tell me."

The fire crackled. The air became thick. My body vibrated.

Duke continued to sip his drink.

We were in a silent standoff, and he wasn't about to tell me squat. I knew my brother. He was untrusting, cold, calculating, and intimidating, and those were only a few of his flaws. He had no reason to trust me, nor I him. But I was realizing why he'd never bothered to pay me a visit. He was as much a stranger to me as I was to him.

I figuratively scratched my head at how we'd gotten to this juncture. I'd always looked up to him. He'd been the father figure in our family. He'd worked hard to find jobs so he could put food on our table. He'd shielded Dillon, Grace, and me from our drunken father, who'd cared more about his booze than his own kids.

It was obvious Duke wasn't going to answer me. It was best to change the subject, or maybe I should leave. But I wasn't ready to give up yet.

I settled into the chair, resting my ankle on my knee. "So, Savannah is in the hospital, fighting for her life."

His glass froze midway to his lips. "Come again." His shrewd facade cracked as his brown eyes became as big as basketballs.

"I was just at the hospital with Jade."

His eyebrows pinched, a deep crease forming. "Jade? You're seeing her again?"

I wasn't there to discuss my nonexistent love life, even though the mention of Jade seemed to perk him up. "She tells me Savannah wanted her to beg you for money for protection inside."

"What hospital is she in?" he asked in a tone that permitted no argument.

"Why do you care? Didn't you and Savannah break up?" Or maybe he was referring to Jade. Surely they weren't an item. Jade hated Duke. Then again, maybe Jade knew how to lie better than she used to. Maybe she was secretly dating Duke, and the only reason she was working for Kelton was to get information on me. Maybe Jade had told Duke about the Feds.

He snagged his phone off the coffee table. "Tell me now." A muscle ticked in his jaw.

He cared. The coldhearted Hart brother cared. Whether it was for Savannah or Jade, I'd gotten a reaction from him.

"Not until you give me answers," I said.

He let out a dark laugh. "Are you serious?"

He could probably find out what hospital Savannah was in, but I had the urge to fuck with him. "Is your hard-on for Jade?" I was being a class A dick. Again, I couldn't give two fucks.

He belted out a laugh. "Jealousy never looked good on you, brother."

*Are we brothers?* It felt as though we were enemies.

"I know you had it bad for Jade. You probably still do." I'd seen how he'd looked at her when she and I had dated. He didn't have to tell me he wanted to fuck her. "So let's not talk about jealousy."

"Why do you even give a fuck? You left her ass behind in high school."

I clenched my teeth. "Are you saying you slept with her?" Maybe he dumped Jade too, and that was the reason she disliked my brother. I gripped the glass, a second away from crushing it or leaping over the coffee table and ramming my fists into his face.

He sneered. "I don't kiss and tell."

I itched to wipe the smirk off his face. It was best that I switched gears, though. I didn't need to end up in the hospital like I had when we were teenagers, although I was broader in the chest than Duke. Still, he could probably deck me in two seconds flat.

"Why do you insist on fucking with my head?" I asked.

"Are you sure I'm screwing with your head or your girl?"

I growled. "Why didn't you fight for me during my trial? Find me a good lawyer. You had the money." I waved my hand around the room. "Still do." The penthouse had to cost about a million, if not more.

He pushed to his feet, that smirk still in place, and moseyed over to the bar. In that moment, he reminded me so much of our old man, and not in the physical features. I resembled my old man in that department, but Duke had his mannerisms—the way he puffed out his chest, the way his expression dripped with resentment and self-satis-faction.

"You made your bed, Denim. It wasn't up to me to fix your shit. How many times did I tell you not to get involved with Alvarez? How many times did I tell you he would bring you down?"

"Then you should've brought me into your money-laundering empire."

He returned with a full glass of bourbon. "Should I check you for a wire?"

I chuckled. "Go ahead. Knock yourself out."

Travers wasn't going to be happy Duke was onto the Feds' plan. I wasn't sure how that new wrinkle would play out for me. With my luck, Travers would think I told Duke then ship my ass back to prison.

His nostrils flared. "What's next for you? Narc on your brother? Work for Tito Alvarez?"

"Why? Do you care?"

Duke kept his feelings close to his vest unless someone royally pissed him off. Then watch out. He could be meaner than our drunk old man.

"Not at all." His tone didn't have one ounce of empathy or sympathy.

I shook my head. "You're a piece of work. What happened to you?"

He shot daggers at me. "What hospital is Savannah in?"

"Answer one question, and I'll tell you. Do you believe I killed Hector?"

"It's late. I have a meeting in the morning."

I squeezed the hell out of my glass. "Why is it so hard to answer?"

He pushed his fingers through his hair. "What do you want from me? Do you want me to tell you I believe you didn't murder anyone? Because that would be a lie. The evidence says otherwise."

I slammed the glass down on the coffee table. "Then tell me what you were doing at Alvarez's apartment the night he was murdered."

His jaw nearly hit the carpet. "What the fuck? Are you for real?"

I couldn't decipher whether he was shocked I knew he'd been there or if he was shocked that I would believe he was capable of murder.

I let him stew while I helped myself to another drink. The first round of bourbon hadn't affected me yet. Maybe my adrenaline was too fucking high.

He lost the snarky attitude, and a minuscule amount of fear jumped free. "Who told you that?"

Tension, thick and strong, filled every nook and cranny in the enormous room.

With my glass full, I returned to stand near the fireplace. I needed the heat from the fire to thaw my rage. Or maybe I should just get stinking drunk and let the alcohol quench my fury. I wasn't a mean drunk. That blue ribbon went to our old man.

"Did you know that gossip is worse in prison than it was in high school?" I asked.

Duke's Adam's apple bobbed. "So you're telling me some con told you I was at Alvarez's apartment on the night he was killed?"

I gulped down a mouthful of bourbon before answering. "Yep."

Duke's eyes narrowed to slits. "Or was it the Feds?"

"I told you I'm not working with the Feds." I wasn't. I'd never told Travers I would do anything, at least not until they gave me something in writing. But deep down, I was never planning to blow the whistle on Duke. Although if he continued to piss me off, I just might slap on a badge and take the reins.

He vaulted off the chair so fast, I barely tracked his movement until he was patting me down like I was getting arrested.

I swung my arms out to the sides, giving him full access to search me. "You won't find a wire if that's what you're looking for."

Edging back, he hardened his jaw.

"Satisfied?"

He clutched the back of his neck. "Did the Feds come to see you in prison or not?" His lethal tone had a crack in it.

"Tell me who told you that, and I'll give you a straight answer."

Duke heaved out a breath. "I'm not revealing my sources."

I cocked my head and shrugged. "Until you can give me straight answers, I'm not giving you squat."

"Then we're done here." He swung out his arm and gestured to the elevators. "Get the fuck out."

"Gladly." The only thing to come of our reunion was that one or both of us would end up in the emergency room, but I had to give it one more college try and attempt to break through his steel wall.

I knocked back the bourbon. "Did you murder Hector Alvarez?"

He lunged, pinning me against the sharp stone frame of the fireplace before gripping my throat. "Until you can act like my brother, I don't want to see you again."

The empty glass fell from my hand. The sound of shattering glass exploded in the vast penthouse.

My eyes bugged out of my head. My lungs burned like an inferno. I clutched his hands, trying to pry them off me. He was a strong motherfucker like Costa. Death loomed as he squeezed the air out of me. I wasn't ready to die, particularly at the hands of my brother.

"Duke," a high-pitched female voice said. "What are you doing?"

She rushed over, wiggling her petite frame between two tall and muscled men as though she could stop an army. "Let go of him."

Duke didn't move a muscle.

The room began to spin.

"Duke Hart," the woman shouted. "Stop. You're going to kill him."

I didn't know if it was her caustic tone or the word "kill" that did the trick, but my brother let go of me.

I bent over, gasping for air and blinking rapidly, hoping to clear the darkness creeping in at a Mach speed.

Small hands gripped my arm. "Have a seat." Her voice was hauntingly familiar.

I inched over to the chair. "You're the woman on the phone."

"I'll get you some water." She dashed off, her red hair flowing behind her.

Duke sat on the coffee table. "You need to leave."

His phone rang, and he practically assaulted it. "What, Harris?" he snapped. "Sure, why not? Send them up." He slammed the phone down. "Well, baby brother, you're in for a treat."

I had no idea what he meant. I was too fixated on the redhead as she glided over with a bottle of water. She must've been in his bedroom when I came up, which would explain his messy hair and bare chest.

If I weren't mistaken, she was none other than Mallory Gomez, Jade's best friend. Maybe they weren't BFFs anymore.

Taking the water, I opened my mouth to ask her when the elevator dinged.

Duke mumbled under his breath as he crossed the room. The redhead bounced alongside him, eager to see who was about to walk off the elevator.

I gulped down water only to spit it up when I laid eyes on Duke's guests.

**16**

---

## JADE

Mallory crushed my hand. I had no idea she was that strong. But I needed a little pain to ground me to my mission.

The elevator sped up to the twentieth floor to Duke Hart's penthouse at breakneck speed. With my free hand, I held my stomach. Nausea threatened to unleash its wrath at any moment. I did some quick breathing exercises to quell the nerves and hopefully the nausea.

"Are you sure you want to do this?" Mallory asked. "You just left the hospital an hour ago. You should rest."

I wasn't in the mood to rest. I was in the mood to tear off a head, decimate a man's balls, and make Duke Hart feel the pain I was feeling.

"I'm good." Those words came out surprisingly strong. I'd been a ball of tears and snot in Mallory's car.

"Then when those doors open, be strong. Say your piece and then leave and never look back at a Hart man ever again."

I didn't plan on it. No matter how badly I ached to be with Denim, nothing good could come of us. I couldn't be with a man who was related to the devil incarnate.

Duke Hart was the bane of my existence. I wasn't going to kill him. Death was too merciful for him. I had no idea what I would do, but maybe the mace in my hand would be a good start. Maybe when he felt the stinging and burning of the pepper filling his eyes, he would wake the fuck up. When he felt the blinding pain of having his balls skewered over an open fire, maybe he would realize he was a class A asshole.

The elevator stopped, and the doors opened with a *whoosh*.

Suddenly, breathing seemed like a monumental task. I inhaled and exhaled, blinking away the last of my tears, or at least I hoped that was the last of them.

I held my chin high. "Let's do this."

Mallory squeezed my hand for good measure.

When we stepped off the elevator, the air jetted from Mallory's lungs. "Cara?"

Mallory's sister clung to Duke, who was standing next to a pillar. His hair was messy, his chest and feet were bare, and he wore an expression that would scare a baby for sure.

Cara's light-red eyebrows hiked to her hairline as she snapped her spine straight. She always had a way of stealing one's thunder. Well, not that night. I didn't care why she had her hands all over Duke or why she was even there.

Hell, I didn't even care when Denim ambled closer, watching me with a steadfast intensity. "Did something happen?"

I held up my hand. "Don't come any closer." It was on the tip of my tongue to tell him he wasn't the brother I wanted right then. But it was best that I stick to my plan. Denim could change my mind with his disarming smile.

He stopped in his tracks. His blue eyes were glossy. He was either buzzed or high. He'd been known to drink and smoke weed prior to prison.

I let go of Mallory and charged up to the imposing human whose heart I envisioned driving a stake through. Inwardly, I laughed. I doubted any type of blade or sharp object would kill Duke Hart.

He didn't move as we stood toe-to-toe.

I craned my neck up. "You killed her," I said without a crack in my voice or a tear in my eye.

He didn't flinch. He didn't blink. The only sign he'd heard me was a muscle jumping along his jaw.

Cara's arms came at me, but Mallory, or maybe Denim, held her back.

Duke deadpanned as his empty brown eyes dropped to my hand.

*Fuck the mace.* I kneed him in the balls. "You killed her. You."

A whoosh of air gushed out of him as the blood rushed to his face. But he didn't drop to his knees or bend over or even cup his balls. He stood erect and stolid, not revealing his true pain.

Dropping the mace, I punched him in the gut, my knuckles meeting abs harder than stone. But no matter how bruised I would be, I would beat him until I bled.

Strong hands gripped the sides of my arms from behind. "Love." Denim's breath fanned my ear.

In that moment, I not only hated the word "love," I hated him. He represented everything bad in my life. I'd let him rule me, even if it was the memory of him and us. I couldn't keep hoping and wishing and praying. Somehow, I had to unlove him.

I hated myself and hated that I was sandwiched in between Duke and Denim. One was coldblooded, and the other had a heart. I wanted to kill one and kiss the other.

My heart went *boom, boom, boom* against my rib cage.

If Mallory was yelling or talking to her younger sister, I didn't hear her.

The only sound in my ears was Denim's breath until he said once more, "Love."

As though that word was the worst swear word in the universe, I spun around and pushed him. "Don't call me that. I am not your love. Not anymore. If you think you can waltz into my life like nothing happened, you're sorely mistaken. You and I will never be. Never, ever, ever."

He raised his hands and edged back, hurt washing over his handsome face.

I couldn't care. If I did, he would hurt me again, and the second time would be more devastating than the first. I had to take a play out of Duke's playbook. I had to be cold. I had to be numb. I had to walk away. It was the best course of action to protect my heart. I had to heal, and I couldn't do that in the presence of any Hart brother.

"Savannah is dead," I screamed. "She's dead because of men like you." Then I turned again and faced Duke. "You are a monster. You drove her to do evil things. Why didn't you see her in jail? Why didn't you take her calls? If you had, she might still be alive."

The man still didn't display any reaction except for that muscle in his jaw, which was moving wicked fast.

I was done blaming myself. Duke might not be the one who'd beaten her, but he'd had an invisible hand in the process leading up to her death.

I sucked in a long breath, and with all the strength I could muster, I punched him in the face.

That freaking hurt. The man was a stone wall.

"Are you going to say something?" I shouted in Duke's face as the tears started again, rolling out like a fast-moving river after a severe rainstorm.

The man only took in breath after breath. His lips were cemented shut.

It was time to go, to leave behind all the bad in my life, and to shed the evil that was the Hart brothers.

Cara stood next to Mallory with shock and awe on her freckled face.

"If you don't want to die," I said to Cara, "leave now and never look back."

Mallory took her sister's hand. "Come on, Cara."

"Sorry, sis. I'm not leaving. I love Duke."

Duke cringed. It seemed he hadn't known that and didn't like hearing she loved him.

Mallory moved her head back and forth. "No, you don't."

*Oh, the irony.* The tables had turned. I was watching Mallory pry her sister away from the very man who had been my sister's downfall.

While Mallory had pulled me out of the depths of hell after I'd reasoned and yelled at Savannah until I'd been blue in the face, I couldn't help my best friend in that moment. My feelings were too raw, and the wound was too deep for me to care about someone else. It was time for a fresh start. A new life. A new place. Maybe after I buried Savannah, I would find my aunt and join her in Africa. Or maybe I would find a cheap apartment on a beach somewhere warm.

Denim studied me, no doubt waiting for some cue from me that it was okay for him to come near me, touch me, or kiss me.

I wasn't giving in, no matter how much I longed for him to press his lips against mine and tell me he still loved me. I was beginning to realize love was fleeting to men like Denim. He would just sweep a girl off her feet, whisper sweet nothings, shower her with kisses, then kick her to the curb.

*Been there. Done that. Got the T-shirt. No more. No, thank you.*

I started for the elevators. My legs were trembling, my hand was bruised, and my heart had disintegrated into a million pieces. I could feel Denim's penetrating blue gaze on my back.

*Don't turn around. Don't give into him.*

I stabbed the button over and over and over, willing the door to open quickly.

"Cara, I swear if you don't come with me now, I'll make sure Mom and Dad cut you off," Mallory chided.

"I don't want their money," Cara said. "And you can't tell me what to do. Not anymore."

*Poor girl.*

"Everyone, out of my house," Duke grumbled in furious undertones.

"Even me?" Cara cried.

"Yes," Duke said. "Jade is right. I'm no good for you."

I tossed a look over my shoulder, scrunching my face. "The man finally speaks."

Sadness flashed in his eyes before he quickly banked it.

Cara rubbed her hands up Duke's chest. "You don't mean what you said."

He pried her hands off him. "Get out."

He was doing her a favor, even though she didn't know that yet. I wished he would've acted like that with Savannah years ago. Maybe then I wouldn't be mourning her death.

Cara sobbed. "I need to get my things."

"I'll have them sent to you." He glared at Cara. "And don't bother coming back either."

She hunched her shoulders, her bottom lip trembling.

Denim just watched his brother kick Cara to the curb, and I couldn't tell what he was feeling or thinking because his blue eyes were empty. *Typical of the Hart brothers.*

The elevator doors finally opened.

No one needed to tell me twice to leave.

**17**

---

# DENIM

The smell of bacon woke me, drifting into the room as I rolled over and stretched. I couldn't remember the last time I'd slept in a queen bed on a mattress that wasn't poking my back or on a pillow that wasn't flat. It was nice not having to listen to men snore, talk in their sleep, have sex, or jerk off in the dead of night.

I sighed, sinking into the comfy mattress as I soaked up the quiet. It was pure gold. Even the decor of bare walls and simple drapes was rich to me.

"Denim," a soft female voice said before she knocked. "It's Maggie. Can I come in?"

Pulling up the blankets to hide my morning wood, I cleared my throat. "Sure."

The door opened, revealing a curvy blonde with green eyes and a smile that could knock any man to his knees. I could see why my brother was smitten with Maggie. Dillon and I had both had hard-ons for her when we were teenagers, but she'd been off-limits. She'd run with a rival gang of ours, and their leader would've cut off our nuts if we'd even tried to woo her to our side.

She padded in and stood near the dresser, adjusting her scarf. "Dillon is cooking breakfast. I have to get to work but wanted to say welcome home. Maybe we can catch up tonight if I'm not late. I'm working on a big story."

"The last time you worked on a big story, you were kidnapped."

She rolled her eyes. "Comes with the job. But this one isn't as risky as the last one on human trafficking. I can't say much, but it involves gang violence."

Raising an eyebrow, I leaned against the headboard. "Gangs, huh? Like the McCauley gang?" Duke had been standing next to their leader in the picture Travers had shown me.

She tucked her hands into her jacket pockets. "Do you know them?" Intrigue weaved through her question.

I probably shouldn't say anything. Travers would have my head if I did, and I couldn't risk anyone finding out I was working with the FBI. Oh, wait. Duke already knew. "Just heard of them. They're more dangerous than the gang I ran with."

"Don't discredit the Creepers," she said. "Tito Alvarez is trying to make a name for himself. He's high on power and money and taking over the city."

I laughed. "What's he up to other than trying to put a bullet in my head?"

She frowned. "Dillon briefly mentioned that to me earlier. Watch your back. Tito is a scary dude. Anyway, he's trying to insert himself into the gun-trade market. Word on the street is he's done with selling drugs."

"Guns?" I couldn't help but think that maybe the FBI had their wires crossed. Maybe Tito should be their target rather than Duke.

"It's a big business," she said. "Boston PD's gang unit can't keep up with the guns coming in and the gang wars going on. But the Feds are now involved because of the large shipments coming in from Europe and South America."

At least the FBI wasn't blowing smoke up my ass. "Where does Duke fit into any of this, or does he?"

Her shoulders tensed. "He's mixed up in something. I just don't know what yet or why he is. Again, welcome home. I got to run."

I didn't get the sense she knew much more than that, although she was close to the cop who'd arrested me for murder. According to Dillon, Officer Ted Hughes was now Detective Ted Hughes, and he was head of the gang unit for the BPD. "Thanks for letting me crash here."

"It's your brother's house. Besides, you're family."

The word "family" sounded odd to me. For so long, my family had been the gangs I'd run with on the streets I'd called home. "Oh, and congrats on saying yes to my brother. I'm happy for you guys."

She blushed. "Thanks. You'll find that special someone one day."

I lowered my gaze to the bed. "I doubt that."

"Jade doesn't want anything to do with you, huh?" she asked.

"You know about Jade? Of course you do. Dillon." When I'd gotten home the night before, Dillon had been waiting up for me. I'd filled him in on every detail since he'd dropped me off at Jade's office building, including getting shot at, the FBI, Savannah, my encounter with our brother, and Jade.

She'd been very clear the night before. She wanted nothing to do with me. I knew now how she had felt when I broke up with her—gutted, hurt, and angry—and I didn't like it one bit.

"Dillon didn't tell me everything."

"It's okay. Nothing really to tell anyway."

Maggie knitted her pretty eyebrows. "You're not giving up?"

I chuckled. "That's a big, fat no. I just need her to make the first move."

"The only way she's going to do that is if you give her some signs."

I had a major fucking sign in my boxer briefs. But I knew what she meant.

The topic of my love life went by the wayside when a voice I hadn't heard in years trickled into the room, and my heart sputtered.

"Where is he?" my sister, Grace, asked.

Maggie smiled. "Someone has been dying to see you."

Footsteps pounded on the stairs, and a tornado came whirling into my room and threw herself on the bed before she wrapped her arms around me. "Denim," Grace squealed.

*Oh my God.*

I hugged her tightly. "Grace? Is that really you?"

The last time I'd seen my baby sister was just before she'd disappeared at sixteen. She'd been swept up in a human-trafficking ring only to escape. Thank God Dillon had been able to take down her kidnappers. Or rather Grace, some ex-military dude that Grace knew, Dillon, Duke, and Maggie had taken down her kidnappers.

Hell, it took Maggie getting snagged by the same people before justice had been served. Our lives weren't the average big house, pristine lawn, and white picket fences. No, the Harts rivaled the Gallagher family from the show *Shameless*. We were highly dysfunctional for sure. We had an alcoholic father, a nowhere-to-be-found mother, drugs, jail, crime, and each of us were just trying to find one spec of happiness wherever we could.

"See you guys later," Maggie said. "Oh, and Denim, don't go anywhere near Tito. He's more lethal than you remember."

Tito's name didn't belong in our conversation at the moment.

Grace tightened her hold on me before she edged back. "I heard he's trying to kill you. Need a bodyguard?"

I raised an eyebrow. "Bodyguard? Who? You?"

She sat on her heels. "I'm tougher than you think."

The last thing I wanted was for her to get involved in my shit. "Let me look at you."

She preened. Her smile warmed my heart. Gone was her baby fat, the acne, and the innocence.

"How old are you now, baby sister?"

She was all woman for sure with curves, toned biceps, brown hair spilling down to her shoulders, and a tattoo of a colorful hummingbird on her neck.

"Can you believe I'm twenty-two?"

*Fuck no.* In my mind, she was still the little runt who'd bounced on my bed at five in the mornings, trying to get me up to fix her breakfast.

I took her hand. "You're beautiful, and you seem happy." Fuck, I prayed she was after being sold to some fucker who'd abused her.

"I am. I have good days and bad. And today is a great day. I've missed you. I'm sorry I didn't come to visit you."

"No worries. Prison sucks, and after what you've been through, you didn't need to see the lowlifes I lived with. On another note, I'm so fucking sorry I wasn't there for you." I kissed the back of her hand.

"No need to apologize. All of us had our own shit to deal with back then, especially Dad."

"Dare I ask about him?" Frankly, I hadn't thought too much about him. Dillon had told me once our old man was trying to get sober.

"He's still drinking. I've only seen him a handful of times, and only because I wanted to get some of my things."

I had no desire to reunite with him, and I didn't want to ruin the day reminiscing about nightmares and asshole fathers. "So, tell me what you're up to."

"Later. We should eat before the big, bad brother starts yelling." She giggled. "Dillon's an army sergeant when he cooks."

"I need to get a quick shower, then."

She touched my hair. "I'm digging the long, badass vibe. Jade must love it."

I threw up my hands. "Does everyone know about Jade?"

She pushed out a shoulder. "We're family. We talk."

I was living in an alternate universe. In what era did the word "family" come into our vocabulary?

The smell of bacon drifted in again. My sister was happy and bubbly and ready to fight my battles, a stark contrast to what I remembered. I was in a room that felt like heaven, with fluffy pillows, a cushy mattress, and a bathroom. If I didn't know I was at Dillon's house, I would've assumed I was at a hotel.

She batted her big brown eyes. "Hurry up. You know how Dillon likes to eat all the bacon."

On that note, my stomach growled. I'd only gotten a chance to eat a measly sandwich after returning from Duke's the night before.

She bounced to the door like she was a teenager again. "I think we should take you shopping to get you some new clothes. Maybe a haircut too."

I laughed loudly. "Shopping, huh? Why not? Haircut, no way."

After the previous day, I could use a day—or hell, a year or more—

to relax and shed six years of that disgusting prison from my skin and out of my veins. Still, I wanted nothing more than to enjoy a day with my sister.

Thirty minutes later, after a hot shower in which the water didn't run cold after two minutes, a good, solid shave, and clean clothes that Dillon had lent me, I was walking into a modest kitchen. It was small, warm, bright, and lived in, unlike Duke's cold atmosphere.

Dillon was reading on his phone at the table by the window. The morning sun sprayed in through the slats in the blinds, and some disk-like contraption moved along the edge of the tiled floor.

"What's that?" I asked. I suspected it was a vacuum, which was odd to me.

"Welcome to the new age of housecleaning," Dillon said, not looking up from his phone.

I got myself a cup of coffee then joined him. Plates of bacon, eggs, and toast were scattered about the picnic-style table.

I plucked a strip of bacon. "Where's Grace?" I hadn't taken that long in the shower.

He set his phone down. "One of my employees called in sick. I asked Grace if she could fill in."

"Darn. No shopping?" It wasn't the shopping I'd anticipated—I just wanted to spend time with my baby sister.

He chuckled. "Is that how you want to spend your second day of freedom?"

"I would shovel shit to hang with her. I feel like I owe her too. I was a terrible brother." I'd never been home to protect her from our old man. If I had been, maybe she wouldn't have taken off, and then she wouldn't have ended up in a sex-trafficking ring.

Dillon made himself a plate. "We all were.

I followed suit. I was famished.

"I think it's best if you stay in today," Dillon said. "Tito might try again."

I shoveled eggs into my mouth. "About Tito, I'm going to head down to see him."

Dillon dropped his fork. "Do you have a death wish?"

"I want to know why he has a contract on my head. Best way to get answers is to confront him."

"You killed his brother, or allegedly anyway."

"Then why wait six years to try and take his revenge? Call me crazy, but I think Duke fits into the scheme somewhere."

Dillon buttered his toast. "Are you saying Duke wants you dead?"

"I'm saying my release from prison has the real killer nervous, and I'm going to get to the bottom of who set me up."

"You're not going to rest until you get answers. Are you?"

"Would you?" I asked through a mouthful of food. "The Harts might be assholes, but we're persistent fucks who will do whatever it takes to get answers. Isn't that what you did to find Grace? You didn't give up. I'm not either." I swallowed a swig of coffee. "This is my life, bro. I'm not going to have a murder charge on my record. Now that I'm out, I can take matters into my own hands."

"Not by walking into the lion's den."

"Sometimes that's the only way to uncover the truth." Although I didn't expect Tito to tell me squat. But I knew his mannerisms. I might be able to read between the lines.

Dillon rose. "Then I'm going with."

"No, you're not. I don't want you involved. You got your shit together. You don't need the hassle of whatever is about to happen."

He laughed, dumping his cup into the sink. "Sorry, bro. Too late. I'm already involved. I have my head of security at the shelter checking on Tito's whereabouts. I've got your back."

A lump formed in my throat. Hardly any of my family stuck up for me except Dillon. He'd been gone for a couple of years in the merchant marines, but ever since he'd returned, he had been visiting me in jail.

I swallowed a mouthful of eggs. "I'm assuming Tito lives in the same neighborhood as he always has."

"He's not. Rafe checked."

If I wasn't feeling loved before, I was now. "You're one step ahead of me."

"I know you, bro. Like you said, we're persistent fucks."

We both laughed.

I finished filling my stomach. "I need to tell Kelton about my encounter with the Feds." I also needed to see if Travers had sent the contract over to Kelton. I doubted the Feds worked that quickly since it had only been twelve hours or so since they whisked me away from the hospital.

Dillon returned to the table. "Do that." He slid the cell phone over to me. "This is yours. You'll need a way to communicate." He pulled out his wallet and produced a credit card and cash. "I added your name to one of my personal bank accounts. You only have a small amount to play with, but take the rest of the day and buy some clothes. Use the cash for whatever. We probably won't hear from Rafe until later this afternoon anyway. Then we'll need a game plan."

My mouth parted as my eyes went wide. "You don't have to do all this."

"I know," he said. "I have a small stash of cash I've made from the stock market, and you're family."

In that moment, the word "family" had a little more meaning to me. "I owe you big time, bro."

"The only thing you owe me is to not go off half-cocked to Tito until I hear from Rafe. Cool?"

That lump in my throat grew bigger, and all I could do was nod.

"Good. I need to use the head."

He left me dazed. I felt warm and fuzzy, which was odd. *Definitely new emotions for me.*

As my mind sliced and diced the events of the morning since I'd opened my eyes, I got stuck on something Maggie had said about Jade. *"Give her some signs."*

I knew the perfect sign.

18

## JADE

Mallory and I left the coffee shop that Denim and I had visited the day before. We'd taken an early lunch. Kelton wasn't due in until noon, and Mallory's boss was in court most of the day.

We strolled back to the office amid businesspeople hailing cabs, window-shoppers lingering to admire the latest fashion, and buses picking up passengers on each corner block. I'd been tempted to walk two blocks in the opposite direction just to see if any cops were still hanging around after the prior day's shooting. But it wouldn't matter. It was too depressing to think about anyway, and I didn't need more grief to pull me down.

The cool fall air was a welcome relief. I'd been sweating for the last few hours. I didn't have a fever, but I felt worn down and spent from crying most of the night. I couldn't shake the image of Savannah laid out in that hospital bed, not breathing.

Mallory closed the top of her coat. "You shouldn't be working today."

"I told you for the tenth time, I need to keep my mind occupied."

I'd stayed at her place, not wanting to be alone. She hadn't either. Mallory had been beside herself after seeing Cara cozied up to Duke. She and Cara hadn't talked much lately. Cara was in college, and

Mallory worked long hours. The only time they did see each other was at a family gathering.

"Have you heard from Cara?" I asked.

"She won't return my calls," Mallory said.

I couldn't blame Cara. I knew firsthand how getting dumped felt—like a punch so hard to the stomach, I couldn't breathe. Denim hadn't been mean like Duke, but a breakup was a breakup.

I hiked my purse higher on my shoulder. "I want to tell Kelton what happened to Savannah and understand what happens next. I want to know if the person who beat her will be charged with her murder." I wasn't sure how the system worked. But I wanted whoever had beaten Savannah to pay.

Wisps of Mallory's auburn hair ruffled in the light wind. "For sure. Maybe we can somehow fit Duke into that scenario." Derision laced her tone.

"You know, what we need is a night out dancing. We haven't been in a long time, and I really need an escape."

Mallory and I had frequented many clubs in our early twenties. It was one of the ways to blow off steam and forget our troubles.

"I don't know," she said. "I should check on Cara, and you should get some rest."

"You can still check on Cara after work. Clubs don't get hopping until later tonight anyway. Let's at least go for a drink." The last thing I wanted to do was be alone in my grungy apartment. I had to stay busy. "Besides, I don't think Duke will take Cara back. Savannah told me once Duke makes a decision, he always sticks to his guns." I hoped I was making her feel better.

My phone rang as we entered the busy lobby of our office building. A crowd was leaving for lunch since it was noon. I plucked my phone out of my jacket pocket and saw Todd's name on the screen.

Mallory glanced down. "Who's Todd?"

*Oh my.* I'd forgotten about him. We'd agreed to chat that day. I lifted my finger to Mallory, signaling for her to wait a second. "Hey, Todd."

"Hey, yourself." He sounded nasally. "Want to get drinks after work?"

"It's not a good day." My heart wasn't into seeing any man at that moment.

The line grew silent as Mallory stabbed the button to the elevator.

"Too bad," Todd said. "I was going to offer to take you to a new club in the city."

"New club?" I prodded Mallory with my eyes. Then something hit me. Todd was more her type, and she wasn't dating anyone. I wasn't a matchmaker, but I could let things fall where they may. "Is there dancing involved?" Not waiting for him to answer, I continued. "Tell you what—text me the name and address of the club. My girlfriend and I might meet you there."

"Cool. I've got to run. Hope to see you tonight." Then Todd hung up.

On the ride up to our office, Mallory said, "You don't need me to tag along. Go and have a good time."

"Oh, no. We're going out, and we're going to take our mind off our troubles." If I had to spend one more moment in my depressing apartment, I would shoot myself. I couldn't let my mind wander either. Otherwise, I would be one big ball of snot.

Mallory crammed herself into a corner of the elevator while others piled in.

I pushed my shoulder into hers. "You might like Todd." I kept my voice low. "He's your type." She liked dark-haired men over blonds and gingers.

"I guess I need to shake off seeing Cara with Duke. It's just been too... I don't know. I saw how he treated Savannah and how she changed because of him."

I hooked my arm in hers. "She won't. Cara's in college. She's not the rebellious type like Savannah. More importantly, Cara isn't going to rob a store or do drugs or any of the other wild and crazy things Savannah did. She's hurt, Mal. She'll be okay." *As long as Duke doesn't take her back.*

"Says the girl who still has a thing for the guy who broke her heart years ago." Mallory's tone was light, but doubt hung in her words.

I was ready to tell her I was over Denim when the elevator doors whooshed open. It was as if they were signaling me to keep my mouth shut. *You will only stick your foot in your mouth. You and Denim are not over.*

Mallory's heels clicked as she left the elevator. "Jade."

"I'm coming." I followed her onto our floor.

Dina lifted her head. "Mallory, your boss is looking for you. He sounds like he's in a bad mood too."

"Oh crap. I thought he was in court all day." Mallory took off like the Flash.

I pressed my hands on the edge of the glass top of Dina's desk. "Is Kelton in yet?"

Her brown eyes lit up. "He is, and he's with some hot new client."

"Please tell me he has brown hair and not blond." I held my breath. The last person I wanted to see was Denim. Maybe I needed to rethink my strategy or employment.

Dina let out a dreamy sigh. "Blond hair down to here." She touched her neck between her collarbone and her ear. "Blue eyes the color of his name, Denim. What a cool name, huh?"

I'd always thought the same thing. According to Denim, his parents had been ready to name him Richard until he came out of the womb with eyes the color of faded blue jeans. His mom was spot-on too.

Dina snapped her fingers. "Jade, are you in there?"

I blinked. "Sorry. I need to get to my desk." Or maybe I could make up some excuse to leave until Denim was gone.

*You can't. Be strong, professional, and cordial. Show him you're not interested in him anymore.* The latter wasn't true. But a relationship with Denim would only end in heartbreak and a river of tears.

Kelton's door was ajar as I set my purse on my chair and blew out a breath.

*I can do this.*

The *tap, tap, tap* of legal assistants banging on their keyboards kept time with my pulse.

Mallory's voice trickled out of the office next to Kelton's. "I can do that. Sir, do you mind if I leave at the normal time today?"

I was intent on hearing her boss's answer until Denim's husky laugh filtered out of Kelton's office. Tingles broke out on my skin, and I was officially, utterly, and royally screwed.

"Seriously, Denim." Kelton was all business. "The Feds have no cause to send you back to prison if you don't cooperate. They may have sped up the parole board's decision, but your prison record is clean for the early release program."

"Dude, the government can do anything. If they can make a murder charge go away, then they can fabricate shit to put my ass back in jail."

Kelton sighed as though he were one second away from shouting at Denim. "I thought you wanted to clear your name."

"Do you know who killed Alvarez?" Anger simmered in Denim's tone. "Even if we did find the neighbor or the person who actually shot Hector, would they willingly speak up or confess?"

"I'll take a look at the offer, but that's as far as it will go. You don't need to sign anything. I'll talk to the Feds as well. Now tell me how things went with Duke."

After walking into Duke's apartment the night before, I could guess that Denim and Duke's reunion hadn't gone well. Or maybe Denim had been dismayed to see me at Duke's or horrified to know that Savannah had died. In a way, I was glad Denim hadn't waited for me at the hospital. He probably would've convinced me not to go to Duke's, and I had no doubt I would've given in. Well, maybe not. I had been beyond angry when I'd left Savannah's room.

I was intent on eavesdropping, but Dina's voice interrupted my trip down memory lane. "These came for you."

I jumped a mile, holding back a squeal. The last thing I wanted was for Kelton to find out I was a nosy nellie. Inhaling, I turned to face Dina.

"Sorry. I didn't mean to startle you." She set a vase of orchids on my desk. "Someone loves you."

I scrunched my face as the sweet floral aroma wafted over me.

Dina touched my arm, showcasing her blue-painted fingernails. "Did you hear me?"

Ever so slightly, I bobbed my head, trying to muddle through who would send me orchids. I knew it wasn't Mallory. For one, she knew what that type of flower meant to me. And two, I'd been with her the whole time. "Thank you."

She studied me for a second. "You look pale."

I was certain I'd seen a ghost. "I think I'm coming down with something." That wasn't a total lie. I didn't feel as heated as I had when Mallory and I had left the coffee shop, but my sinuses were throbbing. I also didn't want to tell Dina about Savannah, at least not until I told Kelton.

Dina edged back. "Well, go home if you're sick. I better get back." She hurried away as though I were contagious.

I opened the card attached to the vase. I blinked once, then twice, as I read each word.

*I know you love orchids, and I hope these flowers bring you a moment of happiness and put a smile on your beautiful face. I'm so sorry for your loss. Xoxo, Denim.*

My knees were wobbly as I eased down into my chair, clutching my chest as though I were having a heart attack. Maybe I was.

After all these years, the man remembered. He remembered that I'd told him how my dad had showered my mom with orchids on their wedding anniversary. He remembered that I, too, would rather have orchids than roses.

I heard Denim and Kelton's voices getting louder, but I was in too much shock to listen.

"Jade," Kelton said. "Is everything okay?"

I shuddered, swallowed my tears, and blinked a few times before I lifted my head.

Kelton and Denim were standing at my desk. The two tall men, about the same height, stared at me with their penetrating blue eyes. Whereas Kelton's were a deep blue, Denim's were a medium shade lighter.

Denim grinned. His smile was sexy and downright heart-ramming when we locked eyes.

"Who sent flowers?" Kelton asked.

I glanced at the card. "They're from a friend." I didn't know if I should out Denim, although Kelton knew about our past relationship.

Kelton tucked a hand into his pants pocket. "Any special occasion?"

I inhaled a quiet breath then told Kelton about my sister.

Kelton tipped his head toward his office. "Let's talk in my office. Denim, we'll be in touch."

"Sure thing," Denim said. "Jade, can I speak to you alone for a minute?"

"I have work to do." I hoped I didn't sound curt. Kelton was all about professionalism, and Denim was a client.

"I need to grab some coffee," Kelton said. "I'll give you a minute, Jade." He wound his way around cubicles until he was gone.

*Traitor.* Yet he didn't know about the war raging in my head over Denim or about the one in my heart.

"Thank you," I whispered to Denim.

He leaned his butt against the edge of my desk, his thigh almost touching my arm. "I'm really sorry about Savannah."

I scooted my chair away from his thigh, which was giving off heat. At least I felt extremely warm.

"You remembered I liked orchids." I couldn't look at him. If I did, I would jump in his arms, ravish his lips, and kiss him until the end of our days.

I sounded like a lovestruck teenager. *Pathetic.* I was supposed to be mad at Denim. I was supposed to be cold and uncaring. I was supposed to walk away. Yet there I was envisioning how his lips would feel on mine—soft, tingly, and mouthwatering.

His gaze slid over me like warm butter. "I remember a lot of things about us."

Butterflies took flight in my stomach as I shivered in delight. I was screwed, but I wanted him to tell me more. I wanted him to tell me every memory he had of us, good or bad. Maybe then he could feel my pain. "What else?"

His tongue darted out to lick his lips, slow and subtle. But that small movement held so much power that heat shot south and settled in my core.

"Can I call you later to check on you?" he asked.

"Not a good idea, Denim."

He frowned. "Give me a chance."

Kelton returned. "Are you ready, Jade?" Then he went into his office.

Sighing, I grabbed my notebook and a pen. "Sorry, Denim."

He leaned in and kissed me on the cheek. "I'm staying at Dillon's if you change your mind or if you just want to talk."

My heart punched my sternum hard as my cheeks flamed. The man was making it hard for me, especially with his puppy-dog eyes.

*Damn him.*

He stabbed a thumb behind him. "I'll see you around."

I guessed he would. After all, he was a client, which meant Denim wasn't going away. Good, bad, or indifferent, I needed to focus on my job and getting justice for Savannah's death.

**19**

———

# DENIM

Dillon and I waited behind a long line of partygoers to get into The Monarch, Duke's brand-spanking-new club that he'd just added to his growing portfolio. According to Dillon, Duke owned a total of three clubs around the city.

The line of mainly women wrapped around the warehouse-style building, and a line of cars wheeled in slowly, searching for a parking spot.

"A meat market, if you ask me," I said to Dillon.

"If this is like Duke's other clubs, you'll see why the place is crawling with eager and hungry women."

I couldn't imagine what he meant. The clubs I'd been in had a DJ, strobe lights, a bar, and strung-out people throwing themselves at each other on the dance floor.

"Do tell."

"Nah," Dillon said. "It's better to see."

*Whatever.* I wasn't there to dance or get drunk or pick up a woman. Duke was my target. Dillon had suggested we pay our brother a visit at his new club since Duke had all but said he never wanted to see me again.

I couldn't say that didn't stab me in the gut because it did. But I wasn't backing down, and Dillon wanted to clear the air among the three of us. Dillon was pissed at how Duke had treated me.

"You know, I can handle my own battles with Duke," I said. "We don't need to be here." Frankly, I didn't even want to go in. It was best if I let things settle for the moment between Duke and me. After all, Kelton had my back with the Feds, so it wasn't like I had to be at Travers's beck and call. He was going to be pissed, though.

Kelton had said the only way I was working for Travers was if I wanted to, but I just wanted to find the fucker who'd set me up, not jump through hoops to throw my brother in prison.

"Yes, we do," Dillon said. "He's going to tell you why he didn't visit you in prison. He's going to sit down and have a drink with us and build that brotherly bond. If he's coming to my wedding, then I want the three of us to be cordial at least."

I couldn't argue with that. "So you're going to invite him?"

"Look, man. Duke is a mess. When he helped me find Maggie after she was kidnapped, I could tell he was struggling with something. I told you that. I'm tired of it. Now that you're out, we need to have his back too."

I didn't disagree. Savannah's death had affected him. I'd seen the sadness in his eyes when Jade had unleashed her wrath on him. Still, it would take more than a few words or drinks to get through to Duke Hart. "Why are we waiting in line? Let's just tell the bouncer we're related to the owner."

Dillon chuckled. "He wouldn't believe us. Every girl in front of us is probably playing that angle. We're almost there. Were the flowers a hit with Jade?"

"I'm pretty sure she doesn't want anything to do with me." I was getting the feeling that no one did other than Dillon and Grace. But I wasn't about to feel sorry for myself. I would show her I still loved her, although a persistent voice in my head said I should walk away from Jade until the danger surrounding me was gone.

I wasn't sure it would ever go away, though. I was related to one of the top criminals in the city if the Feds were right, and that had to bring danger. If Duke's enemies wanted to infiltrate his organization or hurt him where it counted, then his family members could suffer.

Dillon swatted me on my arm. "Did you hear me?"

I threaded my hands through my hair. "No."

"I just got a text from Rafe."

Thoughts of Jade vanished as my ears perked up. I'd been asking Dillon nonstop if he'd heard from his man about Tito's whereabouts.

Dillon brushed a hand over his unshaven jaw, a move he made when he was unsure of something. "Rumor is Tito will be here tonight."

My eyebrows had to be in my hairline. "For real? At Duke's new club?"

I watched as Dillon texted Rafe: *Are you sure?*

Rafe: *My contact is always spot-on.*

I hopped out of line. The night just got more interesting, and I wasn't waiting any longer to get into the club. *Screw Duke.* Tito was my target now.

Dillon caught my arm, hardening his jaw. "What are you doing?"

"I'm going in whether the bouncer lets me in or not. Tito could be in there."

Dillon scanned the area with mechanical precision.

I did the same but only because the Feds came to mind. I was sure Travers or his men were skulking nearby, watching Duke, following me, or maybe scoping out Tito.

"You know, bro. You should get out of here," I said. "Things could get ugly."

"Fuck you," Dillon barked. "I told you—I've got your back. I'm not going anywhere."

I got in his face. "Think about your upcoming marriage, your girl, your shelter, your fucking future. You don't need the hassle." *You don't need to die because of me.*

"Still not leaving." Dillon started toward the bouncer, who reminded me of Stew. He had the physique of a wrestler; large, bulky biceps; a broad chest; and a small head.

Dillon ponied up to the rope with his ID, ready to shove it in the beefy man's face.

The bouncer narrowed his dark, beady eyes at Dillon. "Get in line."

I pulled out my ID too. Maybe if the man saw the Hart name, he wouldn't give us any flack.

He held up his hand to three women, gesturing to them to wait. My guess was they were sixteen or younger, brandishing fake IDs.

*Note to self: Stay away from any ladies inside.* The last thing I needed was to spark up a conversation with an underage girl. With my luck, my ass would be carted off to prison once again.

The bouncer pointed his penlight at Dillon's ID then mine, studying them as though he were confused.

"Let us in," I said.

"Sorry, dude. I have orders not to let you in tonight."

Dillon and I exchanged a surprised look. My brother's eyes were bulging out of their sockets.

The women whined, and one of them cried, "Come on. We're wasting precious time."

Dillon tried to climb over the rope. "Fuck this. I'm going in."

The bouncer blocked Dillon. "I don't think so."

Dillon shrugged at me. "I guess if we're going to get kicked out, we might as well go out in Hart-style fashion." That meant throwing punches and causing a commotion.

As big as the dude was, he couldn't take both of us at the same time.

The people in line aimed their phones in our direction.

Dillon's face lit up. "I'm ready to bash some heads in. It's been a while."

I couldn't blame him. I was tired of getting the word "no" thrown in my face. I was equally exasperated with Duke and his stone-cold, high-and-mighty "I'm in charge and still your older brother" attitude. Regardless, I didn't need a commotion. Tito might run, and Duke could call the cops on us.

I latched on to Dillon's arm. "Wait, bro. I have an idea."

Dillon did a double take, practically frowning. "This better be good, man."

The bouncer even lifted his dark eyebrows.

"Do you want me to call the cops to let them know you're letting in underage women?" I flicked my head to the three teenyboppers who had on two-inch-thick makeup to make them look older. "I'm sure the Feds who are watching us right now would storm the club." Travers would probably jump at the chance to take Duke downtown for questioning and the chance to scare him into talking.

The bouncer scanned the lot.

*Smart man.*

"Good one, bro," Dillon said with a scowl.

The three women started to protest.

"Sorry, ladies," the bouncer said before he turned back to Dillon and me. "If I lose my job, I'm hunting you guys down." He unlatched the rope and allowed us to walk through.

I ignored his threat, as did Dillon. He didn't scare me. Besides, I had bigger threats to worry about.

After Dillon and I each paid the thirty-dollar entrance fee, we entered into another dimension. Men with G-strings danced in cages hanging from the high vaulted ceiling. Others carried trays of drinks to partygoers, and some of them knocked back Jell-O shots with their customers, who were mostly women. I imagined some of the men swinging their hips on the packed dance floor batted for the other team. Some of my brethren in prison would get off on this club for sure.

"See?" Dillon shouted over the punk-rock music. "Not your typical club."

I was about to tell him that it wasn't as elaborate as I'd imagined, but I tossed out that comment when I saw Jade at the bar. Or maybe my eyes were deceiving me. Maybe the woman with black hair spilling down over her low-cut blouse was Jade's doppelgänger.

I slapped Dillon's shoulder. "Bar. Jade is here."

He whipped his head at the L-shaped bar that lined two sides of the club.

I pushed through the throng of stoners, drunks, and sweaty bodies.

One waiter stopped to let a young blonde stroke his hard-on.

*What the fuck is Jade doing here?*

Dillon gripped my shoulder. "Right behind you."

"Look for Tito," I tossed out. "He might be up on those couches on the second floor or at the bar up there."

As large as the space was on the first floor, the second floor was equally as big. The only difference was that I noticed more men above with women walking around either topless or in bikinis.

"Look up at the glass room," Dillon said in my ear.

I stopped near a high bar table along the wall and craned my neck up.

Duke stood behind the glass, dressed in a tailored suit, looking like he was the head of a mafia organization. Suddenly, I was back in prison. The guards there had the same stance as they observed the cellblock.

Man, my mind was a jumbled pile of shit. I had business with Duke, and I had to find Tito, but every fiber in me screamed to get Jade out of the club. If Tito was there, she could be in danger.

I continued on, shoving and pushing across the football-field-sized room. As soon as I cleared a group of teenagers, I skidded to a halt, and Dillon plowed into me.

Jade flipped her silky black hair behind her, exposing a bare shoulder, as she flirted with that dude I'd seen her with at her office building.

Jealousy trampled me, punching me right in the gut.

Jade giggled then swayed. The dude caught her.

*Fuck.* She was drunk.

The dude dragged a finger down her bare shoulder when he should've been lifting her blouse to cover her skin. I understood that the style of her top was one that slid off one shoulder to create a sexy look, and she was fucking sexy, but every guy in the club was probably eyeing her.

I growled, and if it weren't for the loud music, the whole club would've heard me.

"Who's the dude?" Dillon asked.

"Dead," I said.

Jade continued to give the guy her undivided attention, giggling, drinking, and swaying her hips.

I couldn't blame the guy. Jade was every man's dream. Her green eyes alone sucked a man in, cocooning him in her seductive bubble.

"If Tito is here, we need—"

I held up my hand. "I know."

"I'm going to see Duke," Dillon said. "You get Jade and Mallory out of here."

I hadn't noticed Mallory until that moment. She was chatting up a bald guy, and she also appeared to have had one too many drinks.

Jade giggled again at the well-dressed fucker as her gaze floated over him and plowed into me. I swore I faltered where I stood, which was about ten feet from her.

She lost her smile.

*Well, stab me in the heart, why don't you.*

She whispered in the guy's ear before she skirted around a group of teenage boys who sized her up like she was a piece of meat.

The dude tried to stop Jade.

I growled again, mainly at the high schoolers. I was ready to bash in their heads until Jade wagged her finger at me. Instantly, they paled and turned their attention to the dance floor.

"Seriously? Are you following me?" She mashed her red-painted lips into a thin line. I wasn't sure how I heard sultriness in her tone when she was outright angry.

I leaned in. "Lose the feistiness, or I'm going to take you into a restroom and fuck your brains out." My dick was doing the talking for sure. But every time she scolded me, I got hard.

She made a sound I couldn't quite hear over the music and voices, but when she flattened a hand on my chest, her head shot up, and behind the glossiness was pure shock. "Don't say things like that unless you mean it." She pushed her breasts into me.

"You're drunk and grieving. We should leave."

"I'm not going anywhere, certainly not with you."

I traced a line down her neck, shoulder, and arm. Goose bumps erupted on her skin.

The music changed to a slow song, and she started swaying her body.

Yep, she was drunk. My first thought was to throw her over my shoulder and carry her out. That wouldn't go over well, particularly if I was trying to get her back. But she would be safe.

I wrapped my arm around Jade's waist, seating my hand on her lower back. "Jade, please think about leaving." Sugar usually worked over salt, and I didn't want to mention Tito. If we made a commotion, we would draw attention to ourselves.

She pressed her body against mine.

I briefly closed my eyes. I could get so lost in the moment, in her. But I couldn't take advantage of her. I wasn't that type of guy. Although I wasn't beyond losing my load in my jeans. I didn't need to fuck her to get off.

Her hands snaked up my chest. "Tell me the truth."

She was spinning a web around us, and I was about to strip her right there and suck her pussy. It wouldn't be out of the norm considering the way partygoers were fondling the waiters.

"You can't handle the truth," I said in her ear.

She shivered, mashing her body flush against mine. "I can."

"You won't remember." I wanted her coherent when I told her my truth. "Instead you tell me the truth. Are you with that guy?"

She batted those ball-squeezing green eyes over her shoulder. "He's a friend."

I eyed the dark-haired dude, who was watching us intently. "Does he know that?"

"Denim." My name rolling off her sweet tongue was pure sugar, and if it was possible, my dick grew even harder.

I nipped at her ear before I licked at the sensitive spot just below her earlobe. "Angel." I wanted to ask her why she hated for me to call her love but didn't want to ruin the moment. "You don't know what I want to do to you."

She subtly rocked her hips into me. "You want to fuck me." She giggled. "You feel so good. Maybe I want to fuck you."

I grabbed her ass and pressed her hips into my groin, needing friction, lots of it. Then I buried my nose in her hair. "Jade, don't tease. I just got out of prison, and I'll fuck you right here in front of everyone."

She snickered.

I slipped her hand between us, guiding her to take hold of my dick.

She lifted up on her toes. "I always loved your dick, and I want it inside me."

I groaned, thinking of taking her into the bathroom. But as horny as I was, she deserved better, and she deserved to be one-hundred-percent sober. Because when I finally did fuck her, I wanted her to remember every moment, every lick, every thrust, and every kiss I peppered on her gorgeous body.

She swayed in my arms, and it took all my willpower to back away, but I needed to act fast. If Tito was hiding in the club and I was his target, then she was in danger. That was *if* he knew I was there.

"Can I entice you to at least accompany me to Duke's office?" I asked. Duke's office would be safe until we could ensure Tito wasn't there, unless Duke was meeting with Tito.

She tensed. Maybe I shocked her into sobriety. "Duke?"

"This is Duke's new club."

"I'm out of here, then." Her tone was clear and concise.

I sighed, relieved that Duke's name was the key to get her to safety.

Mallory broke free from the guy she was talking to and came over, eyeing me with disgust as if I'd just hurt Jade.

Fuck her. Sure, I'd broken Jade's heart once. I wasn't about to do it again.

But Jade and Mallory blurred when a shot rang out. Glass and liquor bottles behind the bar shattered.

People dropped to the floor or ran for the exits.

Mallory screamed, "Jade!"

Before I could track what was happening, Jade fell to the floor.

**20**

———————

# DENIM

I ripped off my shirt and pressed it to Jade's chest.

She winced, laboring for breath, as tears dropped down her pretty face. "It hurts."

I wasn't a religious man by any means, but I started praying to anyone who would listen. My worst nightmare was playing out before me. The reason I didn't get involved with a woman was because of my enemies. The reason I'd said goodbye to Jade in high school was because of my enemies.

I'd witnessed firsthand how Hector had changed after his number one enemy killed his girl. The hate and revenge had driven him and those close to him crazy, including me.

I gritted my teeth, not only because I wanted to kill whoever had put a bullet in Jade, but to prevent me from losing my shit. I had to be strong for her. I had to show her confidence. I had to show her the wound wasn't that bad even though it was probably life-threatening.

She gasped for air.

The screams and voices in the room dulled as I tuned out everything. I had to focus on what to do next.

*Think, man.*

Dillon! He had some CPR and medical experience from the merchant marines. But Jade needed a doctor.

Mallory crawled over. I had no idea where she'd gone. "Oh my God! What can I do?"

Jade tried to speak as her chest heaved. "Den—"

"Shhh, baby."

"We need to get her to a hospital," Mallory said.

I didn't see that happening anytime soon as I scoured the three exits. There was one on each side of the bar in addition to the main entrance. All were jammed with frantic people pushing and shoving to get out. I did another quick scan to see if I could spot the shooter, but my search came up empty.

The dude from Jade's office building came out of nowhere and sucked in a breath. "I'll go get help."

"Wait," I said to the guy.

His face was pale. "I'm Todd."

I checked the glass room, but I didn't see anyone. Maybe Duke and Dillon had taken cover. The people who had been lounging on second floor were pushing to get down the stairs.

"Can you go up to the glass room and get my brother, Dillon?" I asked Todd.

"Dark shoulder-length hair," Mallory said. "Just yell out his name. Go!"

Todd darted off into the crowd.

My breathing ramped up as I searched heads and faces that time in more detail. Not one was Tito, and nobody resembled the dude who'd shot at me outside Jade's office building.

The shooter had to be on the second floor considering the trajectory of the bullet.

"Maybe I can find a doctor or nurse." One of these yahoos in the club had to have medical experience. "We should move her behind the bar just in case."

Mallory's hair fell out of her updo as she slid her hands in place of mine. "No. She's too injured. Go. Find someone."

She was right.

I kissed Jade on the lips. "I'm going to get help."

The light in her eyes was slowly dying out.

"You'll survive this," Mallory said.

I prayed like a priest she was right.

"Don't leave me." Jade's voice was garbled.

Tears were on the precipice of falling out of my eyes.

I hated to leave her, but I had to find help. "Keep a good pressure on her wound," I said to Mallory.

I kissed Jade again, hoping to assure her I would be back, or maybe to calm my own nerves. "You're going to make it." I vaulted up. My heart was in my throat, and I didn't feel like my blood was moving through my veins.

*Move your fucking legs, man.*

I dashed to one of the bar exits. They weren't as crowded as the main entrance, and I might have a clear path once I was outside to find someone. I kept on high alert, looking for any sign of the gunman.

"Anyone in here a nurse or doctor?" I asked, pushing through the crowd, not caring that I was plowing people out of the way. "My girl has been shot."

As if I'd spoken magical words, a swath opened up as people shook their heads.

One gal gave me a sad look and started to help me push deeper through the throng.

I couldn't even believe I'd only been out of the joint for two days. I was already falling into the criminal world, and I was taking Jade with me.

"We need medical help," the young brunette shouted.

The bottleneck finally opened up more at the door. I bolted out and into a small parking lot with only four cars. I ran for Jade's life onto the side street and rounded the building when someone grabbed me from behind.

"Denim Hart, remember me?" the man said.

I whirled around and stumbled, relief taking over my body. "Lou. Where's Duke? I need help." The short, squat dude worked for my brother.

"Take him," Lou ordered.

I didn't have time to react before someone threw a bag over my head. I fought the man, trying to squirm out of his hold, but it was hard since I couldn't see a fucking thing. Rough hands shoved me into a car. I fell flat on my face and could tell I was in a tight back seat.

"Get up," a voice I didn't recognize said.

"Hurry up," Lou called out. "Cops are on the way."

*I am going to fucking kill Duke.*

I pushed at my captor. "I need to get help for my girl."

"Your girl is dead," the dude said.

I headbutted him. "You're fucking dead."

He let out a savage laugh. "I doubt it. You'll be dead before you can say boo."

I fumbled to get the bag off my head until my captor shoved a gun into my side.

"Make another move, and I'll put a bullet in you like we did your girl."

My breathing became more rapid. My insides were on fire. And my heart splintered into a million fucking pieces. I would never get the chance to tell Jade how sorry I was for everything or to tell her how much I still loved her. Suddenly, the hate and revenge Hector had possessed for the asshole who killed Tanya were running through my veins.

"Lou," I called. "What's going on?"

The guy jamming the gun into me laughed again. "Lou can't help you."

I pulled on the bag for nothing more than to loosen the tension around my neck in an attempt to quell the claustrophobia kicking in.

The man rammed the gun into me harder. "I told you not to move, asshole."

"Just take this bag off my head." My voice was strangled because the acid in my throat was ready to come out.

The dude laughed. "Shut the fuck up, or I'll put a bullet in your knee."

"Why not kill me?"

"Oh, I tried to the other day on the street."

He was the dude in the red ball cap. "So, do it now."

"Plans have changed. It seems the boss wants you alive for a bit longer."

My brain was not connecting the dots. *Whoever wanted me dead doesn't now?* I couldn't imagine Tito having second thoughts about killing anyone, unless he wanted to kill me himself.

My phone rang, and the dude dug into my pocket. "Seems Dillon is looking for you," the asshole said before a cold air swept in. "We don't need anyone tracking you."

"Did you just throw my phone out?"

He roared with laughter. "I can't wait until you see what's next."

"I'm shaking with excitement." *Not!*

As we traveled to wherever the fuck we were going, I prayed—not for me, but for the bastard responsible for shooting Jade. Because when I had the chance, vengeance was going to be sweet and rewarding, and afterward, I would walk back into prison with open arms.

**21**

---

# JADE

**M**y eyelids opened, and my ears slowly started to register beeps and dings. The sound had pierced through my brain fog, or maybe it was the dull throb of pain in my chest that had woken me.

"Jade," Mallory squealed. "You're awake." Her warm hands landed on my arm.

I shuddered, and tears stung my eyes. "It hurts to breathe." My brain scrambled to form a coherent thought.

Mallory's big blue eyes came into view. "I know, honey. You just had a bullet removed from your chest."

I squinted at the bright light overhead before examining myself just to be sure that bright light wasn't some indication I was on my way to heaven. An IV was tethered to the back of my hand, and a hospital gown covered my body. That was all I could see aside from the hospital room. I tried to lift my hand to touch Mallory so I could make sure she was real. "I'm not dead," I said to ground myself in reality.

Tears floated in her eyes. "Nope. You're in one piece. Thank God."

I licked my dry lips. "Thirsty." My mouth felt as rough as sandpaper.

Mallory had a cup with a straw in it in front of me in less than a second.

The cool liquid slid down my throat, clearing the pebbles of sand. I sucked the cup dry.

She returned the empty cup to the dresser next to my bed. "Do you remember what happened?"

"Things are hazy, but yeah. I was talking to Denim one minute, and then I was on the floor." I grimaced at the memory of how hard it had been to breathe.

Tears flowed down her cheeks. "I was so worried."

"Where's Denim? Is he all right?" My gaze bounced around the small room, but all I saw was a window and a small alcove with a counter.

Mallory paled. "I don't know. He went to get help, and no one can find him."

My heart punched my ribs. Surely he didn't walk away like he had in high school. I didn't want to believe he'd just taken off, but I couldn't shake the feeling he'd run as far away from me as he could.

Then fear so strong stole my breath. "He's dead. Just like Savannah." As soon as I said it, I knew I was right. Everyone in my life was dying.

Mal shook her head, rubbing my arm. "We don't know that."

Tito wanted him dead. The only reason he wasn't there was because Tito had kidnapped him. But that didn't make sense when a guy had been shooting at Denim the other day.

I swallowed, holding back the need to bawl my eyes out. He'd sent me flowers. Hell, he'd kissed me.

"How long have I been here?" I asked.

Mallory looked as miserable as I felt. Her silky hair was oily, her face was ashen, and dark circles stained the underside of her eyes. "Three days. You've been in and out of consciousness with all the pain meds."

"Denim's been missing for three days?" My theory was becoming real. Tito had probably dumped his body in the Boston Harbor.

"Dillon and Duke are looking for him."

"Duke? Bull."

"You need to rest," Mal said. "Don't worry about Denim. His brothers will find him."

*Don't worry? Is she insane?* I would never get the chance to tell him how I felt. Why was my life full of drama and mayhem? I was being tested for sure. But I had a second chance at life. Apparently, I wasn't ready to join my family in heaven. Therefore, I decided I wouldn't waste a single moment of the life I had left. If Denim was alive, I wanted him to know how I felt. Life was too freaking short.

Mallory was talking, but I wasn't listening. I tuned her out and let my eyes drift shut. I was having a hard time staying awake all of a sudden. Maybe when I woke up, I would be back in that club, pressed up against Denim, listening to his husky voice tell me he wanted to fuck me. I was going to replay that scene over and over and over again. It might be the only thing to keep me from freaking out.

I couldn't lose another person I loved. Maybe I was bad luck. Maybe I should become a hermit and keep people away from me. Denim thought I wasn't safe around him, but he wasn't safe around me, and maybe Mallory wasn't either.

My eyelids flew open. "How is Todd?" I'd completely forgotten about him.

"He's fine, just a bit shook up. I'm going to get the nurse to let her know you're awake." Her tennis shoes squeaked on the floor as she headed toward the door.

"Mal, was anyone else hurt?"

She gave me a feeble smile. "You were the only one." She bumped into Dillon as he inched into the room, looking frustrated and worn out.

He sidled up to my bed and gave me a weak smile. "Welcome back."

"Did you find Denim?" I rushed out.

His Adam's apple bobbed. "No."

"Maybe the Feds have him."

"He's not with the Feds," Dillon said. "They're waiting to talk to you."

"Me? All I can remember is talking to Denim, and then I was on the floor." I was sure they didn't want to hear how Denim had kissed me.

A muscle jumped in Dillon's unshaven jaw. "We believe Tito Alvarez took him."

"I do too. But if we're right, that means he's dead. He can't die, Dillon."

He grasped my hand. "You still love him, don't you?"

Tears slid down my cheeks. "I do. I want a chance to tell him. But I'm also afraid. He ripped my heart out. I'm afraid he might do that again." I didn't know why I was puking up my feelings to Denim's brother.

Dillon squeezed my hand. "Give him a chance. He's not the same person you knew, Jade. Well, he is. He still cares. He still has a big heart. And he would die for those he loves. But he's not getting involved in selling drugs or running with gangs."

"I know. He told Kelton and me how he wants to start a family. Between you and me, when I heard him say that, my stomach fluttered in the hopes that I was in his equation." Again, I was foaming at the mouth, telling Dillon my deep, dark secrets about Denim. Maybe the medication was the cause of me spilling my guts.

"Take things slow. When I first saw Maggie again after several years, I wanted to start up a relationship with her, but I couldn't bring her into my mess. Us Hart brothers have a way of pushing away those we love to protect them."

"You did that to Maggie?"

"Sadly, I did. But she wasn't having any of my shit." Dillon's brown eyes flashed with love for his girl. "Jade, my brother doesn't die easily."

I laughed, albeit weakly. "Are you in my head?"

He smirked. "I see the fear in your eyes. It's the same look you had as a teenager when you came to the house and Denim wasn't home."

That was true. Sometimes I'd worried he was dead from a gang fight. Other times, I had worried he would die at the hand of his alcoholic father.

"Duke has every one of his men out looking for our brother."

I cringed at Duke's name. "If Tito is behind the shooting, was he at the club?"

"We didn't see him. We think it was one of his men. Maybe the same one who shot at you guys on the street."

"They're following us," I said almost to myself.

Dillon checked over his shoulder before regarding me. "I don't trust the hospital to keep you safe. We need to get you out of here."

My eyebrows knitted together. "What? This is probably the safest place to be."

"I don't agree. Anyone can get ahold of an employee badge, and if they really want to get past security, they will. Anyway, Duke and I think you're the target, and Tito has had a man following you since before Denim was released from prison."

"I don't understand."

Dillon scraped a hand over his chin. "We believe Tito wants Denim to suffer for killing Hector, and you're Denim's weakness. My brother still loves you, Jade. He might not admit that, but he would die if anything happened to you."

I couldn't argue with his reasoning. "So why now, though? Why wait until he's out?"

"Tito actually didn't. He had a man inside try to kill Denim."

I'd remembered Denim saying something along those lines when we'd been at the diner that Tito had put a hit out on him.

Mallory glided back in and resumed her spot opposite Dillon. "What did I miss?"

Dillon took his hand away from mine. "As soon as we can get you out of here, you'll be staying at Duke's. Until then, I have a man who will be watching you while you're here. I'll be here too."

"No. No. No," I said. "I'm not staying with Duke." The heart monitor went nuts.

Mallory rubbed my arm. "I don't like it either, but Tito can't get to you in Duke's penthouse."

"Traitor." I wanted to remind her how she despised Duke. Then I turned to Dillon. "Honestly, do you want me to kill your brother?"

Dillon chuckled. "He's an ogre, but he has a heart."

I scrunched my face, and that small act hurt like hell. "A black heart. Anyway, I have to work. I can't be hiding. And I have to bury Savannah."

"I'm sorry about Savannah," Dillon said. "I can't force you. But please consider staying with Duke. He's got the men, and his penthouse is a fortress."

I appreciated Dillon's concern. "I can't hide away. I have a life." *Albeit a depressing one.* "I have a job." Although Kelton had told me to take time off since I'm entitled to bereavement leave, but I didn't want to. I had to keep my mind occupied. Otherwise, I would go completely insane.

"Kelton told me he gave you time off for Savannah," Dillon said. "He agrees you need to be protected as well."

"I'm not taking time off," I volleyed back. "Look, I want to help find Denim."

"You're in no shape to do anything," Mallory said. "And if you want to work, then I'll bring your laptop to Duke's."

I glanced at my BFF, the same woman who hated Duke probably more than me at the moment.

She nodded. "I'll work from Duke's too. We can both drive him nuts."

Dillon was holding back a grin.

I wasn't. But I doubted I could do much of anything until I didn't feel like I'd been run over by a Mack truck. Still, if Mal was at Duke's with me, at least she would keep me from throwing him out the window.

"I need to make a phone call," Dillon said. "Then, Mallory, you can take a break."

Mallory laughed, shaking her head. "This woman isn't leaving my sight either."

"You should go home and get some rest," I said. "Dillon will protect me." I wanted more time alone with Dillon. He was making me feel better emotionally. I was beginning to feel as though I were part of a family, which I hadn't had since before the house fire.

"You two work it out. Either way, I'll be back." Dillon left.

I grasped Mal's hand. "You need a shower and a good night's sleep. Go home. I'll be fine. Tito isn't going to kill me."

"Why are you so sure?"

"Because he's gotten what he wanted." I hated to say he'd killed Denim. The more I voiced that thought, the more I was afraid it would come true, and I prayed I was wrong.

**22**

---

# DENIM

Puddles of water were scattered around the trash strewn on the floor of the barren warehouse. A hint of fish hung in the air, or maybe it was the stench floating off my sweat-soaked body.

I groaned even though I couldn't feel my legs. The only pain resonating in my brain was the burning in my muscles or the intense friction of the rope cutting into my wrists as I dangled from the ceiling. My mouth was parched. Every limb and muscle hurt like a bastard, and I could barely open my eyes.

I was in hell—the kind from which a person didn't escape.

I licked my split lips, and the metallic taste of my blood gave me a small jolt to wake the fuck up and get out of there. I wasn't sure how, though. My ankles were tied, and my toes barely touched the cement floor. I drew in a breath and choked from the disgusting dead fish smell lingering in the air.

"Boss, he's coming to," a baritone voice said.

I knew that voice. My gaze flitted from one side to the other, searching for Lou Romano. My vision was blurry, and I couldn't see past my swollen nose or cheeks.

"Hey." I sounded rough and ragged. I cleared my throat. "Hey," I said a little louder. "Tell my brother to be a man and confront me himself." I hadn't seen Duke yet. I was sure my brother was behind my kidnapping and the contract on my head. After all, Lou Romano worked for him.

When I'd first arrived—I was guessing four or five days ago—I had been knocked out. The minute I'd gained consciousness, I had been knocked out again by three men who got their rocks off on using me for their own entertainment. I'd asked to see Duke, but the men had laughed and continued to play the torture game.

I pulled on the rope around my wrists, but the act only served to make it cut deeper into my skin.

"You're not getting out of those," Lou announced with excitement as his footsteps grew louder.

I blinked several times. I was sure I had blood in one of my eyes, hence the blurriness.

Lou Romano entered my vision. He was short in height with a short neck and pointed chin. He was known on the streets as Pliers.

He cocked his head to one side then the other. "You're one tough motherfucker, Hart. Then again, you always were." True to his nickname, he plucked a pair of pliers from his back pocket. The metal glinted in the dim light spraying down from above.

"If you're trying to scare me, you'll have to do better than making love to those pliers."

He dragged a dirty fingernail over the handles. "You were always a cocky fuck."

A ragged laugh escaped me. "How's my brother, Duke?"

He opened and closed his pliers. "Peachy."

Despite knowing that Duke was behind stringing me up and beating the crap out of me, I was too out of it to care. But then I gulped down a mouthful of air. If Duke was responsible for my plight, that meant he was responsible for shooting Jade.

I thrashed around. "Get my brother," I shouted, but my voice was only a whisper. I would gladly kill if Jade didn't survive. The idea of Jade dead caused my gut to spasm.

"Now I see the fear," Lou said.

I spat in his face. "Tell my brother to get his ass in here, or out here, or wherever the fuck we are." Given the fishy aroma, we had to be near Boston Harbor.

I pulled down on the ropes, but it was pointless. If I could get free, I probably couldn't run. I couldn't feel my damn legs, let alone my arms. The only thing I could feel was the sweat dripping down my face, back, and chest. Or maybe it was blood.

Lou laughed again. "In due time. But first, I have my orders."

I growled, baring my teeth. "When I get free, I'm going to tear you apart limb by limb after I drive a knife through my brother's heart."

He belted out a sinister laugh, which bounced off the cracked cement walls and echoed loudly. "I can't wait to hear you scream." He dragged the pliers down one side of my face. "I think I'll start with your teeth. Then your fingernails."

Keys jangled behind Lou. "Hold up." It was another voice I knew well.

Growling, I writhed as Lou clamped my upper lip between the pliers, squeezed as though he were fighting with a nail that wouldn't come out, and pulled hard. I grunted, fighting to hold in the pain.

Lou knew I was in hell, and the fact that I didn't squeal like a pig didn't matter. Lou let out a satisfying and hearty laugh.

*Fucker.*

"Just a taste of what's to come."

"Lou," Tito Alvarez barked.

Lou backed away with a smirk that was cold, calculating, and downright creepy as fuck.

My mind juggled to understand what was going on. Lou worked for Duke, or I thought he did. Maybe Tito worked for Duke too. Maybe they were one big, happy family.

Tito twirled his keys on his finger and strutted closer, as if he didn't have a care in the world. I briefly wondered if the blood on his white T-shirt was mine. I didn't remember seeing him, but I hadn't been coherent. For all I knew, he'd beaten me when I was down, which he had been known to do with his victims.

He crossed his skinny arms over his chest. "It's good to see you, bro." He said every word like he meant it, and I would've believed him if it weren't for the dark glare he was giving me.

"Do you kill your brothers?" I fired back.

"That's your department," he was quick to respond. "I hear your girl isn't going to make it."

I spat in his face. "So you admit shooting her?"

"She wasn't the target. You were."

"Why? Because I killed your brother?"

"I know you didn't kill my brother." He sounded like he knew who had.

Confusion and shock melded together, making my eyes nearly pop out of my head. "How do you know I didn't kill Hector?"

"You're not a killer. Never were. Hector left that part of the job to me."

"So what the fuck is this all about?" I gritted my teeth.

"Lou, go shine your pliers. I need a moment with Hart."

Lou snarled but obeyed, taking his pliers with him.

"So he works for you now?" I asked. "Or do you both work for Duke?"

Tito slipped his gnarly fingers into the pockets of his ripped, soiled jeans. "Fuck. I don't work for Duke. He's the reason you're here, though."

"So you hired Costa to kill me because of Duke? You had some guy follow me the day I got out of prison and try to off me? Then you tried again at the club? Do I have the facts right?"

He snarled. "You just don't die, do you?"

"Fuck you. Why am I here, man? In one moment, you're trying to kill me, and in the next, you're kidnapping me. Be done with it already."

"I had a change in plans," he said. "If you're dead, I won't get what I want."

Tito was a persistent motherfucker, but he never thought before he acted.

I pushed out all the air in my lungs. "What do you want?"

He plucked out his phone, punched in a number, and waited until the line rang. "Let's ask Duke."

I used Lou's word. "Peachy."

The line rang again, echoing in the empty warehouse.

"Alvarez." Duke's voice came through loud and clear. "Where the fuck are you?" My brother's tone was calm as though the two were as thick as blood.

Tito had a satisfied grin on his ugly face. "Don't you want to know how your baby bro is doing?"

I stared at the phone, seething as sweat poured off my body. "How's Jade, Duke?" I rushed out, not sure if he could hear me since my voice was low and raspy.

Silence filled the line except for Duke's heavy breathing. "What do you want?" he finally asked. This time, his tone was scary as fuck.

Tito tapped his chin with his finger. "You know what I want—a seat at the table."

Maggie was right when she'd said that Tito Alvarez was trying to make a name for himself. *He's high on power and money and taking over the city.*

"Do you think the leaders will open their arms for a lowlife gang leader who puts contracts out to off people?" Duke asked. "That's not how the organization works. We don't call attention to ourselves. We stay legit and under the radar. Until you learn that, you have no place at the table."

Inwardly, I was laughing like a crazy man at how Duke was reprimanding Tito as though my brother were his old man. For the briefest of moments, I was transported back to when Duke would yell at Dillon and me for doing stupid teenage crap like smoking weed or drinking our old man's liquor.

"Duke," I called. "Is Jade o—"

Tito mashed his lips into a thin line. "I want into your organization like the other gang leaders. Bring me in, and I won't kill your brother."

"I don't care about Denim. I haven't for years," Duke said in a serious tone.

He hadn't given me the time of day in over six years. But a tiny voice in my head said to trust him. *Trust him like you did when you were a boy. Trust him with your life like you did when you ran in a gang with him. Trust that he values blood over money and riches.*

Trust could wait until he answered me about Jade. "Duke?"

He didn't acknowledge me. I was relieved Duke wasn't the one who had been trying to kill me. But what the fuck? He could at least say something to me.

Tito plastered on a satisfied grin. "You won't bat an eye if I shoot him right now, then?" Tito produced a gun from his lower back.

"Look, Tito," Duke said. "You've already got one kill under your belt. Kill Denim, and I can promise you that you'll never have the chance to play in the big-dog arena." Then the line went dead.

Duke's words stung like a swarm of angry bees. *One kill? Does that mean Jade is dead? Or is Duke baiting Tito?*

Tito kept the gun aimed at my temple. "I guess he doesn't care about you. Let's see how Duke reacts when I deliver your dead body to him."

I had to think fast. My problem was that my brain hurt as much as my entire bloody body. Still, my past relationship with Tito had to count for something. I certainly didn't want to die, not before I had a chance to confirm whether or not Jade was dead. But I couldn't think about Jade at the moment, or I would explode, and I had to get out of there.

I swallowed a ball of dirt. "Why is it so important to get a seat at the table? What table?"

Tito loved power. He loved being in charge. He hated that Hector was revered by those who'd worked for him and even by people who hadn't.

His arm was steady, his finger primed on the trigger. "I know you're trying to stall me."

Tito was also a hothead, and the feat had always gotten him into trouble. Hector had had to clean up his messes several times.

"You're right. I am. Honestly, I have no fucking clue what's going on here. In one breath, I think Duke is trying to kill me. In another, you are. The tables keep switching. Frankly, I'm fucking tired. I didn't get out of prison only to die." My voice was even.

The skin around his nearly black eyes loosened, but the gun was still trained at my head.

"Tito, you know me. We've been through shit. We can work this out." Hector had talked Tito down from the ledge many times. Hopefully, I could do the same.

"How? Are you going to get me into Duke's organization?"

"Tell me more, man. I can help. I'll talk to Duke." Duke wouldn't listen to me, but I needed to make Tito believe he would.

Tito lowered the gun.

Inwardly, I thanked someone above.

"Word on the street is Duke made a deal with the Colombian cartel about two months ago. He would be their front man to move drugs and guns through Boston. But the only way to do that was to engage some of the bigger gangs in the city. So Duke invited leaders from certain gangs to sit down and negotiate a plan where everyone at the table would benefit."

"And Duke didn't pick you."

I couldn't argue with Duke's choice not to do business with Tito. It wasn't that he was a lowlife as Duke had said, but Tito drew too much attention, particularly if he didn't get his way. I didn't know much about Duke's business dealings, but I knew my brother. He was big on trust and little on attention.

Tito tucked the gun in the waist of his jeans. "I have more connections than most of the gangs. Fuck, I could get rid of one shipment in the blink of an eye."

"Are you bragging or serious, man? Because, look, Duke has little patience for someone who talks the talk. He wants someone who gets shit done."

He scratched his head of dark hair. "You know I get shit done. The Creepers have made more money than ever since I've been at the helm."

"Give me something to work with, and I'll take that to Duke."

He glanced at the floor then up at me. "Throw him a bone?"

"A big fucking bone, man. Otherwise, he won't bite."

He bobbed his head, his mind wandering. "I can do that."

"Then cut me loose, and I'll get you that spot at the table." The last sentence came out a little too fast. Whether I could or not, I only needed him to believe me.

He laughed. "Your brother doesn't want anything to do with you."

"Duke was blowing smoke up your ass. He cares." Not one part of anything I'd just said was true.

"Why should I believe you?"

"Believe me or not. But if you deliver my dead body to my brother, you can hang up any chance of getting in. You've already got one strike against you."

He considered me for a long minute, if not more, chewing on his bottom lip. "Lou! Get your ass in here!"

I closed my eyes as several cuss words fell from my lips.

Lou rushed in, looking excited to start torturing me.

"Cut him down," Tito ordered.

Lou pouted like he'd just lost his pliers. "Why? I had plans for him."

"You can take out the rage you have for Duke on someone else," Tito said.

Lou dug into his boot and pulled out a switchblade. Then he reached up and cut the rope.

I fell like a rag doll to the ground then quickly scrambled to get the rope off my ankles.

Lou stomped off like a little boy who hadn't gotten his way.

Tito leaned against a square beam. "Give me a couple of days, and we'll be in touch."

I pushed to my feet on shaky legs and managed to walk up to him without falling. Before he had time to blink, I punched him in the jaw. "You better pray my girl is alive."

He spat on my boot. "Get the fuck out of here before I change my mind."

"One last question. If you know I didn't kill your brother, do you know who did?"

"Not a fucking clue. But if you ever find that person, I want to know."

Not likely, but he didn't need to know that. That person was all mine, and if the Feds were right and Duke had been at Hector's the night he was killed, Tito would never, ever know, at least not from me. I might be pissed at Duke, but I would deal with him myself.

I gave Tito a two-finger salute as I limped my way to fresh air.

"Hey, Hart," Tito called.

I didn't bother to turn around.

"If you don't come through, I will kill you and everyone you love."

I had no doubt in my mind he was serious. But I didn't fail at much, and if Jade wasn't breathing, I would kill him first.

## 23

# DENIM

The scent of salt water lingered in the night air as I headed down a deserted street, away from Boston Harbor, away from the rundown warehouse I'd been beaten to a pulp in, away from hell.

The more I walked, the more pain seized every limb in my body. The adrenaline was vanishing, and my legs were about to give out. My head hurt like someone had bashed it a few times with a baseball bat, and a dull pain throbbed in my ribs and stomach. I swished saliva around in my mouth to get the sandpaper feeling to go away, hoping to coat the dryness in my throat too.

I stepped off a curb and faltered as dizziness set in. I wasn't going to make it another block. I bent over, bracing my hands on my knees and scanned the neighborhood. There had to be life somewhere nearby.

A cat screeched, but that wasn't what I was hoping for. I blew out a breath and straightened. I had to find a phone.

I held my growling stomach as I crossed the street. I hadn't eaten in days, which only added to the weakness I was feeling. I spotted a light in the field one block down. I squeezed my eyes shut then oriented my vision and looked again. Flames shot out of a trash can, and two men were hovering over it.

Suddenly, I shivered. The sweat on my body was still there, but with a brisk wind picking up and breezing over me, I felt as though I'd just stepped out of a warm bath and into a winter storm.

I swallowed, licking my lips as I pushed on. Maybe one of those guys had a phone. I sped up my pace as fast as my weak legs would allow. But my efforts were about to fail when I reached the chain-link fence surrounding the field. Winded, I bent over once again to catch my breath.

*Come on, Denim. Kick your ass into gear. Think of Jade. You need to see her.*

I didn't even know if she was alive. *Fuck.* I latched on to the fence. Then I lowered myself to the ground. I needed a minute to clear the dizziness. Otherwise, I would fall flat on my face. I closed my eyes, willing my muscles to cooperate and my head to clear.

Then two men's voices carried with the wind, floating past me as my head spun like I'd drunk a fifth of bourbon. My ears perked up, and my eyes flew open at the rumble of an engine.

Slowly, I swiveled my head toward the car inching toward me. No doubt the occupant was looking for someone or something. Maybe he'd lost his cat.

Then I stiffened. Maybe Tito was looking for me. Maybe he'd changed his mind about letting me go. I wasn't sure I gave a fuck, though, with the way I was feeling.

The headlights grew brighter, blinding me until the car pulled up to the curb. Before I could comprehend who the driver was, the man was squatting down in front of me.

"What the fuck?" Dillon's voice made my heart sputter.

I was a tough motherfucker, but in that moment, tough wasn't in my vocabulary. I wanted to throw my arms around my brother and not let go.

Dillon helped me to my feet. "You look like shit."

"Feel like it too, bro." My voice was rough.

He helped me into the passenger seat before he ran around the hood of the car and hopped in.

"How did you find me?" Not that it mattered. I was grateful I wasn't hanging like a slab of meat drying out in some cold warehouse.

He threw his car into gear and sped down the road. "Tito called Duke and told him where to find you."

It made sense. Tito wanted Duke to know he hadn't killed me to make sure he still had a chance of getting into Duke's organization.

I slumped in my seat, popping my head back, ready to pass out for eternity. But I couldn't. "Jade. Please tell me she's alive."

He reached over and touched my arm. "She is, bro. The bullet hit the right side of her chest, above her breast. The doctor said she was lucky. She'll be in the hospital for a few more days. I got her well protected. No one is getting past Rafe."

I let out a groan that blasted my ears. "Thank fuck." I closed my eyes as warmth started to spread throughout my body. "How long has it been since the shooting?" I'd lost track of time and hadn't bothered to ask Tito.

"Five days. We've been looking everywhere for you. Duke had his goons out. I had Rafe combing the streets and checking in with his contacts when he wasn't guarding Jade's hospital room. Hell, I even had my bud Hunter, who works for a security firm, looking for you. Not to mention, the Feds have been worried."

I let out a strangled laugh, opening my eyes. "They probably think I bailed on my parole."

Dillon merged into traffic, heading into the Back Bay near Beacon Hill. "They questioned Jade, but she had nothing to tell them. Anyway, I called Kelton a few minutes ago while I was scouring the area. His place is close by, and he wants to chat. However, I think I should take you to the emergency room."

I flipped down the visor and checked myself out in the small mirror. Christ, I did look like I'd been in a war. My eyes were black and blue. A cut was bleeding on my brow, and my lips were dry, cracked, and split in one area.

"I'm fine. I just need a hot shower and some food before I see Jade. I'm starving."

I didn't want her seeing me in the state I was in. I might scare her, and that was the last thing I wanted to do. She'd been through enough.

"You can shower at Kelton's."

After several lights and turns, Dillon was parallel parking on Louisburg Square, where million-dollar townhomes were the norm. "I have Rafe guarding her. And believe it or not, the Feds have someone watching her too."

Travers had probably employed the same person who'd been watching her when she was at the hospital for her sister. I made a mental note to thank him at some point.

I got out of the car, albeit slowly. "Beacon Hill. Wow."

Dillon met me on the sidewalk. "Well, Kelton is a lawyer. It's this way." He pointed behind where he'd parked.

Dillon and I walked side by side, not saying a word. When we reached number twelve, I climbed the stairs behind Dillon. He was primed to knock when the green door opened.

Kelton grinned at Dillon until his blue eyes landed on me, and he lost his smile. "What the?" He waved us in before pushing his fingers through his black hair. "I'll have Lizzie get a first aid kit."

"Let's hurry this show up. I want to see Jade."

Kelton closed the door. "You're not seeing Jade tonight. Visiting hours end in a couple of hours, and you need a good night's rest."

I wanted to say we would see about that, but my stomach grumbled at the aroma of something delicious wafting in the air.

Dillon chuckled.

"Lizzie is making lasagna," Kelton said. "Follow me."

He didn't have to tell me twice. *Eat, shower, then see Jade—in that order.* I didn't need sleep, and if I had to, I would sneak into the hospital.

"Nice place." I whistled as I followed Dillon and Kelton, taking in the rich design of the elegant curved staircase, a massive crystal chandelier dangling from the ceiling, a formal dining room big enough to entertain at least twenty guests, and a library that would rival the public one in the city.

I squinted at the bright recessed lights overhead when I entered a spacious kitchen drenched in dark cherrywood, stainless-steel appliances, and white marble countertops.

A woman with black hair and big gray eyes set the pepper shaker down on the counter and came over to me. "I'm Lizzie." Her expression held concern. "I'll get the first aid kit."

"If you don't mind, can I use the shower first?" I needed to get the blood, mud, and stench off me.

"I'll show him the shower," Kelton said to his girl. "Afterward, we can tend to his cuts. It doesn't look like you need any stitches."

I would bet some of the wounds were healing already.

"Come on." Kelton started to backtrack the way we'd come in. "I have some clothes that might fit you."

Following him, I took in a deep breath, and my body odor could knock out a bear.

After I'd taken a hot shower and donned the clean clothes Kelton had lent me, I was again walking into the kitchen.

Lizzie, Dillon, and Kelton stopped talking.

Lizzie popped up from a barstool, grabbed a mug, and poured coffee into it. "Here. This will help."

Any liquid would help. In the shower, I'd drunk as much water as I could. I took the mug. "Thank you."

Kelton waved a hand, gesturing to a stool next to Dillon. I noticed he'd changed out of his suit and into a Boston College T-shirt and jeans, similar to the clothes he had let me borrow.

Lizzie removed a pan of lasagna from the oven. "I hope everyone is hungry."

I didn't care if she fed me dirt. I would eat anything at the moment.

Kelton wrapped his hand around a bottle of beer. "First, I'm glad you're okay. I hear Tito Alvarez flies off the handle. Why did he let you go?"

I gave Dillon a sidelong glance. "I told him I could get him into Duke's organization."

Dillon choked on his drink. "You what?"

"It was either that or die. Sorry, bro. I'm not ready to die."

Lizzie was doing something at the stove that I couldn't see.

Kelton sat up straighter, his expression blank. "How do you plan on doing that?"

I shrugged. "Not sure." I hadn't even thought past getting food in my stomach or seeing Jade. "But if I don't, he won't hesitate to kill me and those I love."

Dillon shook his head.

Lizzie set the hot pan of lasagna on a trivet in front of us. Then she kissed Kelton on the cheek. "I'll be upstairs. I'll let you guys talk."

He wrapped a hand around her waist and kissed her on the lips. "Thanks, Lizard."

I raised an eyebrow at her pet name. It was cute and unique, sparking an idea of what I could use for Jade since she didn't like me calling her love.

Lizzie bounced out of the room while I dove into the lasagna, not displaying any manners. I piled a heaping serving onto my plate and took one bite, savoring the cheesy gooiness. My stomach rumbled with pleasure. I took another bite, sighing. I had to eat slowly. Otherwise, I ran the risk of getting sick.

Kelton and Dillon began to fill their plates.

"Agent Travers tells me Duke is hooked up in the gun trade," Kelton said.

"You talked to him?" I asked, chewing the out-of-this-world lasagna that had a perfect combination of spices, cheeses, and meat.

"That's one of the reasons I wanted to see you," Kelton said. "I ran into him when I was visiting Jade earlier at the hospital. He was there asking her questions. Anyway, I made it clear that he needs to stop making idle threats. Your parole is well aboveboard, and the only way you can go back to jail is to violate your parole in some fashion. You are not obligated to help him take down Duke. However, if you want to clear your record, you might want to consider working with the Feds. The offer he gave me is good. There's no hidden agenda or threats whatsoever."

"It's up to me, then?" I asked for no other reason than to roll that idea around in my head. "I guess my question is, what specifically does Travers want me to get from Duke?"

Kelton wiped his mouth with a napkin. "According to the letter, the Feds want a time and place of the next gun shipment coming in. Get that info, and they'll seal the deal with you."

I let out a crazed laugh. "Duke isn't going to give that to me."

"That's a fact," Dillon said in between bites. "Duke knows the Feds are watching anyway. It's impossible for Denim to come through."

*Exactly.* The only way my name was getting cleared was to find out who killed Hector, which was an impossible feat in my mind if I couldn't find the neighbor. But my conundrum at the moment was that I had Tito breathing down my neck. I was in a catch-22. And I cared more about keeping Jade alive than clearing my name.

**24**

---

# JADE

Six days had passed since I'd gotten shot. Seven since Savannah died. I was ready to get out of my hospital bed and breathe in some fresh air or do something. Sitting idle was driving me nuts. I had to do something to keep my mind busy and not think about whether Denim was dead or alive.

Tears pooled in my eyes as I stared at the bathroom door in my private room, which Dillon had insisted on. He'd even had one of his security guards who worked at the shelter guard my door. I felt like I was back in Savannah's room in the ICU.

Regardless, I appreciated his concern. "We need to be careful. I can't let anything happen to you. Denim would never forgive me."

"Do we know if he's alive?" I'd asked several times. Actually, every time Dillon, Rafe, or Mallory came in, that was my first question. I'd even asked Kelton when he'd come to visit, knowing full well he didn't have any answers.

I'd also bombarded Agent Travers when he'd peppered me with questions. His response had been, "We have our men out looking for him." Then he'd said, "I hope he didn't violate his parole."

I'd almost punched him for his last sentence. The jerk was worried about him violating parole. He'd given me the impression that he was hoping Denim actually *had* so the FBI could send him back to prison.

Regardless, the more time that ticked away, the less of a chance there was that we would find Denim alive, at least that was the usual police rule with missing persons.

Thankfully, the pain meds kept me groggy and sleeping most of the time. When I'd been awake, Mallory and I had talked about a burial service for Savannah. I'd tried to call my aunt, but I'd gotten her voice mail, and I hadn't wanted to leave bad news on a recording.

I flicked on the TV. The room was too quiet. Mallory was working, Dillon had an errand to run, and Rafe was standing outside my door. He didn't come in much. Every now and then, he would poke his head in, and I would laugh. It wasn't like I was about to disappear. Sure, I could jump out of the window, but I was five stories up, and I wasn't a daredevil. Nor did I have anything to run from, at least not yet.

When Rafe wasn't on duty and Mallory wasn't talking my ear off about work, Dillon sat with me and sometimes stayed the night. I enjoyed reconnecting with Dillon. He'd filled me in on his life. I was horrified to hear about his sister ending up in a sex-trafficking ring. He'd explained the harrowing experience of searching every part of the city for Grace for four years. I couldn't imagine how hard that must've been, always wondering if he would find her dead or alive. I'd cried when he'd gotten to the end of the story where he'd found her.

I couldn't help but think how Savannah could've easily been snatched by some creepy dude and put up for sale, although prison was hell too, just a different kind of hell.

Regardless, I knew that by telling me about Grace, Dillon was trying to put me at ease. "My brother doesn't die easily," Dillon had said without a hint of doubt in his voice.

When someone wanted a person dead, they would go to great lengths to make it happen. Tito had tried twice within days, and if my belief that things happened in threes were true, then Denim might be a goner.

I focused on the TV rather than Denim. The ribbon at the bottom of the screen caught my attention. "Update on the recent shooting at The Monarch."

I turned up the volume.

A pretty blonde from the local news channel waved to the club behind her. "We're standing outside The Monarch, a brand-new club that opened last week, where the recent shooting took place. We've tried to contact the owner, but a representative for the club declined to take our call. Police still haven't found the shooter, but witnesses have described a man in his late twenties with dark hair. We also learned earlier that the woman who was shot will make a full recovery. We'll have more updates on the news at eleven. Coming to you from downtown Boston, I'm Maggie Marx, KBCA News."

So that was Maggie. In our long talks, Dillon had gushed about his bride-to-be and how she worked for a local news channel.

"She's gorgeous," I said to myself.

"So are you," a husky voice said.

My heart stopped at the sound of Denim's voice. I darted my gaze to the doorway. When I did, my mouth came apart. Tears catapulted out so fast, I couldn't stop them.

His beautiful blue orbs popped amid the blackness ringing his eyes. His cheeks were swollen, and several cuts were scattered around his face.

"You're alive." My voice cracked.

He strutted in with a sense of purpose as though I were the last woman on earth and he needed me to save him.

Little did he know that he might be saving me. He might be giving me hope that we had a future together. I was deathly afraid he could or would break my heart again. Yet in that moment, with the way sparks were flying and the heat between us was sizzling, I would give him a hundred more chances.

He grasped my hand and brought it to his lips. "Hey, beautiful."

He must have been looking at a different woman, because the last time I'd looked in the mirror, I'd screeched. My black hair was oily and matted to my head. My green eyes were dull, and my skin was ashen. I had managed to give myself a quick sponge bath, but I desperately needed a shower—a long, hot one that went on for days.

Denim showered kisses on the back of my hand, igniting a string of tingles that zipped up my arm, down my chest, and settled in my belly.

"Tito didn't kill you. Wait, was Tito the one who tried to kill you?"

Denim gave me a lopsided smirk. "He tried."

I tugged my hand free and tucked his blond strands behind his ear. "I'm so happy you're alive. Tell me everything. How did you get away? Does Dillon know you're okay?" Although I wanted to know the answers, I didn't want to talk. I wanted to stare into his eyes and absorb him and the way he was looking at me with so much love and devotion.

His grin grew wider as he leaned into my touch. "I'll tell you later. Right now, I just want to look at you. I've been worried out of my fucking mind about you." He stared at my lips hungrily, marking his time like a wild predator eyeing his next meal.

Goose bumps popped to attention at the very idea that he could devour me. He'd done just that when I'd first met him.

*The bell had rung, and kids spilled into the halls. I'd hung behind in chemistry lab to ask the teacher a question. Afterward, I bolted out of the class to get to my next one. Only I didn't get far. I plowed into a hard chest and would have fallen on my butt if it weren't for the hottest boy in school catching me.*

*"So sorry, baby doll." His voice was raspy and gentle.*

*I let out a squeal.*

*He chuckled, guiding my chin up until our eyes met.*

*My mouth went dry, and my pulse banged hard against my skin.*

*"I'm Denim. And you are?"*

*I'm in love. But I didn't say that. I couldn't even speak.*

*His beautiful blue eyes penetrated through me with temptation and sin, and my brain shut down.*

*We stood there in the hall as kids ran by us, carving out our own private space.*

*My tongue snaked out to lick my lips.*

*He flinched.*

*"I'm Jade," I finally said.*

*His gaze had roamed wild and free down to my chest and back up.*
*"Gorgeous. Absolutely gorgeous."*

He groaned, snapping me out of my trip down memory lane. He bowed his head until his lips were a tiny fraction from mine.

My pulse ignited in a steady *boom, boom, boom.*

Before I let my brain get ahead of my body, I pressed my lips to his.

He groaned again, a sound that shot spikes of ecstasy straight to my clit.

His lips were familiar yet new as he thrust his tongue into my mouth. He took like he once had so many years ago when I was his. Actually, I'd always been his. He'd never lost me. I had never given my heart to another man since him. In some twisted kind of fantasy, I'd always hoped we would reconnect one day.

He flattened his hand on my face, nipping my lips and my tongue, groaning and moaning with me.

Memories came roaring back of Denim and me stealing a kiss in between classes, hiding in closets at school, under the bleachers, and anywhere we could find to devour each other.

He broke the kiss. "We shouldn't do this."

I could feel my eyebrows coming together. "Why not? Is it because of me or prison?"

I might've been tipsy the other night, but I hadn't forgotten the heat between us or our conversation. In particular, I remembered the part where he'd said, *"Jade, don't tease. I just got out of prison, and I'll fuck you right here in front of everyone."*

A laugh rumbled from deep within the caverns of his belly and broke free, echoing around the room. "Truth?"

I rolled my eyes. "Since when do you not tell the truth?" One of his defining traits was his honesty. Not only that, the man always said what was on his mind, regardless if it hurt or not.

He placed my hand on his heart. "Feel this."

I was usually one for romance, for sweet nothings, and a dozen roses—not roses, orchids—but I wouldn't mind wrapping my fingers around his hard dick and showing him what he'd been missing.

His soft blue eyes glistened. "I'm not going to play games. I've had six years to pick apart everything I did wrong, and the biggest mistake I made was letting you go."

At the time, I hadn't believed his reasoning. I hadn't believed I could get hurt if we stayed together. Now I was slowly seeing that maybe he was right, but that didn't change how I felt for him.

"You hurt me, Denim. So tell me why I should give you another chance."

"Because I'll never walk away from you again," he said as sure as we were breathing. "I don't want another woman, Jade. I've never stopped loving you."

I wanted to throw myself at him and confess the same to him, but a small whisper in the back of my mind told me to proceed with caution.

*He's mixed up with his former drug buddy. He's working with the Feds. His life is still dangerous. What's to say he won't push you away again? Or that I won't get shot at again? Or worse, killed, the next time someone wants to use me as revenge against him?*

Someone clapped behind him. "What a wonderful speech."

Denim's jaw turned to cement, and he let go of my hand as he spun on his heel. "Rude much, Travers?"

Agent Travers stepped into the room. "Jade, nice to see you again." His sweet demeanor with me was a sharp contrast to the crassness in his tone when he spoke to Denim.

Aside from asking me about the shooting at the club, Travers had also grilled me about Duke. I didn't have anything on Duke either. Besides, the man wouldn't tell me his deepest, darkest secrets. In addition to Travers, Boston PD's gang unit had asked me questions, including if I knew whether a gang was responsible for the shooting, in particular the Southside Creepers, which was led by Tito.

"You look like shit," Travers said to Denim.

"What do you want that you had to interrupt a private moment? You've already spoken to my lawyer. I'm not obligated to help you."

Travers flicked his head to the hall. "A word alone."

"I don't keep secrets from my girl. Besides, she works for my lawyer. Go for it."

He was right. I couldn't divulge the specifics with anyone except Kelton. Still, I felt as though I were the one intruding.

"Given the events at the club, I was hoping you will take the deal."

"My brother isn't going to tell me about gun shipments or anything about his business. I keep telling you that. Besides, he knows you and I have been talking."

Travers's nostrils flared. "How does Duke know that?"

Denim held up his hands. "You tell me. I hardly said hi to my brother when he dropped that bomb at my feet. Maybe your men are getting sloppy."

"Careful, Hart. I can bring you in for obstructing an investigation."

Denim growled low. "You have no grounds. Stop with the threats. I did my time and followed the rules for the early release program. The only thing you did was speed up the parole board's decision."

Travers narrowed his green eyes. "They weren't going to give you parole given the fight you got into."

I grasped Denim's hand and squeezed, hoping to tame the anger I could see brewing in his pinched features.

"Whatever, man. Look, I'm tired. My body has been through hell, and right now I just want to spend time with my girl."

"I thought you wanted your record wiped clean?" Travers asked.

Denim blanched.

As much as I despised Duke, I couldn't fault Denim for not wanting to send his brother to prison.

Travers started for the door. "The offer still stands."

"Travers," Denim called.

I couldn't see Travers's face with his back to us, but I would bet he was sporting a smug grin.

"I'll take your offer with one caveat," Denim said.

Travers pivoted on his shiny loafers. His expression was blank. "I'm listening."

"What if I can get you someone else?" Denim asked.

"Unless this someone else has something to do with gun trafficking, it's of no use to me."

Denim shoved his free hand through his hair. "Give me two weeks to get you someone better before you revoke the offer."

Travers considered Denim. "You've got one."

"Or what?" Denim asked.

"The offer is gone. And maybe I'll arrest Duke by then."

Denim flinched. "On what charges?"

"Now why would I tell you that?" That smug grin I was sure he'd had earlier was front and center. "One week." Travers sauntered out like he'd won the war.

Denim roughed his hands through his hair. "Fuck my life."

"I bet Travers is lying about arresting Duke. Just the way he said 'maybe' sounded like he's hoping he can arrest Duke. Or he wants to scare you and Duke until you both crack."

"Enough about Duke. I want to look at you. Where were we? Oh yeah." He leaned in and kissed me like a man possessed.

At that moment, Travers, Feds, gangs, Duke, violence, and almost getting killed flew out of the room. I was right where I wanted to be.

## 25

## DENIM

I roamed the sprawling penthouse for nothing more than to expend some pent-up nerves. I hadn't wanted to leave Jade, not after the kiss we'd shared. But I'd gone ahead and opened my big mouth and told Travers I would get him someone else he could skewer other than Duke. I wasn't sure I could come through within a week or if Duke would agree to help me, but I had to try. I had to get Tito out of the picture. Then I wouldn't have to worry about Jade's safety—or mine for that matter—and above all else, I could have the murder conviction wiped from my record.

Dillon stood in front of the floor-to-ceiling window, gazing out at the cityscape. "I wouldn't want to live here. The view is great, but this place is lifeless. Does Duke even spend time here?"

I checked down the hall. "I think with a woman's touch, it would be warmer and more inviting."

The doors to the other rooms were shut. I was tempted to snoop to see what Duke had in those rooms, like a desk, filing cabinets, or some clue that would tell us more about our brother—the same brother I felt like I barely knew anymore.

But I decided not to go digging. Duke wasn't beyond throwing me out the window. I also suspected Duke had hidden cameras. I didn't see any in the living room or kitchen area. But that didn't mean he wasn't hiding the cameras in his recessed lighting or some James-Bond-type device that looked like a normal fixture or piece of furniture.

More importantly, if I wanted him to trust me, I had to make sure my actions were aboveboard in case he was watching us.

I joined Dillon, skirting the island and then the dining table. The fall weather was slowly morphing into winter, and I couldn't wait for the snow. I wanted to cozy up to a fireplace in a log cabin in the mountains with Jade and hibernate for the winter. Now that was a perfect idea if she would only take me back. We still hadn't finished our conversation since we'd been rudely interrupted by Travers, and then Dillon had walked in.

I wouldn't blame her if she didn't want me. I didn't deserve her. She was pure and perfect, and she should be with someone who hadn't been in jail for murder or had an enemy or enemies who could use her to get to me.

But she had a magnetic pull on my heart, and I was done pushing her away. Whether she was with me or not, she would always be a pawn to anyone who wanted me dead. I crossed my fingers she would take me back. If our mind-blowing, dick-squeezing, heart-pumping kiss was any indication of how she felt, then I stood a good chance.

Dillon waved a hand in front of me. "Earth to Denim."

I stared at myself in the reflection in the window. My face looked like the monster in *Frankenstein*. I had two black eyes, a split lip, and my upper torso still throbbed in pain. If it weren't for four Advil, I might not be upright.

"I'm here. What was the question?"

"It's nothing," Dillon said.

I glanced at him. "You look worried." *Or maybe tired.* Like Duke, Dillon didn't wear his emotions on his sleeve, but as his brother, I could tell. It was barely noticeable, but he got faint little lines in the corners of his eyes when he was concerned.

"In a way, yeah. I don't agree with what type of business Duke's in, but he's still our brother, and I don't want to see him go to prison."

Deep down, I hoped Duke knew what he was doing or that he had a back door he could escape through if things went haywire for him. He would survive in prison, but I didn't wish that on him.

"I don't either, bro. Come to think of it, maybe that was the reason he never bothered to visit me in the joint. He didn't want to see where he could end up one day." It was the only thing that made sense to me.

The sun was tucked behind buildings as dusk set in. The traffic below was heavy. Pedestrians entered and exited the shops and hailed cabs.

Dillon lifted a shoulder. "Do you really think Duke will roll over for Tito?"

"Not at all. But I promised Tito I would get him a spot at the table, and if we can convince Duke to help us formulate how to take Tito down, I think he'll bite. Plus, handing Tito to the Feds will get him off my back and maybe keep the Feds away from Duke for a little while." I didn't think the Feds would give up on Duke even if they put Tito away. But that was for another day.

Dillon scratched his arm. "Don't get your hopes up."

"When it comes to Duke, I don't."

Dillon checked his phone. "Duke's late."

Duke had given the bellman the okay to let us up to his place to wait for him.

"Did you get a chance to tell Jade how you feel?" Dillon asked.

"Kind of. But after Travers left and you came in, I didn't get a chance to finish. Now we're here." I'd thrown a lot at Jade, caught her off guard, and if I knew her, she would want time to think. I would wait for as long as it took. "I need to keep her somewhere safe. The shit with Tito could go south. And Grace, man. Tito will pick off everyone I love if he doesn't get what he wants."

"Then we need to make darn sure he does," Dillon said on a growl. "Grace can't get mixed up in this shit."

"No fucking kidding." I hadn't been there for Grace, but now that I was a free man, I would do whatever it took to make sure no one ever hurt her again. "What about your shelter?"

Dillon shook his head. "I'm not putting the women in jeopardy. Grace will be safe at my house. She can handle herself. Maggie can too. I'm worried about Jade. She isn't trained in combat or guns or fighting. Anyway, Duke agreed Jade could stay here."

I could feel my eyebrows lifting. "For real? Wait. She won't stay here. She hates Duke." I was shocked my brother had offered. After Jade had let loose on him the other day, I didn't expect Duke to be hospitable.

"You're going to convince her," Dillon said. "She gets out of the hospital tomorrow."

I wanted to argue with him that he shouldn't get involved, but we'd already been down that road. Yet I had to say it one more time. "Don't get involved with all this shit. I'm a big boy. I survived prison. I can handle this." I had no idea where Jade lived, but Duke's penthouse wasn't a bad idea to keep her safe.

Dillon grinned. "You can't handle Duke. Sorry, bro. But I can."

"How? Duke isn't going to roll over and let you pet his belly."

Dillon choked out a laugh. "He will."

The elevator dinged just before the door slid open.

*Perfect timing.*

Duke strutted in. His light-brown hair was slicked back, his jaw was clean-shaven, and he was wearing his normal scowl. He headed for the kitchen, loosening his tie.

I balled my hands into fists as I stalked toward him. "Did you want me to die? Tito was about to put a bullet in my head, man." Steam filtered out of my nose.

Dillon rushed up and blocked me. "Fighting will get us nowhere."

Duke opened the fridge door. "Tito wasn't going to kill you. He's bragging that you're going to get him a spot in my organization, though." He punctuated the word "*my*."

*Fucking Tito.*

Growling, I went over to the island.

Dillon trailed, staying close, making sure I didn't lash out at our brother. I wanted to, but Dillon was right as always. Fighting only led to bloodshed and two pissed off brothers, and we needed to figure out how to deal with Tito. Then Duke and I could work out our differences.

Duke carried three bottles of beer over and set them on the marble counter. "Denim, how are you going to do that?" He sounded genuinely curious, not condescending or patronizing.

Dillon slid onto a stool, taking a beer.

"If we don't give the fucker what he wants, he *will* kill me."

Duke twisted the cap off his bottle. "None of my associates want to deal with Tito Alvarez."

I sat next to Dillon. "They don't have to." I held up my hand before he cut me off. "Hear me out. The FBI has a hard-on for you. They think that because I'm your brother, you'll divulge your business dealings about gun trafficking or whatever it is you're doing."

Duke sipped on his beer. His face was expressionless. He just sat attentive and quiet as a mouse, which was kind of unnerving. He reminded me of our old man, who would always listen to our excuses when we did something wrong. Then after we'd finished talking, our old man would strike with a belt, his hand, or a beer bottle. Whatever he had close by was what he'd used to beat us.

"I informed Agent Travers earlier that I would get him someone other than you. What if we gave them Tito? Tito mentioned he can throw you a big bone to gain your trust. Let's meet with him and hear what he has to say. Then we can formulate a plan from there."

I gave myself a mental high five. For one, Duke wasn't kicking us out or yelling. He wasn't being an ass, and he seemed like the Duke I knew before I'd gone to prison.

Duke pulled off his tie, nodding. "I would like nothing more than to get that bastard out of my way and my life."

I would second that. Jade and I didn't need to be running forever and always looking over our shoulders.

Duke set his beer down. "I need to get out of this suit. Then we can talk through some scenarios and set up a meeting."

That had seemed too easy.

"Cool," I said. "Agent Travers gave me a week. We need to act fast. Otherwise, the offer to clear my record vanishes." I sighed. "Oh, and he mentioned he *might* arrest you. I suspect he was just trying to get a rise out of me, though."

Duke didn't flinch. "He can't. He doesn't have shit on me."

"Are you sure?" Dillon asked. "I would hate to see my other brother go to prison. That shit is getting old."

*Amen to that.*

"The Feds could raid me now, and they won't find a fucking thing. If they think they have something, then the most damage they could do is hold me for questioning." Duke spoke every word with confidence.

The Feds wouldn't arrest Duke unless they had something concrete. If he wasn't worried, I wasn't either. Besides, I had my own shit to deal with, and knowing Travers, he was probably pissed he had no control over me. So he'd thrown out an idle threat to see if I would bite.

Duke unbuttoned his shirt. "Denim, it's best if you stay out of this. I can handle Tito. You've been through enough."

My heart tripped at his last line. He did care. It was the perfect opportunity to ask him why he hadn't visited me in prison, but I didn't want to get off track, and part of me knew when I finally got him to tell me, I wasn't going to like his answer.

"I need to be involved. If things go south, he's coming after me, Jade, and those I love." It was up to me to make sure I protected Jade.

Dillon took a swig of beer and played his ace card. "That means Grace, bro." His tone was soft, calm, and packed a wicked punch.

Duke went ramrod straight and paled for a mere second before he banked his emotions. It was good to see him react even if it was fleeting.

"I'll be right back," Duke said as he headed down the hall.

"I should get the ball rolling and call Tito."

Dillon slid his phone over to me. "Use mine. I know you don't have one anymore."

I hadn't had a chance to get a new one since Tito cut me loose.

I wasn't sure if Tito had the same cell number he'd had when I'd last been a free man, but I gave it a shot.

Tito answered on the first ring. "Who's this?"

I put the call on speaker. "Duke is willing to listen." I pictured the twisted look on his face as surprise barreled through him. If I knew Tito, he hadn't had faith I would come through.

After two beats of silence, he said, "You work fast, Hart."

"I want you off my ass. Do you have a problem with that?"

Tito growled. "I liked you better before you got all reformed."

He liked me better when I was obeying his brother and following orders, or better yet when his brother would put him in charge.

"Do you want in or not? Because this is your only chance."

"Fucker," he mumbled. "Give me two days."

I was tempted to use Travers's line and tell him he had one, but I had some things to take care of, including getting Jade from the hospital and to a safe place. "Do you have that big bone I suggested?"

"That's none of your concern," he said in disgust.

"I beg to differ. My ass is on the line here, and I need to prep Duke. If your bone doesn't involve guns, Duke walks." I assumed Tito knew that, but I wasn't taking a chance. He had mentioned the Colombian cartel, drugs, and guns. But Travers wanted guns.

"I know what Duke and his associates are looking for, asshole. I'm not a fucking idiot. We'll be in touch." The line went dead.

Duke strutted in and resumed his spot across the island from Dillon and me.

"Tito wants to meet in two days," I said. "And it seems he's working on a gun deal."

Duke's eyebrows climbed to his hairline. "Is that so?"

Dillon picked at the label on his beer bottle. "Why are you surprised?"

"Tito only deals drugs," Duke said. "Unless…"

"Well, the suspense is killing me," I said.

Duke took a swig of his beer. "McCauley and I believe Tito has been trying to broker a deal with the Mexican cartel to get a foothold in the gun trade."

"Does your organization deal in just guns?" I asked. I'd never known Duke to dabble in drugs.

Duke gave me a cocky grin. "Sorry, bro. The less you know, the better."

He was probably right. With my luck, the Feds would string me up and torture me until I talked.

Dillon nursed his beer. "We'll meet with Tito, find out what he has, and then what?"

"You're not coming," I said.

Dillon narrowed his brown eyes. "Fuck if I'm not."

Duke raised his voice. "Boys."

As if Dillon and I were teenagers again, we snapped our attention to Duke, ready to obey him.

"The only thing we can do for now is listen to Tito," Duke said.

I bounced my knee. "The Feds were very specific on getting info on a gun shipment."

Duke bit his lip. "Chill. I'm sure if Tito wants in as bad as he says, he'll deliver that. It might not be within a week. All you need to do, Denim, is keep the Feds informed. If they know there's a big carrot at the end of the road, they'll wait."

Duke's patience was admirable. Mine, on the other hand, sucked the big one at the moment. "Why are you so calm?"

"I'm five steps ahead of the Feds. I know they've been watching me. I'm just as anxious to get Tito off my back as you are. If I don't, there'll be an all-out war on the streets between the Colombian and Mexican cartels. The Colombians don't like when anyone moves in on their territory, and they've carved out one in this city. I, for one, don't want to see that happen. So we need to practice patience."

"I don't care about a war. I care about Jade and Grace and staying alive." I wanted to say I was in this predicament because of Duke. The bullet Jade had taken was because of Duke. But pissing Duke off any further would only alienate him, and I needed him.

Duke's face darkened. "I'm well aware of the stakes. But going off half-cocked isn't going to accomplish anything. How many times have I taught you that?"

I didn't have a comeback, and frankly, he was in charge and had been at the criminal game longer than I had.

Silence bounced around the room until Dillon spoke. "Do you think Tito had Savannah killed?"

Duke's hardcore exterior crumbled into a look I couldn't put my finger on.

Tito had hired Costa to kill me. So it was possible he'd hired someone to kill Savannah.

"You loved her," Dillon said as a matter of fact. Of course Dillon would see what I couldn't.

Duke skirted the island and slowly walked in the direction of the bar as though his legs were trembling.

Dillon and I looked at each other, and I shrugged. Dillon nodded, confirming he was right.

A minute or two ticked by before Duke returned with a full glass of bourbon. Whatever emotions we'd seen in him a moment ago had been banked. I zeroed in on his eyes, but they were clear. I'd never seen my brother shed a tear in his life, and true to form, he wasn't now. But he was wrestling with something heavy. Our reunion the other night was beginning to make sense.

Duke had never been one to tell us his feelings. Even when he was dating Savannah, he'd never displayed affection toward her around me. He wasn't one to show how jealous he was or how in love he was. He always kept women at arm's length.

I wasn't a doctor, but I would guess his women issues might stem from our mother abandoning us. Hell, I wouldn't be surprised if our old man was rubbing off on him too. I'd been at Duke's twice since getting out of prison, and both times, he was sucking down the alcohol like it was water.

Duke set his glass down on the island, drilling his gaze into me.

"What?" I asked.

He sighed as he shoved his hands through his hair. "You're not going to like what I have to say."

I wasn't sure how the love he had for Savannah would upset me unless he was about to tell me he was in love with Jade. Come to think of it, that look he'd had a moment ago was the same look he'd had when Jade stormed in the other night to tear him a new one.

Without breaking eye contact with me, he said, "I think I know who killed Hector."

*Well, fuck me.* I had things all wrong.

My jaw practically slammed onto the counter. My brain suddenly froze into one solid piece of ice with one thought—I had spent six fucking years in the joint, and my brother knew who'd killed Hector. A sharp pain ricocheted through my chest.

Dillon swung his gaze like lightning from me to Duke. "Talk, man. Or Denim is going to use your head as a punching bag. I might too."

I hopped off the stool, ready to send my eldest brother through the fucking window. Instead, I took a breath and blinked several times to get rid of that vision as I clenched my hands into fists. I was seething, breathing hard, and began pacing.

"Savannah was at Hector's the night he was killed," Duke said evenly.

My pulse pounded in my ears. *Savannah?* I knew she'd done drugs, but I didn't know she'd bought from Hector. I sure as hell hadn't sold to her. When I'd dated Jade, I had promised her I wouldn't sell to Savannah, and I never had.

Duke sighed. "I didn't know she'd been there until two months ago. She called from prison, begging me for money. I knew if I didn't at least talk to her, she would continue to call me. So I went to see her. I told her you might be getting out, and she cried. She said you should've never been sent to prison." He swallowed. "Then she told me what she saw that night."

Madness enveloped me. My head was spinning. My blood was boiling. I dug my nails into the palms of my hands just to be sure I was still alive.

"She'd just entered Hector's building when she heard a gunshot," Duke said. "Scared, she bolted and hid in the shadows across the street. She didn't want anyone to see her. A few minutes later, she saw Tito leave the building."

I stopped pacing, and every limb in my body locked up tightly.

*What the fuck? What the actual fuck?*

My tongue was stuck to the roof of my mouth, and something large and sandy was lodged in my throat. Savannah could've saved me from going to prison, or at the very least, my case wouldn't have been so open and shut.

I swished saliva from side to side to get my tongue working.

"Who else knows this?" Dillon asked.

There was no way Jade knew. She would've forced Savannah to go to the cops with that information. Or maybe she wouldn't have. She hated me for leaving her.

Duke shrugged. "As far as I know, no one but her and now me."

I was breathing fire. My mind tried to form a coherent thought other than a jumbled mess of speculation and revenge. In that moment, my veins burned like an inferno because I wanted so badly to put a bullet into Tito's head.

*Hold up. You don't know if he actually did it.*

Something careened through me, thawing my brain. "Why do the Feds think you were at Hector's that night? Is that fact or fiction?"

Duke didn't flinch. "I have no idea. Savannah did have my car that night. Maybe the Feds reopened your case, knowing you were up for parole, and wanted to get you to help them. They discovered that tidbit and used it to get you all fired up." He took a breath. "Besides, if I was there and someone saw me and told the cops or Feds, they would've questioned me around the time of the murder. No one did."

I set my jaw, trying to figure out if he was telling me the truth. "You told me you believed I killed Hector." The heated words we'd exchanged during our reunion were flashing like a neon sign before me.

"You pissed me off," Duke said as a matter of fact. "I swear on Grace's life I didn't kill Hector."

Dillon regarded me. "He's telling the truth."

I studied Duke. He didn't have that cold scowl, but rather he had a pleading look. Given the way he'd paled when Dillon had thrown out Grace's name earlier, I knew he wouldn't use Grace as a crutch to lie.

I grabbed the back of my neck as I returned to my seat. "Tito set me up. Motherfucker. And I bet he paid the neighbor to take a hike or worse, killed her, so she wouldn't tag him for the murder. Yet I'm curious why Savannah didn't come clean when it happened. Her testimony could've saved my ass."

"She was afraid for her life," Duke said.

"So it makes sense, then, that Tito had Savannah killed in prison," Dillon added.

Duke dragged a hand along his jaw. "Maybe, but not because she saw him. Otherwise, he would've killed her six years ago."

"Not unless he found out recently," I said. "Prisons are notorious for eavesdroppers. Anyone could've overheard your conversation."

Regardless of our speculation, one thing was certain—Tito was going down. And I knew exactly what I had to do.

**26**

----

## JADE

I set my bag on a queen bed in Duke's guest room.

Denim had convinced me I would have full reign of the penthouse without Duke, and honestly, I hadn't protested much. Coupled with Savannah's death and getting shot, I felt like a rag doll. I was surprised I'd made it from the cab into the elevator and then into the penthouse. If it weren't for Denim holding me, I might've collapsed.

Clutching my chest, I sat down on the plush mattress. The doctor had cleared me to go home with the caveat that I take it slow. I'd learned the bullet had hit a muscle above my right breast. He'd said muscles take longer to heal. His parting words were, "Only do what you can."

I didn't need to do much in the way of physical activity, except I needed a shower desperately. I'd been a bit embarrassed to be so close to Denim. My body needed a good scrubbing, and my hair needed to be washed a hundred times to get all the oil out of it. But a shower might have to wait. I wanted to sleep. I'd taken a pain pill before I left the hospital. I gently eased back in bed until my head was on the pillow. Maybe I could catch a quick nap before Denim returned.

He had a meeting with Kelton and errands he had to take care of.

He'd promised I was safe in the penthouse. I wasn't afraid. Heck, I was too tired to be frightened.

"If you need me, I left my new cell number on the kitchen counter," Denim had said. "Duke's number is there too. He's staying at The Monarch."

I didn't care where Duke was as long as he wasn't in my face. I was beyond angry with him for what had happened to Savannah. A sharp pain stabbed my heart every time I thought about her. I kicked myself in the ass for not trying harder to help her.

I knew Savannah would have never straightened up or changed unless she admitted she had problems—drugs, lying, stealing, and of course, Duke Hart. He hadn't killed her, but he'd had an indirect hand in her demise. I would never forgive him, which might pose a problem if I decided to take Denim back.

I would be lying if I said I didn't want Denim. More than anything, I wanted us to pick up where we'd left off. I wanted to kiss him again. I wanted to start a family with him.

He was right. We didn't need to play games. We both knew each other. We both knew what we wanted. So why shouldn't I give us another chance?

*He'll break your heart again.* I wasn't listening to the devil in my head. It was time I threw caution to the wind and saw where the road took us. I would like to believe that, as adults, our heads were screwed on better. Denim was a different man. I had seen that the instant he'd walked into the meeting room in prison, the instant we'd locked eyes.

We weren't teenagers with raging emotions that drove our actions. We'd both had time to grow, think, and decide what we wanted, and I wanted Denim Hart, every freaking inch of him, despite the danger that surrounded him. I knew he would protect me, and I felt safe with him.

Denim and I deserved a second chance. We deserved to start anew and see where our relationship took us. If we didn't try, we would both wonder what if, and I was tired of playing the what-if game. Life was precious and short, and I shouldn't waste it because I feared the unknown or feared having my heart shattered.

Suddenly, I wasn't tired. I eased off the bed and padded across the plush white carpet and into the en suite bathroom. I flicked on the light and found myself standing in an enormous room.

The glass shower tucked in the corner was larger than the entire bathroom in my dinky apartment.

I found the towels in a small closet in the other corner and started the shower. It was time to shed a lot more than the grime coating my body. It was time to let go of the past. I stripped down and examined myself in the mirror over the stone sink. I touched the large bandage on my chest, making sure it was secure. The nurse had given me a small bag of medical supplies, including waterproof bandages.

I couldn't look at myself any longer. Hopefully when I emerged from scrubbing myself clean, I wouldn't look like death.

Three hours later, I was squeaky-clean, my hair was dry, and my skin was soft. I'd made coffee, taken inventory of Duke's sparse kitchen cabinets, and now I was curled up in bed. In a way, I felt like Julia Roberts in *Pretty Woman.* I hadn't taken a bubble bath, but staying in such an expensive place made me feel pampered.

I'd just closed my eyes when footsteps clamored down the hall. I jolted up and threw off the blankets to see who was there, and a moment later, Denim graced the doorway.

I didn't move, but not because I was surprised he was there. I was buck naked. It felt nice to have my bare skin on the thousand-thread-count sheets.

He leaned against the doorjamb and raked his heated gaze over me, taking his time when he landed on my breasts.

On command, my nipples hardened.

He licked his lips, pushing his hands through his hair.

Instantly, I imagined him pushing his hard cock into me.

"Do you normally sleep naked?" His voice was husky.

I swung my legs over the side of the bed. "Nope. I was waiting for you." *Bold much, Jade?*

His eyes blazed, hungry and heated, as he popped off the doorjamb. "Is that so?" He stalked over with a boyish smile, but there was nothing boyish about Denim Hart. He had broad shoulders, a strong jaw, arms built to protect, hands made to bruise, and lips born to tease, tempt, and drive a woman into a delicious rage.

I grabbed my nipples. "I'm all yours."

One eyebrow went up. "Don't fuck with me, Jade. Because when I'm finally inside you, you're mine. No one else. Not even that douche you were with at the club. This is it for me. You're it for me."

Sitting on the edge of the bed, I planted my feet on the floor and opened my legs. "You should know I'm not the type to play with your head." I slid my hand between my legs.

He ripped open his shirt, and buttons flew in all directions.

I giggled, but the sound died when he was standing before me. His blue eyes hypnotized me, ensnaring me into his seductive web, and I couldn't look away.

He took the hand I had in between my legs and guided it to his dick. "Feel that. Years of waiting for you." Then he placed my hand on his heart. "You asked me why you should believe that I won't hurt you again. Feel this. My heart beats for you and only you. It will never beat or pine for another woman. I thought letting you go was protecting you. I was so fucking wrong. The only one who can protect you is me. So I'll ask you again. Are you sure you want us, me?"

I tugged my hand from his wildly beating heart and tucked my fingers inside the waistband of his jeans. "I've never been more sure of anything." I swallowed as I traced my fingers up the dips and valleys of his six-pack. "I'm still in love with you. Never stopped. But…"

He tensed, his abs tightening beneath my hands.

"If you hurt me, I will kill you." I wasn't teasing. I would die a thousand deaths if he walked away again.

He didn't laugh either. Instead, he traced the outline of the bandage on my chest before his fingers landed on my chin. "If I do, I'll give you the knife." His tone was deathly serious and so was the look in his eyes.

As if those were the magic words I needed, I started to undo his belt.

He stopped me. "Maybe we should wait until you're healed. I don't want to physically hurt you."

"I've taken pain meds. And I know you'll be gentle." I was sure the doctor wouldn't think sex was taking it slow. But I trusted Denim. "You're in bad shape too."

His face was bruised pretty badly. He'd filled me on his ordeal and the torture he'd endured at the hands of Tito and his men.

"Nothing I can't handle." He shucked his jeans in seconds with expert precision as though he'd practiced that move fifty times.

I watched in quiet fascination and intensity as my body heated in all the right places.

When he was fully naked, lust burning in his eyes, blond hair wild around his face, and his dick hard, ready, and bigger than I remembered, I whimpered.

*Is he truly the Denim I remember?* It didn't matter. Teenage Denim had been hot and swoony. Twentysomething Denim radiated strength, power, and a healthy dose of passion I wasn't sure I was ready for.

Or maybe I was ready because I was holding out my hands, and my eyes were fixed on his cock. When he stepped in between my legs, I wasted no time wrapping my fingers around his silky, smooth shaft.

He groaned, a sound that awakened every butterfly in my stomach.

Suddenly, my brain scrambled like an out-of-control satellite signal. It'd been years since I'd given him a blow job, years since I'd done much in the way of sex. I wasn't sure I would be as good as I'd been at seventeen.

He curled long fingers around his shaft as if to show me how it was done.

But I didn't need a lesson, although watching him stroke his long, thick erection was a sight to behold. With his free hand, he reached out and rolled one of my nipples in between his fingers.

I purred, my eyelids drifting shut. And before my brain kicked into gear, my hand was traveling down my belly until I was circling my clit.

Denim tapped my chin. "Open up, beautiful. I want to see sparks in those emeralds as you come for me."

It was then I realized just how close I was to reaching that crescendo of unadulterated bliss. I wanted to stop, to wait, to make it last, but I was too far gone. All those images of Denim and me I'd had in the shower had been foreplay.

I did as he commanded and opened my eyes to find him on his knees, watching me intently, passionately.

I continued to pleasure myself. My body was on the brink of something fantastic, something that had been dormant in me for years.

Sliding his gaze down my body one inch at a time, he rubbed his calloused hands along my thighs. "You're more beautiful than I remembered."

I wanted to shove my hands in his hair and guide him down to my throbbing clit. But he beat me to it and lowered his head.

My pulse thrashed at the image of his tongue all over me. But I didn't have time to envision anything. My hips bucked the moment his lips closed over my nub. I moaned so loudly, I had no doubt the city outside could hear me.

Then he stopped cold.

"No," I whimpered. "Please." I wasn't beyond begging. It had been far too long since I'd felt him and the euphoria of us.

He chuckled, kissing the inside of my thighs, my stomach, everywhere but the one spot I needed relief. "I'm so happy to see you're still impatient."

"Ass."

And just like that, we were teenagers again, bantering in the throes of passion. He would always tease me to the brink of pure, delicious pain.

"Remember this?" He licked the back of my knee.

I giggled and moaned. "Ass."

He licked the back of the other knee.

I couldn't describe the sensation except that it sent tingles to every part of my being, and Denim Hart knew how to play me perfectly.

I was ready to explode, and as I'd done so many times over the years, I played with myself.

He shook his head. His eyes were hooded, and his grin was sexy. "I want to take care of you." He buried his head in my pussy, nipping, licking, and sucking.

I squirmed and let out a huge sigh, clutching the comforter in my hands.

He moaned as he stuck two fingers inside my channel, not missing a beat as he flattened his tongue on my nub.

I bucked my hips, and when I did, he sucked hard.

I let out the scream of all screams, and my body went slick with sweat.

Denim kept his lips seated and licked with gentle strokes as I rode out the best orgasm in forever.

When I finally came down, I sat up, breathing heavy. My cheeks were burning, my mind was clear, and my heart was full.

Denim had disappointment written on his face when he rose.

I blew out a breath. "What?" I couldn't imagine why my orgasm would make him pout.

He stroked his dick, and his pain was so evident as he eyed my pussy. "I don't have any condoms."

"I'm on the pill." The pill helped to regulate my monthly periods so they weren't so heavy.

His shoulders relaxed. "I promise I'm clean."

Letting my legs fall open, I scooted back on the mattress as he climbed onto the bed. When his hands were on either side of my head and his dick was primed and ready to enter me, he leaned down, hovering over my body with uncertainty in his eyes

I cupped his face. "I'll be okay." I wasn't in any pain.

"You're not exactly healed." His voice was strained.

"How about if I get on top?"

He beamed. "I always loved you on top."

That I had forgotten.

We traded positions, but before I straddled him, I had to taste him.

He lifted up on his elbows, his chest rising as he watched me.

I crawled down his body and wrapped my lips around his dick.

He drew in a loud breath as his eyes drifted shut.

When I took him deep, he almost flew off the bed. "I'm not going to last."

I swirled my tongue around the head of his cock, teasing, licking, and nipping.

He threaded his hands through my hair and groaned. "I need to be inside you. Come here."

I climbed on top of him, and he guided his cock to my entrance. Our eyes locked. My heart was beating off the charts, and sweat coated our bodies.

He gave me a nod like I needed a gentle push. I guessed I kind of did. The last time I'd had sex was a one-night stand years ago. The only thing that had been inside me since then was my vibrator, which was nothing like the real thing.

My chest was rising and falling as I seated myself onto him. The moment he was completely buried inside me, I stilled. There was a pinch of pain, but once that passed, I squeezed.

Denim's lips parted. "Fuck me now, beautiful. Otherwise, I won't have any control. I'll flip you over and fuck your brains out. And I don't want to hurt you."

I giggled. "Ever the gentleman."

He gripped my hips, his eyebrows creasing as he urged me to move.

For a split second, I felt powerful. I had the reins, and I could command him at will. It was my turn to see him come undone.

I pressed my hands to his hard pecs and began rocking my hips.

A loud grunt rumbled out of his chest as his fingers dug into my hips. "Faster, baby. Faster." He bucked and thrust.

I rocked hard and fast as his dick hit that sweet spot inside me. My core went liquid. My body hummed, and I didn't want to stop, but I was losing steam.

"Flip us," I said. "You won't hurt me." I would deal with the pain later if he did because I wasn't stopping.

Carefully and without breaking us apart, he rolled me over then froze. "Are you okay?"

I bobbed my head. "Now fuck me like you mean it."

"Yes, ma'am."

I giggled.

Pressing his hands into the mattress and keeping his chest off mine, he became a madman, pounding into me hard and fast. It was a beautiful sight to see the boy who had developed into a virile man about to come completely undone.

He dipped his head, and his hair brushed my chest. Tingles sprouted like flowers on the first day of spring.

He sucked a nipple into his mouth, circling his tongue around without losing momentum in the least. I squeezed around his cock as the friction climbed higher and higher and higher.

Then he let out a growl. "Fuuuuuck." His biceps bunched, his abs tightened, and his head fell back. "I can't stop."

"Keep going. I'm close."

He kept pumping in and out until his name dropped from my lips, light and breathy. An explosion of stars danced before me as our gazes clung to each other with a quiet message of love, desire, and forever.

When I finally shuddered in a heap of pure bliss, I was ready to pass out.

He curled up alongside me, brushing my sweat-dampened hair from my forehead. Then he peppered kisses up and down my chin. "I do love you, Jade." He sounded sad all of a sudden.

But I was too spent to probe, and I didn't want to ruin the moment. I snuggled against him, tangling my limbs around his, and closed my eyes. We could talk more in the morning.

**27**

---

# DENIM

J ade looked peaceful as she slept. Her black hair was wild around her head, her hands were tucked underneath the pillow, and her soft snores hummed in the room.

Careful not to wake her, I eased out of bed with an erection that I was sure would be permanent with her at my side. I wanted to roll over and make love to her again, but she needed the rest, and I had to meet Travers. The only way to take down Tito was to do it the legal way, which I knew, but I sure as fuck wanted to gut him with a steak knife. Yet if I gave in to my urges, I would end up back in prison, and that wasn't happening.

My feet had just sunk into the carpet when Jade stirred.

*Damn.*

"Where are you going?" she asked in a sleepy voice, which was sexy as hell.

My dick grew harder if that was possible. I leaned over and kissed her on the cheek. "Sleep. You need to rest."

Hell, we'd had one epic night that would be embedded in my brain until the day I died, and not because of the sex. That was great, and we'd only had one round. I didn't want to put her through too much physical activity. She'd said she was fine, but I could tell how tired she was.

What had made the night epic was the love we'd never lost for one another. It was as though we'd picked up right where we'd left off eight years before.

I wanted more nights like that of holding her, talking, making love, and falling asleep with her in my arms. I wanted to show her the world, swim with her in the ocean off some tropical island, and curl up in a cozy cabin in the mountains in the dead of winter.

*No more city life. No more Titos of the world. No more crime. No more running.* After I cleared my name, I was hightailing my butt out of the city with Jade on my arm. Neither of us had anything or anyone holding us back.

She propped her head in her hand. "Let's spend the day together. We can order in and watch movies."

I hadn't told her yet about the plans Duke and I had with Tito. I hadn't told her what Savannah had witnessed outside Hector's apartment. I felt it wasn't my place to share that information since Duke had heard it firsthand from Savannah.

Jade might not believe Duke, but she needed to hear the story from him. Besides, the more I thought about what Savannah had seen, the more I believed Tito had had a hand in his brother's murder. However, I couldn't shake a few nagging questions. *What was Savannah doing at Hector's that night?* Hector hadn't been the only drug dealer in town, and surely she'd had her own dealer. I also wasn't one-hundred-percent sold on why she hadn't gone to the cops. She'd known I'd gotten pinched for the murder. Savannah had had a ton of faults, but I didn't see her cowering, especially knowing Duke had the men to protect her. Although Tito wouldn't have hesitated to kill her if he knew she'd seen him.

But I might be wrong on all counts. Until I could get the truth on who the murderer was, I didn't want to say a word to Jade because it would only upset her. She was mourning her sister and trying to heal. She didn't need any more turmoil at the moment.

*If you can't get Tito to talk, then what? You can't ask Savannah.*

Someone in Tito's circle had to know something about why he'd been at Hector's and what had happened. But it wouldn't matter. His men wouldn't throw him under the bus, and they certainly wouldn't tell me shit.

Jade waved a hand in front of my eyes. "Denim, you checked out." She felt my forehead. "You're warm."

I chuckled. "Hot is more like it." I lowered my gaze to my cock.

She licked her lips. "Well, let's take care of him." She gave me the most beautiful, sleepy, seductive smile.

Then my phone buzzed on the nightstand.

She flopped down onto the pillow. "You don't have a job. You don't have to be anywhere. So who's calling?" Frustration threaded through her tone.

I kissed her on the cheek. "Patience, baby doll. I'm in for the long haul."

My phone continued to buzz.

She stuck out her bottom lip. "I want you inside me."

If I fucked her, I would be late, and I didn't want to piss off Travers. I needed his help if I wanted to clear my name.

My phone stopped vibrating.

Jade batted her long lashes, her big green orbs eating me up. "See? Now come back to bed."

My phone pinged with a text.

Travers: *You're late.*

I checked the time. I wasn't late. We were meeting at eleven, and it was only nine thirty.

Me: *We agreed eleven.*

Travers: *I left you a voice mail last night, changing the time.*

Me: *Sorry. I'm just seeing a voice mail now.*

Travers: *Can you be here in thirty?*

Me: *On my way.*

Travers had picked a hole-in-the-wall breakfast joint four blocks from Duke's place, so I had no problem getting there in time.

"I'm meeting Travers," I said to Jade. "Rain check?"

Her phone rang, and she scrunched her pretty nose. "Sure. I guess someone is trying to tell us something." She collected her phone from her nightstand.

I kissed her quickly before bolting into the bathroom. Within ten minutes, I was showered and dressed.

I found Jade in the kitchen, making coffee. I wrapped one arm around her from behind, and with the other, I moved her long hair to the side. "I'll call you later." I peppered kisses on her neck.

She leaned into me. "No rush. Mallory is on her way. She's going to work from here and keep me company."

I didn't know what time I would be back, but I was glad Mallory would be there with her.

After one long, tongue-twisting kiss, I said, "Don't go out, please. Until I can get Tito off our backs, I don't trust him."

She turned in my arms and tucked my wet hair behind my ear. "Is that why you're meeting with Agent Travers? Do you guys have a plan?" She sounded relaxed, happy, and content.

I brushed her nose with mine, inhaling her. She was sweet, and she was all mine. "We do." Or I did. I wasn't sure yet if Travers would jump on board or not. "I love you."

She tensed.

I edged back, studying her. That smile she'd had a moment ago was gone, and in its place was pure fear. "What's wrong?" I'd expected her to shower me with kisses when I told her I loved her, not freak out.

"That tone in your voice." She shuddered. "That's the same tone you used when you broke up with me. I love you, but…" She looked away.

With my fingers on her chin, I gently guided her to look at me. "Hey, never again. What you're hearing in my tone is concern and hope that we can take Tito down once and for all." I cupped her face with both of my hands.

Her eyes were wide, intense, and insanely green. "I'm serious, Denim Hart. I will hunt you down this time and kill you." Her tone was rock-hard. "My heart can't take losing you again."

I understood her trepidation. I understood we were diving in too fast. But I didn't want to waste another minute, day, or year without her. I'd been a fuckup at eighteen, and I would like to think that I'd matured and reformed, even though I hadn't killed anyone. Prison had taught me maturity and had given me ample time to dissect my wants and needs, and I needed Jade like I needed water to survive.

"I understand it will take time for you to trust me again, to trust that I won't walk away. I know words are just words, but I'll show you." I started by pressing a kiss to her jawline, her chin, her nose, her ears, and even that sensitive spot behind her ear. I repeated those steps until she became putty in my arms. Then I nipped at her bottom lip, tugging with my teeth. If we kept going, I would miss my meeting with Travers, but I needed to show her I was serious.

She smiled. "You should go before I strip you naked."

"Baby doll, I do love you."

"I know," she said. "Now go before the FBI shows up here and arrests you."

After one last quick kiss, I headed out.

Travers was sitting in a booth when I walked into the restaurant fifteen minutes later. As usual, he was dressed in a suit and shiny loafers, with his hair slicked back.

I slid into the seat across from him. "Where's your partner?" I hadn't seen Brock since I'd met him in prison.

He deadpanned. "We're not here to talk like buddies, and I don't have time. What do you have for me?"

The waitress sashayed up, blowing strands of her brown hair out of her eyes. "What are you having?" She poised a pen over her pad, ready to take my order.

"Coffee. Nothing else," I said. When she glided to the next table, I regarded Travers. "I'm meeting with Tito Alvarez later. I want you to wire me up."

He reared back. "You're mighty zealous."

"I believe he murdered his own brother, and I'm going to get him to talk."

Travers held up a hand. "You're going to get him to talk about a gun shipment, not a murder. Right? I'm FBI. A local murder isn't my jurisdiction. Talk to the Boston PD."

I rolled my eyes. I wasn't a complete idiot. I knew he couldn't arrest Tito for a local murder. "I'll get you a time and place of a gun shipment. But I need to have his confession of the murder on tape legally. And do you really want the local cops in on this?"

I could seek out the cop who'd arrested me. Dillon knew Officer Ted Hughes well. Apparently, Ted was like a father to Maggie. I tucked that tidbit in my back pocket and made a mental note to text Dillon. I had to cover all my bases in the event the Feds wouldn't play.

My goal was to clear my name, and with my newfound information that Tito could've murdered his brother, I didn't need the neighbor as a witness.

*If Tito doesn't talk, you might.* I would cross that bridge when I got to it.

Killing two birds with one FBI agent would be cleaner and easier than bringing in more cops. We could satisfy Travers, and I could finally see the real murderer go to prison.

"Let's not forget you're acting as my parole officer," I continued. "Aren't you supposed to help me?" The main role of a parole officer was to help ex-cons with things like finding a job and a place to live. They were even supposed to help the person deal with old problems, and Tito was an old problem.

His expression was far from pleased. "Who will be at this meeting?"

I knew he was salivating to hear Duke's name. "Myself, Duke, Tito Alvarez, and one of his guys." When I'd called Tito the day before, we had agreed to keep the meeting small.

Travers perked up. "Duke, huh? I'm surprised, Hart. You mean I might get Duke after all?"

I shrugged. It was possible. But our meeting was to discuss guns, and that alone wouldn't put Tito or Duke behind bars. However, I wasn't about to piss off Travers by goading him. He would learn soon enough that Duke wouldn't be present when the guns came in.

"I just want to be clear about something," I said. "The written agreement you'd sent to my lawyer stated that I needed to give you a time and place of a gun shipment. If I do, my record will be cleared. Is that accurate?" When I'd stopped by Kelton's office the previous day, I'd read the formal agreement a few times to make sure I understood what was expected of me. Then Kelton had explained that as long as Tito delivered the time and place, then I was in the clear. The letter didn't call out any names in particular either.

Travers sat back. "That's correct. Are you confident Tito will give you that info?"

*Not at all.* "Honestly, I'm not sure." If I could at least get Tito to confess to the murder, then I wouldn't need the Feds holding their terms over my head. "Are you in to wire me up or not?"

"This is your one shot," he said. "But you better get me that info."

I shook my head. He was a Class A dick, still making idle threats. "I'm trying here, Travers." The fucker had to see that. "I want you off my back. I want to go home and make love to my girl. I want to find a job. And above all else, I want my friends and family to know I didn't kill anyone." The people in my life already knew that, but still, having a clean record was more important to me than guns and drugs.

**28**

---

# JADE

After Denim left, I made myself busy in the kitchen, trying to keep my mind off our conversation. I knew he loved me, but that didn't mean he wouldn't walk away again. Doubt was my worst enemy, and I knew his actions would speak louder than his words. His actions the last couple of days had been nothing short of a boy who was in love with a girl.

I shrugged off the niggle of doubt, and as I prepared a mug of coffee, I replayed the night before over and over and over in my head. His lips had been sinfully inciting, his tongue masterfully pleasing, and his dick huge and gratifying. I'd wanted to go for round two, but he'd declined. I had almost pouted, but I understood he'd wanted to let me rest. I had a feeling he was hurting from all his cuts and bruises too.

In addition to the great sex, if anything could erase my uncertainty, it was how Denim and I connected. It was as though we'd never broken up. We had talked about high school, when we'd first met, and the good times we'd had. He'd asked me about my life, and I'd asked him about prison. He'd held me the entire night, and I doubted he'd gotten any sleep because every time I'd moved or turned over, he was caressing my arms or kissing my head.

Sighing, I brought the mug up to my mouth, and another shiver racked my body as my stomach growled. I realized I hadn't eaten much in days.

I set my coffee down on the counter and rummaged through the cabinets. Then I remembered that Duke had no food in the house. I was in the mood for a hearty breakfast of bacon, eggs, and even pancakes. I'd barely touched any of the hospital food they'd given me.

I could dash out and pick up some groceries. But on second thought, Mallory was due there in an hour. She could stop by the coffee shop near our office. I would settle for an egg-and-bacon sandwich or even one of their fresh bagels.

I collected my phone from the counter and sent her a text to ask if she would bring food.

Mallory: *For sure.*

Then with the coffee mug in my hand, I set out to explore more of Duke's abode. My bare feet slapped on the hardwood as I traveled down the wide hall to the other five rooms aside from the one I was staying in.

But as I tried to open each door, I found the first two locked. The third door was a guest bathroom. The fourth door was also locked. I was about to give up and return to the kitchen when I noticed the last door at the end of the hall was ajar, something I hadn't noticed when I'd arrived the night before. However, as tired as I'd been, I hadn't noticed much.

With my curiosity piqued, I pushed in the door, slowly and tenta- tively. I didn't think Duke was home. Denim had told me Duke would be staying at his club, The Monarch.

I poked in my head. "Hello," I called out.

No one answered.

I trudged into the black-and-red room, complete with a king-size bed, large-screen TV hanging on one wall, a dresser, a couch, and a doorway to an en suite bathroom.

"Duke," I said again as I wound my way into the bathroom.

He wasn't there. I even stuck my head into his walk-in closet and was met with a room bigger than the one I was sleeping in.

Suits galore hung on one side. Shoe racks adorned one wall.

Drawers and two dressers took up another wall. I seriously could live in this closet. He even had a comfy chair nestled into the corner.

I walked around, inspecting his suits as I traveled through the large closet. I stopped at one dresser, set my coffee down, and peeked in the top drawer. A gun and two clips sat next to a handful of watches. I closed the drawer and moved on. I had no need for a gun and wasn't surprised Duke had one either. I glanced around, and when my gaze landed on the other dresser, I sucked in a sharp breath.

I hurried over and picked up the picture.

Savannah and Duke were sitting by a pool with the ocean in the background, and both were smiling. They looked happy and in love. It was odd to see his straight white teeth or a happy glint in his light-brown eyes. He looked relaxed and warm, nothing like the coldhearted man I knew. What had my eyebrows flying up was the way he was holding Savannah like she was his everything.

I stared at my beautiful sister. Her brown hair was piled on top of her head in a messy bun, her skin was sun-kissed, and she was wearing her quirky smile.

I fumbled to figure out what had gone wrong between Savannah and Duke. My sister wasn't the easiest person to get along with, but Duke's outer exterior said he wasn't either. Maybe they'd been made for each other.

I briefly closed my eyes, staving off the need to cry. My sister would never get the chance to fall in love again.

I didn't hear Mallory until her voice made me jump.

"Snooping isn't your scene," she said somewhere behind me. Then she whistled. "What a freaking closet."

I placed the picture back in its spot, dashed away a lone tear that had escaped, and turned around. "I think I had Duke all wrong." I uttered those words more to myself than Mallory as I collected my coffee cup.

But true to Mallory's form, and her opinion of Duke, she said, "Nonsense. You're sounding like Cara now."

I pressed my stomach against the edge of the center island that traveled down the length of the closet to where Mallory was fingering Duke's suits. "How is she?"

She set big blue eyes on me. "How are you?"

"Don't deflect, and I'm fine."

"You don't look fine." Her gaze drifted past me. "Is that Duke and Savannah?" Her long legs ate up the space between us. Then she studied the picture, whistling again. "One picture doesn't tell the truth."

As much as I despised Duke, I had to believe he had some emotional structure beneath his critical coldness. After all, he was a Hart, and Dillon and Denim were nothing like their older brother.

"Maybe not," I said. "Let's get out of here." With my luck, Duke would walk in, and he didn't need to know we'd been snooping.

Mallory and I padded down the hall to the kitchen and settled at the island. I dove into the egg sandwich she'd brought me.

She made herself at home and got coffee. Then she produced two laptops from her bag. "Here. I know you're on leave, but in case you get bored, you can check emails at least."

It wouldn't hurt to do some work. That way, I could keep my mind off Denim, Savannah, and getting shot.

In between bites, I asked, "Are you going to answer my question about Cara?"

She opened her laptop then twisted her auburn hair up on the top of her head before securing it with a clip. "Cara is in London with my folks. She's still upset, but maybe she'll meet someone better while in London."

Mallory's dad traveled the world as a sales manager for a company that rented generators used to power the Super Bowl and other sporting events like the PGA. Her mom often accompanied him on his business travels.

"So how is Denim? And where is he? I was sure you two would be between the sheets." She waggled her pretty eyebrows.

I blushed. "I wanted him to stay in bed with me, but he had a meeting with the FBI."

"Mm. You sure he isn't meeting with Tito Alvarez?"

I cocked my head, chewing the delicious egg-and-bacon sandwich. "He didn't mention it. Should I be worried?"

She lifted her dainty shoulders as her fingers flew over the keys. "Not sure. But I did overhear him talking to Kelton yesterday about some meeting with Tito today."

"Today?" I asked through a mouthful of food, tensing.

"Kelton advised Denim of the legal way he could take down Tito. I wouldn't worry."

That was easier said than done. The last thing I wanted was to lose Denim when I'd just gotten him back. But Denim was working with the FBI. Surely they would keep him safe. Unless Denim lied and was meeting with Tito rather than Agent Travers.

*Don't get upset. He's trying to protect you.*

Mallory pulled out an envelope. "Oh, this was delivered to the office via courier this morning."

I examined the envelope that had my name and office address on it. I wasn't sure who would know where I worked other than my immediate friends. Or maybe the contents had something to do with one of Kelton's cases until I saw *personal and confidential* printed on the envelope.

"Well," Mallory said. "Open it."

So I did. Inside was a sheet of paper with words typed on it and another envelope addressed to me from Savannah. My brain froze as a chill tiptoed up my spine.

"What is it?" Mallory asked.

I gulped down a mouthful of air. "It's from Savannah."

Mallory's eyes bugged out. "For real?"

I held my breath. Savannah had never written me a letter from prison. Savannah had never written, period. I'd been the one to keep a diary as a teenager.

She'd teased me about it many times. "Why would you spill your guts on paper? What if someone found it who you didn't want reading it?"

"No one ever will," I'd replied. I'd kept my diary in a shoebox hidden in my bedroom. My parents had never been the type to snoop, and neither had Savannah.

I read the letter that accompanied Savannah's first.

*Dear Ms. Kelly, my name is Ellie Rogers, and I was a friend of Savannah's. She wanted me to give you this envelope if anything ever happened to her. I stopped by the address she'd given me a couple of times, but you weren't home. Your kind neighbor, who I begged by the way, mentioned you worked for Davenport Law Firm. Anyway, I'm so sorry for your loss. I adored Savannah. If you get a chance, please let me know if you are having a funeral service for her. I would love to be there. Kind regards, Ellie.*

She went on to leave her address and phone number at the bottom.

I looked at Savannah's envelope then at Mallory. "I'm not sure I can open it."

"You got this, girl. I'm right here too. Can I see that one while you read Savannah's?"

I slid Ellie's letter over to her then walked over to the window and opened Savannah's. My hands trembled as I removed the two-page letter.

Swallowing down my nerves, I began reading.

*Dear Sis,*

*If you're reading this, that means I didn't make it out of prison alive. You're probably wondering why I would even write a letter like this to begin with. But I felt the need to lay out the truth. Because if I'm dead, then the truth might never come out.*

*I would like to start by saying I'm sorry. I'm sorry for not listening to you. I'm sorry for taking advantage of you. I'm sorry for so many things. I know you're probably wondering why I didn't tell you that when you came to see me. It's hard to talk when others around me are listening. I had to be careful with what I said.*

*My tears were spilling over like Niagara Falls.*

*As I mentioned on your last visit, I need money for protection. There's a group of girls, or a gang, who has it out for me. At first, I didn't think twice about it. You know me. I'm a fighter. I've fought my own battles and have needed no one to do that for me. But prison isn't high school. The women inside are bigger, meaner, bitchier, and have no regard for human life. It's been tough to stay alive every day for the last two years, and everyone inside needs protection. I know you might not comprehend that, but it's true.*

*But the main reason I'm writing this letter is because I need you to know something. For the last six years, I've been carrying around a secret, and I didn't know if I could ever come clean. I didn't know if I would ever be able to say what I'm about to say to you.*

*I know you've never stopped loving Denim, which is why I could never bring myself to face you and why I treated you horribly.*

*Denim Hart didn't kill Hector Alvarez. I was at Hector's the night he was murdered.*

I shrieked, holding my stomach.

Mallory ran over to me. "What is it?"

"I need to sit down." I hurried over to the couch. The letter was burning a hole in my hand and my freaking heart. I set the letter on the table then blew in and out several times.

The sound of a running faucet trickled in my ears, and a moment later, Mallory handed me a glass of water.

I eyed the bar. "I think I need something much harder."

She stuck the glass in my face. "No. You're on pain meds."

I took the glass of water but didn't drink.

She sat next to me and pointed at the letter. "May I?"

Nodding, I decided to drink the water. Maybe it was enough to kick-start my brain or get rid of the numbness blanketing my body. Beneath my shock, so many emotions sizzled—anger, hurt, excitement, hell, and everything under the sun.

Mallory read the first page to herself, and when she finished, she also shrieked, but not as forcefully as I had.

"Can you read the second page to me?" I asked.

She swallowed then began.

*"I went to Hector's to actually find Denim. I wanted to talk to him about you. I'd overheard him talking to Duke about how he missed you. So I was going to convince him to call you to see if you two could*

*rekindle things. He wasn't at his apartment, and I knew if he wasn't there, he was probably at Hector's.*

*"Yeah, Duke and Denim attracted trouble and the wrong kind of people. It's true that the world Denim and Duke live in is no place for sweet people like you. I also know that Denim saw firsthand how Hector lost the love of his life to one of his enemies, and that scared the fuck out of Denim, which was the reason he broke up with you. I only know that because, again, I overheard him talking to Duke one day.*

*"Anyway, I had just entered Hector's building when a gun went off. Scared, I ran out and hid in the shadows across the street. Denim didn't come out of the building that night. Tito Alvarez did. I don't know what happened. But the next thing I knew, Denim was getting arrested. I never had a chance to talk to him.*

*"You're probably wondering why I didn't go to the police. Oh, I thought about it and decided I should do the right thing. But after Hector's neighbor gave her statement to the police and disappeared shortly after, I clammed up. I didn't want to face the same fate as the neighbor, and I would've if Tito ever found out I saw him. He's a monster, sis. He has no regard for human life."*

Closing my hands into fists, I was ready for vengeance.

*"I hope you understand I had to keep my mouth shut. Well, I did tell Duke when he came to visit me two months ago. He didn't know until then. I kept calling and calling him until he broke down and finally came to see me. When I told him the story, he was livid, but he said he could've protected me, which was why I couldn't get him to take my calls after I told him. But the only person who could protect me was me."*

I grabbed Mallory's arm. "I need a break." I wiped tears from my face with the sleeve of my robe.

"Only two short paragraphs left," she said through her own tears.

I blinked. I might as well push through.

She scooted closer to me and finished reading the letter.

*"Sis, I could go on for days and tell you more about me, apologize, cry, and beg for your forgiveness, but it doesn't matter if I'm dead. However, I would like for you to do one thing for me. The two women*

*in the gang who have been beating me were Greta Sanchez and Louise Collier. They were operating on orders from Tito Alvarez. I don't know how he found out I knew about him being at Hector's. I never told a soul except Duke.*

*"In closing, please make sure Tito and these two women pay. I also want you to use this letter as my confession to Denim. I want him to know how very sorry I am. Duke will never forgive me, but I do hope Denim understands.*

*I do love you. I'll say hi to Mom and Dad.*

*Your rebellious but loving sister,*

*Savannah Kelly*

*P.S. I'm going to give this letter to a friend of mine who visits me frequently. I'll ask her to send it only if anything happens to me. Her name is Ellie Rogers, and if you ever get the chance to look her up, please thank her for me."*

I bawled my eyes out. My heart literally hurt, and I wanted to hug my sister. I wanted to hold her and tell her I loved her. Sadly, I would never get to again.

Mallory drew me into her embrace, smoothing a hand down my hair and back. "Let it out." She sniffled.

"Did you happen to overhear where Denim was meeting Tito?" I asked through a river of tears.

"No. Sorry," Mallory said.

"I'm not hiding in this place. It's time I get answers." *Or maybe revenge.*

# 29

# DENIM

Duke had a bottle of bourbon in his hand as he strutted over to a round table positioned in the middle of the room. A spotlight shined down as though we were about to get up on stage and act out our parts. In a way, we were.

Duke's part was to keep his mouth shut so he wouldn't incriminate himself. My role was to ask the questions and get Tito talking and spilling what information he had on the Mexican cartel and the shipment of guns. I knew how to jerk Tito's chain, although it wasn't very hard to do with him.

We'd agreed to meet at Duke's club mainly because we wanted Tito to feel welcomed on Duke's turf and at Duke's so-called table.

Tito hadn't blinked an eye when I told him to meet us at The Monarch. Sure, he wasn't totally ignorant. We knew he would bring men. But Duke had two guards posted at the back door to ensure Tito only entered with one of his men.

Opening and closing my hands, I walked around the first floor of the club, trying to tame my nerves. I didn't give a shit about guns or power. I wanted a confession out of Tito. But I wasn't banking on him confessing. He'd kept the secret of Hector's murder locked tight for six years.

Travers wouldn't be pleased if I tried to get Tito to talk about murdering his brother rather than the time and place of a gun shipment, but I didn't give a rat's ass.

I grabbed a bottle of water from behind the bar, the same bar that had taken a bullet like Jade. Most of the mess had been cleaned up except for the shattered wall-length mirror that hadn't been replaced yet.

"You think it's wise to drink?" I asked.

Duke let out an evil laugh. "You think it's wise to wear a wire?"

I lifted my arms up and out. Then I pointed at my neck. The Feds had inserted a small listening device into the collar of my shirt. Duke was onboard with throwing Tito to the Feds, but he did not like the wire.

"Tito will give them too much information," Duke had said prior to one of Travers's men suiting me up.

I met Duke at the table then closed my hand over the listening device. "Why are you all of a sudden worried? You said the Feds had nothing on you."

He pushed out his shoulders and ran his hands through his thick crop of hair. "Are they listening?" His voice was barely audible.

I closed my hand over the device tighter. "I doubt it." If they were, it would be muffled.

"McCauley is having a cow." He kept his voice so low, I could barely hear him. "Tito has something on him that I wasn't aware of. If he starts flapping his jaws about McCauley, I could get pinched in the crossfire."

"As in dead or as in jail?"

Duke stretched his neck. "Let's just say either one. Because if things go south, I'm afraid I'll be the one murdering the fucker before he walks out of here."

We were in this mess now, and if we backed out, Tito wouldn't think twice about following through on killing me and those I loved. I couldn't worry about Duke and his partner, McCauley. I had to think of myself.

Regardless, I might beat Duke to the punch if my self-control broke. The vengeance was careening through my veins, hot and light-ning fast. Night after night, I'd lain in my prison bunk, thinking about what I would do if I ever found the person who'd set me up—killing, strangling, and torturing came to mind. But if I wanted a future in which my living quarters didn't include bars and cements walls, I had to temper my retribution. I had a beautiful woman on my arm, one who I hoped would be my wife one day. No way was I messing that up.

I wished Dillon had joined us. He had a knack of being the level-headed one, but he had no business in our fight. His job was to keep an eye on Jade. I didn't trust Tito. If he didn't get his way, he would defi-nitely use Jade as his pawn in his lust for power.

The bell to the back door rang.

Duke knocked back the rest of his bourbon. "Here we go."

Letting go of my collar, I focused on the hall along the bar.

One of Duke's men called out, "They're clean, boss."

Footsteps clobbered down the short hall until Tito and Lou came into view.

"I meant to ask you, bro—what happened between you and Lou?" I whispered.

"The fucker stole from me," Duke responded.

I shook my head. "You're better off without him."

Lou scanned the club up and down, making sure he checked every nook and cranny. "No other men, Duke?"

Duke threw him the middle finger. "Just sit your ass down, Lou." His tone brooked no argument.

"Fuck off," Lou spat back. Literally, spit sprayed from his mouth. "I don't take orders from you anymore."

I held back a laugh.

"Got a problem, Denim?" Tito snarled as he pulled out a chair.

I was tempted to follow in Duke's footsteps and tell Tito to sit his ass down, but we were there to do business, not exchange barbs or heated words. The only thing I wanted to hear from Tito was him confessing to killing his brother.

*Keep the end game in mind.*

"Let's get down to business," I said evenly.

Tito took inventory of the room. "Why do I feel like someone is lurking in the shadows? If you so much as have the cops watching, I will finally kill you, Denim."

Maybe Tito wasn't a moron after all.

I opened my hands. "Why would I do that? I just got out of prison."

Duke growled. "Sit your ass down too, Alvarez. You wanted a seat at the table. Here we are. Talk."

Tito stuck his middle finger up at Duke as he obeyed.

Duke's jaw was cement. "That's no way to gain entrance or my trust."

Tension hung in the air, thick, tight, and ready to snap.

"You have the floor, Tito," I started. "Let's talk gun shipment." It was best to start with that rather than whether or not he'd killed his brother. Maybe I could get him in a good mood by letting him think he was playing with the big boys and then catch him off guard.

Tito clasped his hands together and set them on the table. He eyed Duke. "First, I'm not giving you any information until I know for sure this meeting isn't a way to placate me."

Duke sat up straighter. "Now why would I waste my time pacifying you? You want to work with me, then give me something I can take to my colleagues."

Tito regarded Lou.

I had to hand it to him—he'd been smart to bring Lou along. After all, Lou knew Duke well.

Lou nodded, his fat neck rolling under his chin.

"I want fifty percent of the proceeds from the sale of the guns," Tito said.

Duke sat back and laughed. "You're not calling the shots."

"Then who is?" Tito asked. "And if it's your partner, why isn't he here?"

Inwardly, I sighed. The more Duke kept talking, the more he would back himself into a wall with the Feds.

The back doorbell rang.

Surely that wasn't Travers wanting to raid the joint. We hadn't gotten a single ounce of anything he could use to send Tito or my brother to prison.

I narrowed my eyes. "I told you, Alvarez, not to bring any more men."

"Fuck off, Hart," Alvarez said. "I have two men waiting in the car. Unless they have to take a piss, I have no clue who's raining on our parade."

Duke and I exchanged a perplexed look.

My guess was that it was Dillon. He was as stubborn as Duke and me.

Hushed voices filtered in, but I couldn't make them out except for the hint of a female voice.

Lou slapped Tito on the arm. "I got a bad feeling, boss."

Tito pushed to his feet. "I think this was a mistake."

Nonplussed, Duke said, "You walk out that door, you won't have another chance."

My phone vibrated in my back pocket.

I had to agree with Lou. Something wasn't right. I pulled my phone out and read the text.

Dillon: *Jade isn't at the penthouse.*

My stomach dropped to my booted feet, and then I heard Jade yelling, "If you don't let me in, I will knee you in the balls."

I didn't have time to figure out why she was there or how she knew I was at the club. I hadn't had time to call her because I'd only had a short window between meeting with Travers and meeting with Tito.

Jade ran in with Duke's men hustling behind her. Red rimmed her eyes as though she'd been bawling, her lips were thinned, and she was breathing heavily.

My brain was clambering to understand what had her about to explode.

"Sorry, boss," the big, burly guy said to Duke.

Tito beamed from ear to ear. "Well now. You're looking beautiful as ever, Jade. How's the chest?"

She sneered at Tito, audibly growling. "I take it you're Tito Alvarez?" She marched up to Tito. Her hands were closed into fists at her sides, ready to inflict some serious damage. I'd never seen her so enraged.

I slid closer in the event that Tito had plans to hurt her in any way.

She held up her hand. "Denim, stay back. This is my fight."

My brows climbed to my hairline.

Jade kneed Tito in the junk, and hard too. "That's for shooting me."

He squealed like a pig, doubling over as he gripped his balls.

Duke laughed, Lou winced, and I smirked.

"Fuck," Tito managed to get out in a high and strained pitch.

Then she clutched onto Tito's hair before he could straighten, pulled on it hard, then rammed her knee into his face. "That's for killing my sister."

I choked. How did she know? The only people who knew were Dillon, Duke, and me.

I looked at Duke, and he shrugged. I didn't think Duke would've shared that with Jade. Maybe Dillon had spilled the beans trying to stop her from coming here.

Wait, I'd told Kelton. But he'd promised me he wouldn't say a word until we had the facts.

Blood oozed out of Tito's nose as he lifted an arm in the air. "I get it."

Jade let go of him. "You don't fucking get it."

Tito straightened. "Are you going to let her beat me, Hart?"

I couldn't tell whether he was talking to me or Duke because he didn't take his eyes off Jade.

I inched closer to my girl. Tito didn't have any weapons on him, but he might decide to use his fists. "Jade, let me handle this."

Movement caught my eye in my peripheral vision. Mallory inched in and hovered around the bar, watching Jade.

Jade snarled at me. "Not a chance. Don't you want revenge too? He killed his brother and framed you."

Lou gasped. "You killed your own brother?"

Tito took a step back. His dazed, dark, guilty expression ricocheted off Lou, Duke, me, then Jade.

I didn't have time to find out how she knew because I was focused on Tito. "Well?" I tried to keep my voice steady and my body from lunging at the motherfucker. "Did you kill Hector?"

Jade pushed him on his ass.

Tito grunted as his backside hit the floor. He glared at Jade.

I was frozen as I watched Tito, waiting for him to say something.

"Tell me, asshole," Jade shouted at the top of her lungs. "I want to hear that you're responsible for my sister's death."

Jade's elevated voice kick-started my legs, and I closed the distance between us. "I want to hear how you killed your own brother."

Lou shook his head. "That's fucked up."

Tito seemed to crawl into himself as though he wanted to hide, which was odd with the big personality he had. I'd never seen him cower. But the defeat written on his face disappeared as he rose.

He brushed his hand down his jeans. "You don't have any proof." His cocksure attitude was back as he jutted out his pointy chin.

Jade shuddered as she tossed a look over her shoulder at Mallory and held out her hand.

# 30

# JADE

**M**y hands shook as I unfolded Savannah's letter. I'd gotten lucky that Tito was even there. The only reason I was at The Monarch was to ask Duke where Denim was meeting Tito. I hadn't even been sure Duke was part of that meeting.

Nevertheless, I was ready to see Tito suffer long and hard. Mallory had tried to stop me, but I was too far gone to listen to her or anyone. I had one mission—get revenge for Savannah.

Tito watched me, unmoving, with dots of fear in his dark eyes. *He better not move.* I was ready to shoot him dead with the gun I'd taken from Duke's bedroom. The guards hadn't frisked me. One had tried until I kneed him in the groin, so the other one had backed off.

I'd never had the urge to hurt another human being, but I itched to do something to this man who was evil and didn't deserve to live.

The club was deathly quiet except for the rustling of the paper and the pounding of my pulse in my ears.

I skimmed down to the lines I wanted Tito to hear and started to read aloud.

*"The two women in the gang who beat me were Greta Sanchez and Louise Collier. They were operating on orders from Tito Alvarez. I*

*don't know how he found out I knew about him being at Hector's. I never told a soul except Duke."*

I held up the letter in front of Tito. "Be a man and take charge of your actions."

He cocked his head, and blood trickled down his upper lip. "Those girls won't talk."

An odd sound erupted from me. Tito was going to come clean before we left this club, before he had a chance to run or disappear, and before he had a chance to kill me or Denim.

I checked on Duke, who was standing as stoic as ever. If he weren't standing, I would've bet the man didn't have a heartbeat. "Did you throw Savannah under the bus? Did you have a hand in her death?"

Denim, who was slightly behind me and off to the side, sucked in a sharp breath.

"He probably did," a short, freaky-looking older man said. He was glaring at me, or maybe he was in awe of me. *Whatever.* He gave me the creeps.

I made a mental note to thank Denim for breaking up with me. He was spot-on. I didn't want to be with a criminal, not ever. If Denim had any ideas of joining Duke in his business—whatever that was—I was walking away and not looking back.

"Well?" I asked Duke again. "Are you and this thug in bed together?"

Shockingly, a laugh rumbled out of Duke. "Fuck no."

It was then that I finally looked at the man who had my heart in the palm of his hand, the man who had been imprisoned for a wrong he didn't commit.

Denim was tense, his jaw was set, and he also appeared ready to hurt someone. A sharp pain gripped my chest. The man had lost six years of his fucking life.

"Look." Tito's voice scraped my nerves, sending raging chills down my spine.

With the letter in one hand, I dipped my free hand in my coat pocket and wrapped my fingers around the handle of the gun. I wasn't a killer. Yet if he didn't come clean, I was ready to take the law into my own hands.

I regarded Tito with my hackles raised.

One side of lips curled, and he puffed out his chest as if he'd won this battle, which was laughable. He hadn't won anything. "You have nothing but your sister's word."

"Do you want to hear more of my sister's words?" Even though it was a question, I wasn't asking.

I read another part to him.

*"I'd just entered Hector's building when a gun went off. Scared, I ran out and hid in the shadows across the street. But Denim didn't come out of the building that night. Tito Alvarez did. I don't know what happened. But the next thing I knew, Denim was getting arrested. I never had a chance to talk to him.*

*"You're wondering why I didn't go to the police. Oh, I thought about it and decided I should do the right thing. But after Hector's neighbor gave her statement to the police and disappeared shortly after, I clammed up. I didn't want to face the same fate as the neighbor, and I would've if Tito ever found out I saw him. He's a monster, sis. He has no regard for human life."*

The gun in my pocket felt heavy and exhilarating at the same time. I lifted my eyes to stare at Tito. "Last chance."

Tito looked at the short, creepy guy as though he could save Tito. Then his attention swung to Duke and Denim. None of them were bouncing on their feet to help. He set his dark eyes on me. "Or what?"

I swallowed an elephant and pulled out the gun, aiming it at Tito's heart. I had no idea if I could successfully shoot him since I'd never shot a gun before. "Or I shoot."

"Jade." Denim's husky voice drew closer. "Don't. He's not worth it." He touched my trembling arm gently. "Angel, lower the gun."

A tear slid down my cheek, burning a path until the salty tear was sliding into my mouth. "He is worth it. For Savannah. For you. Don't you want him to pay?"

His hand inched down my arm. "He will pay."

More tears clouded my vision, and I shook my head. "No."

"You're not a killer." Denim's hand was on my wrist. "Give me the gun."

All I saw was my sister fighting to stay alive. All I saw in front of me was the thug who had stolen six years of Denim's life.

Tito stared at me, his dark eyes pleading. "Hart, you better get that out of her hands."

His grating voice seemed to blast in the deadly quiet room, and in that moment, I didn't think. I closed my eyes and squeeze the trigger.

The blast hurt my ears, and I practically fell into Denim.

Mallory screamed.

Before I could open my eyes, Denim had the gun out of my hand. "Duke, take Jade, please."

My heart punched my ribs, trying to get out of my chest. To my dismay, Tito was still standing without a scratch on him with a smile that reminded me of the Joker in *Batman*.

My nostrils flared as Mallory rushed to my side. "Come on. You don't need to go to jail for that asshole."

Duke was behind me. "Mallory's right." His voice was tender, causing me to falter.

"I'm staying right by Denim's side." I narrowed my eyes at the man I was helplessly in love with. "I'm not a weakling. Tito is going to confess, or I'm going to beat him senseless."

Tito laughed like a madman.

The creepy guy said, "Boss, let's get out of here."

Denim trained the gun on Tito then Lou. "Neither of you are going anywhere until we finish our business. Now, Lou, I suggest you sit your ass back down."

Lou obeyed like a good little soldier.

Denim swung his arm and aimed the gun at Tito. "Talk, or I will shoot, and you know I won't miss."

"Hart." Tito's bravado was gone, and in its place was the fear I'd seen on him earlier. "You're not a killer."

"But you are." Denim had both arms outstretched, holding the gun like a trained cop. "Talk, motherfucker."

"You're not going to shoot me," Tito retorted.

Before I took a breath, another loud boom rebounded around the club.

I flinched, my heart in overdrive.

Mallory let out a squeal, and Duke ushered her to the bar.

Tito shrieked as he stammered, clutching his knee. "Fucking bastard. I'm going to end you once and for all."

Denim cocked his head, pointing the gun at Tito. "Not the words I want to hear. One more chance, or I will put a bullet in your skull."

*Oh my God!*

Instantly, the cloud of rage in my head vanished. Maybe it was the blood soaking Tito's jeans or the notion that Denim could go back to prison for good. Whatever was making me see clearly, I couldn't let him go back to prison if he killed Tito.

I lightly placed my hand on Denim's back. "Denim, we're both not thinking straight."

Denim inched closer to Tito. "Last chance."

Tito raised his hands, wincing, sweat glistening on his face. "Okay. Put the gun down. I didn't mean to kill Hector." Defeat threaded through Tito's words. "It was an accident. We got into an argument over a supplier, and he wouldn't listen to me. The next thing I knew, I had his gun in my hands, and he was dead."

Denim took another step closer to Tito. "Then what? You dumped the gun in my backpack?"

Tito nodded, pain etched on his ugly face.

"Say it," Denim said through gritted teeth.

"I did," Tito whispered. "I knew that was your backpack. I couldn't let my family find out what I'd done. Hector was the prodigal son."

Every ounce of air in my lungs escaped in a loud rushing sound, and I faltered. That cloud of rage was back, and before I could stop myself, I lunged at Tito, tackling him to the floor.

His back hit the ground with a thud as his hands went around my neck. "Savannah deserved to die," Tito snarled.

I sank my teeth into his hand.

He cried out. "Bitch."

Strong hands gripped my arms. "Angel," Denim said.

I wasn't an angel. I was the devil at that moment. I wanted Tito to suffer for what he'd done.

Denim pried me off Tito, and once I was on two feet, I spat in Tito's face. "You are a monster, just like my sister said." Tears burned my eyes, but I wasn't going to cry. Not yet. I wasn't sure Savannah's written confession or Tito's verbal one was enough to put him away. It was his word against ours, and Savannah wasn't there to tell her side of the story.

*You have more evidence to put him away than the police had for Denim when the jury convicted him. And you have witnesses. Tito will pay in prison.*

"Why did you kill Savannah?" I asked. I knew why. I just wanted to hear him say it. "She never did anything to you. She kept your secret for years while Denim paid for your actions."

Duke was at my side. "Answer her. Or you'll feel my wrath next."

Tito stumbled to his feet, his eyes widening at Duke.

With Duke as scary as he was on one side of me and Denim with a gun on the other side of me, Tito should be scared, although I didn't see the gun in Denim's hand anymore.

Tito's Adam's apple bobbed. "One of my girls overheard her talking to Duke." He spat blood on the floor. "I couldn't let her live."

Duke took one step toward Tito when an army of law enforcement surrounded us with guns at the ready.

Duke and Denim raised their arms up in the air as though they'd made that very move a million times.

Tito didn't move.

I snarled at Tito. "I hope you rot in prison for the rest of your life."

A man behind me with a baritone voice said, "He will."

As if those two words were a balm to my severed heart, I sagged in relief.

# 31

# DENIM

A cop frisked me, removed the gun from the back of my jeans, then cuffed me. Other cops did the same to Duke, Lou, Tito, Mallory, and Jade.

*God. Jade.*

The bravery she had exhibited when she'd walked in was gone. In its place was fear.

A pang of hurt spread through my chest. The last thing I ever wanted to see was her in cuffs.

Officer Ted Hughes, tall and mean as fuck, helped Jade to the table. "Sit here." His tone permitted no argument.

Another officer did the same with Mallory, Lou, and Duke.

Then Ted Hughes waltzed up to me and sized me up with a snarl that made the hairs on his mustache twitch. "Denim Hart. I was surprised to hear you got parole."

"I'm surprised you showed up today," I said in a nice tone. The last thing I wanted to do was piss off the man. With my luck, he was still going to lock me up for shooting Tito, but honestly, I didn't give a rat's ass. I would gladly spend time in jail as long as Jade didn't. She wouldn't survive in jail, nor would she have forgiven herself if she had shot Tito dead.

"Dillon is a good friend," Hughes said.

"Where are the Feds?" They were the ones who'd put a wire on me. They were the ones taping everything.

"I'm right here." Travers strutted in, scanning the club with his normal scowl.

"Did you get everything on tape?" I asked Travers.

"You fucker. You set me up?" Tito's voice cracked.

I gave him a crisp nod as a weight was lifted off my shoulders. "You're lucky I didn't kill you."

"You're dead, Hart." He flicked his chin at Duke. "Both of you."

Duke's nostrils flared. "Careful, Alvarez. You're incriminating yourself in front of the law."

A cop escorted Tito and Lou out of the club.

Hughes smoothed his fingers over his salt-and-pepper mustache. The man had gone a bit gray in the six years since he'd arrested me. "We have enough to put him away for life."

Jade sobbed, and my heart splintered.

"Can you take the cuffs off me?" I asked Hughes. "Unless you're taking me to jail."

"You did shoot someone intentionally, and he was unarmed," Hughes said as a matter of fact.

I would've kept shooting Tito until he came clean, but I didn't say that. "I didn't kill him. Besides, don't I get a pat on the back for taking a true murderer off the streets?"

"Hughes," Travers said, "we agreed I could have my go at Denim before you take him in. We have some unfinished business."

I should've been worried, but I wasn't. Tito had confessed, and while I hadn't gotten him to give up a time and location on his gun shipment, I didn't need the FBI anymore.

Hughes pinched his chin. "When you're done with Duke and Denim, let me know. I need to question the others anyway." He sauntered off toward Jade.

I glanced over my shoulder at my girl and mouthed, "I love you."

She smiled weakly. I was sure she was worried about whether or not she was going to spend some time behind bars. But she didn't have to worry. She hadn't done a thing but bring the gun. If she hadn't, I wasn't sure Tito would've talked.

I cleared my throat. "Are you going to say something, Agent Travers?"

He briefly closed his eyes, no doubt trying to temper his anger, which was evident with the muscle ticking along his jaw. "You didn't get me what I wanted."

"I tried." I packed as much sincerity in those two words as I could. Because I had tried.

Duke stood by me and listened.

An exaggerated sigh escaped Travers. "I should penalize your girl for interrupting things."

I growled low, grinding my teeth together. "Careful, Travers. I wouldn't want to have my lawyer contact your superior for harassment."

He laughed. "I like you, Denim."

"Could've fooled me."

"I'll get what I want." He glanced at Duke. "It's only a matter of time before your brother fucks up."

Duke kept his mouth shut even though I could detect an air of smugness around him.

I shrugged. "Not my business." I had other unpleasant words to fire at Travers, but we were ending on a good note, so I zipped my lips.

"Ted," Travers shouted. "He's all yours." Then Travers said to Duke, "A word alone."

My brother didn't protest as he followed Travers to a quiet spot away from the traffic.

My pulse sped up as worry cinched my gut. I couldn't remember if Duke had said anything to incriminate himself before Jade stormed in. Then again, Duke had been well aware of the consequences.

Dillon came out of nowhere. "Hey."

"How did you get in?" I imagined the club had cops everywhere outside.

He flicked his chin at Ted. "It helps to know the man in charge. You okay?"

A slow smile emerged as my muscles loosened. "Never better. I owe you, bro."

"You don't owe me shit. It was easy to get Ted on board. He and his gang unit have been wanting to take down Alvarez for a long time. And Agent Travers didn't protest either. What do you think he's saying to Duke now?"

Travers looked as though he were reading Duke the riot act, and my brother wasn't showing any signs he was the least bit frightened.

"He's throwing out threat after threat after threat," I said. After all, that was Travers's MO. Jade was still immersed in conversation with Ted, as was Mallory. I scratched my wrists. The fucking cuffs were irritating my skin. "You think Jade will spend the night in jail?"

Dillon lifted a shoulder. "Not sure. But if I know Ted, unless there's a good reason to bring her or any of you in, then he won't waste his time. He hates paperwork."

"Can you call Kelton just in case?"

Dillon nodded as Duke sauntered up, hands still in cuffs, while Travers stormed out.

"That went well," Duke said, not fazed in the least about his conversation with Travers. "How does it feel to have your life back?" he asked me.

"It's sinking in slowly." Once I had a place of my own, a job, and Jade on my arm, then I would feel more of a sense of peace.

As if he knew what I was thinking, Duke said, "I want you and Jade to take the penthouse."

Dillon's jaw came unhinged.

Mine did as well. "I don't want handouts, man." I got the vibe he was feeling guilty.

"This isn't a handout," he said. "You need a place of your own until you can get on your feet."

"He's staying with me," Dillon said.

I liked crashing at Dillon's, but he was getting married, and I couldn't impose too much longer. I could stay with Jade, or we could get our own place. "Why are you suddenly offering?"

Duke's chest heaved. "I didn't help you when you went to prison. I didn't visit you. I'm sorry about that. I want to show you I'm not a complete asshole."

A wide smile broke out on Dillon as though he were proud of Duke.

"Why didn't you visit me?"

Duke sighed. "Honestly, to protect you. The shit I'm in brings all kinds of threats. So I didn't want to put any of your lives in jeopardy. It might not be what you wanted to hear. You might be thinking you're a big boy who could take care of himself, but that's not the way I see it. I'm the older brother. I'm the one who's supposed to protect you." He flicked his chin at me then at Dillon. "And Grace. It kills me every day that I kept her at arm's length. If I hadn't, I might've been able to prevent what happened to her." It sounded as though Duke was on the verge of tears, although he wasn't showing any visible signs.

"Well, it fucking hurt, bro," I said. "You could've at least taken my calls and told me that."

Duke's voice sounded pained when he spoke. "As much as I wanted to, I couldn't show I care."

I knew that feeling well, which was the reason I'd cut Jade out of my life. Apart from that, I wasn't one to hold a grudge, and if the shoe was on the other foot, I probably would've done the same thing.

Dillon gripped Duke's shoulder. "If you want to redeem yourself, start by getting out of the shit storm you're in."

"Walk away from the cartel," I added in a low tone just in case anyone was listening.

Most of the other cops had cleared out.

Duke leaned in closer to Dillon and me. "If I do, you two might as well get my funeral arrangements ready because you can't walk away from the cartel."

I couldn't believe I was about to ask this. "Anything I can do to help?"

He feigned a smile. "Build an honest life for you and Jade. Marry her. Have kids. And stay away from me. Both of you. Because if I screw up, my enemies are coming for you and everyone I care about."

He'd never spoken truer words. But I had to help in some way.

"I know a dude in prison who can set you up with a new name and passport."

"So do I, bro. I'll be fine. I've made my bed."

No matter how hard Dillon and I tried to help him, he wasn't going to let us. Duke was as stubborn as they came.

"I'm not taking your penthouse," I said.

"Too late," he fired back. "I already put it in your name. And before you protest, saying yes is helping me." He gave me the impression he was shoring up loose ends in the event he was killed.

A knot formed in my gut. "Okay." Sometimes there was no arguing with Duke. When he had his mind made up, he wasn't changing it.

Ted took the cuffs off Jade, and before I could track her, she was throwing her arms around me. "Officer Hughes isn't taking any of us to jail."

*Thank fuck.* I was more relieved she wasn't going.

Ted came over and took the cuffs off Duke then me.

As soon as my arms were free, I tugged Jade to me. "You okay?"

She flashed her green eyes up at me. "I'm so sorry."

I edged back and cupped her face. "Sorry?"

She sniffled. "You went to jail for something you didn't do. Savannah could've helped you."

"She couldn't. She did what she had to do to protect herself. Tito would've killed her."

She buried her face into my chest and cried.

I rubbed her back. "Shh. Everything will be okay now." I rested my chin on her head, inhaling her coconut shampoo. "We can move on with our lives." No more Tito. No running. No fear for Jade's life. And no fucking Travers. With my name cleared, that meant no parole.

I squeezed Jade to me as my body began to shed six years of hell, one muscle at a time.

Mallory ambled over, looking less pale than she had earlier. "Well, that was fun. Not."

Jade left me to hug Mallory.

Ted combed his mustache with his fingers. "For now, go home. If I need any of you, I'll find you." Ted regarded Dillon. "Can we chat?"

Dillon and Ted walked away.

Duke ambled around the bar. "Anyone want a drink?"

I wasn't in the mood for liquor, but rather a sexy, black-haired, green-eyed beauty. I wanted to hug and kiss and do many other naughty things to her until we couldn't breathe.

**32**

---

# JADE

The rain came down in sheets, pounding on the roof of Dillon's car as he drove Maggie, Denim, and me to the church. We were having a small service for Savannah.

I bounced my knee while the scenery outside the backseat window sped by. Every time I blinked, I saw flames after flames after flames. I remembered Savannah's screams vividly. I had been choking on smoke, and Dad had been yelling at me to get my sister out of the house.

I blinked several times to erase the memories. It was eerily chilling that I was burying Savannah around the time of my parents' death.

I captured a fingernail in between my teeth. "Why does it rain on funerals?" I mumbled to myself.

"The rain is God's tears," Maggie said from the passenger seat. "He's crying for them just like we are."

A chill blanketed me as I let her words seep in. At Mom and Dad's funeral, there had been a drizzle of rain, not a steady stream of hard rain. Still, I liked Maggie's reasoning. In fact, I loved her reasoning. It was poignant yet uplifting and comforting, and for some odd reason, the pain in my chest eased.

"Thank you for that," I said to Maggie.

I'd finally met her after Tito was arrested. She'd been covering the big showdown for the local news station. We hadn't had a chance to get to know one another yet, however before we'd gotten in the car, she'd invited me to her wedding.

I'd accepted. The last time I'd been to a wedding, I was ten. Mom had dragged Savannah and me with her to a friend's wedding. It had been a happy occasion, and it would be nice to see happiness again.

After I buried Savannah, I planned on doing things that made me happy. I'd taken the first step and said yes to Denim when he asked me to move into Duke's penthouse with him. I hadn't batted an eye. I'd thrown myself at him with a kiss that said "hell yeah," and not because of the lavish apartment on the top floor of an expensive building, which was icing on the cake, but because I had Denim back and things were looking up.

As for Duke, he was getting The Monarch ready to reopen. However, in the three weeks since the club incident, I hadn't seen Duke. I was hoping to see him at the service. I wanted to thank him for paying for the burial service, and I still needed to get some things off my chest with him.

Denim reached over and pried my hand from my mouth. "You've been surviving on your nails," he teased.

I batted my eyelashes his way. His face was completely healed, showing no signs of the beating he'd taken from Tito and his men. He had a couple of scars, but they made him look more badass amid his close-shaven beard than ever before.

I was feeling a ton better from my gunshot wound. I, too, had a scar forming above my right breast. Denim had said it was a sexy battle scar. To me, it was a stark reminder that I wanted nothing to do with criminals.

Denim had promised me he wouldn't regress or fall into his old ways.

"Not even if Duke needs your help?" I'd asked.

"No. Duke is on his own," he'd said. "I'm not going back to prison."

I believed him. He'd enrolled in online courses to finish his degree in business, and he'd been out job hunting. He hadn't had any luck yet, but I was confident he would find something soon.

I was back at work and loving my job with Kelton Maxwell. In between working long hours, I was learning the paralegal role with Mallory's help.

Denim kissed the back of my hand. As he did, his blond locks toppled forward, grazing my skin. "Angel, you okay?"

Tingles sprouted. "I'm good."

Denim grinned, his blue eyes clear, happy, and loving. He seemed like a new man now that his murder conviction was about to be erased. If it were even possible, he looked sexier than he ever had. Maybe it was the suit. I thought suits looked yummy on men, especially if it was tailored, and Denim was wearing one of Duke's expensive suits—black pants and jacket, dark-blue shirt, and a gray tie to complement the ensemble.

"Thank you," I said.

"For what?"

Dillon flicked on the blinker. "We're here."

"I'll tell you later." I didn't want to go into detail in front of Dillon and Maggie.

Once we were parked, Dillon climbed out, darted around the car to the passenger side, and held up an umbrella for Maggie.

"Are you ready?" Denim asked.

"Not really."

He grabbed the handle of his umbrella, hopped out, and held open the door for me.

I slid along the buttery leather seat and took his hand. Once we were cozied up under the umbrella, we rushed into the church.

Mallory was waiting just inside, wearing a simple black dress that fell to her knees. Her hair was tied back in a low ponytail, her mouth was pinched, and crinkles lined her forehead.

Before Denim lowered the umbrella, Mallory was throwing her arms around me. "I'm sorry it's raining outside. I've been so worried about you." She knew all too well rain had a tendency to trigger bad memories.

I hugged her tightly. "I'm okay." I truly was. Denim was part of the reason. Honestly, if I didn't have him to hold me at night, I probably would've stayed in bed that day.

She inspected every inch of me. "Are you sure?"

I smiled with lingering tears. "It's time for new beginnings."

Denim stole me from Mallory, cocooning me in his strong arms. My back was pressed against his front. "It sure is." He kissed me on the ear. "Jade is in good hands now."

Mallory jutted out her chin. "If you hurt her again, you better leave town because I'll find a way to overturn your murder conviction."

"You'll make a good lawyer one day, Mal." Denim wasn't the least bit concerned by her threat.

"Damn straight," she retorted.

A gust of wind blew in, signaling the entrance of a young lady with bright amber eyes and blond hair. She smiled at me. "Jade Kelly?"

"You must be Ellie." I walked up and gave her a hug. "Thank you so much for coming. And for being such a great friend to Savannah."

She squeezed me. "She was special."

I'd learned when I'd contacted Ellie to invite her to Savannah's service that she and Savannah had met just after my sister graduated high school. Both of them were into drugs, but Ellie had gotten clean early on.

Someone touched my back. "Jade?"

I pivoted on my heel. "Todd, you managed to get away from work. Thank you."

He smiled, showing his overlapping tooth. "So sorry for your loss."

Ellie touched my arm. "I'll see you afterwards." She left to find a seat.

Mallory joined Todd. The two had gone out a couple of times in the last few weeks. I didn't know if they were serious, but it was nice to see my BFF dating. "We should get settled. Kelton is inside with a few others from the office." Mallory grabbed Todd's hand.

Warmth spread through my chest because I knew I had the best boss in the world. True to his word about how family came first, he'd given me more time off than I was allowed. But I hadn't taken more than a week. I was the type who had to keep busy.

Denim ambled up, and we were about to follow Mal and Todd when the door opened, bringing in more cold air along with Duke.

I hadn't been sure if he would show.

Denim and Duke exchanged a brotherly hug. "Thanks for coming, bro."

I touched Denim's arm. "Can I have a word with Duke alone?"

Duke regarded me with suspicion.

"I won't knee you in the balls," I teased. That day with Tito in the club, I had been a madwoman, and I couldn't fault Duke for being a little uneasy around me.

Duke's features relaxed with a hint of a smile.

Denim kissed me on the cheek. "Good luck, bro." He sauntered off, chuckling.

When Duke and I were alone in the small entryway of the church, I said, "Thank you for paying for the service."

He bobbed his head and swallowed. "Jade, I never wanted anything but happiness for Savannah." Sincerity weaved through his words.

"What happened between you two?"

"Our relationship was volatile. We were oil and water."

I angled my head. "But you loved her?"

"I guess. Does it matter?"

Duke was a hard man to read, and I was dreaming if I thought he would give me a straight answer. The fact that he'd wanted nothing but happiness for Savannah said it all. So I dropped the ten-question interrogation.

"You're right," I said. "We should go in. Thanks again for helping and for everything you've done for Denim."

"Jade, do me a favor?" His tone was a plea, or maybe I was imagining things. The Duke I knew would never plead with anyone. "Take care of Denim." He sounded like he wouldn't see Denim again.

My heart splintered. "Without a doubt." I hooked my arm in his. "Shall we?"

He stiffened as though he didn't want to go in.

"I got you," I said. "So do your brothers." Tears began to flow down my cheeks.

Duke sighed then closed his hand over the one I had on his arm.

As we walked to our seats, I couldn't help but feel a pang of sympathy for Duke. He was in too deep with the cartel, and according to Denim, there were only two ways out—prison or a body bag.

More tears began to spill as I eyed the coffin. Soft music floated from the overhead speakers, and heads turned.

I nodded at Kelton and at the others who were there to pay their respects.

Once we were seated in the front row, and I was sandwiched in between Duke and Denim, I slumped my shoulders, exhaling.

Denim entwined his fingers with mine. "You okay?"

I squeezed his hand. "I love you," I whispered. I couldn't begin to describe how I was feeling except protected and loved.

He leaned closer to my ear. "Ditto, angel."

We were starting anew, and after the funeral, I had to focus on Denim and me. We had no one and nothing standing in our way.

Tito was in prison and, according to Kelton, would be for quite some time. We had a nice place to live, and I had the one man I'd never stopped loving back in my arms. I hoped that man would one day be my husband, partner, lover, best friend, and the father of our children.

# EPILOGUE

## DENIM

The holidays were never a great time of year for me. Growing up, my siblings and I didn't get much under the Christmas tree. I'd always told myself that when I had a family one day, I would shower them with gifts galore. I wanted my kids to believe in Santa Claus. I wanted to see the excitement on their faces when they ran into the living room on Christmas morning and saw the presents under the tree. I wanted to see them tear the wrapping paper to shreds and their eyes pop wide when they finally saw what Santa had brought them.

The sun was barely up as dawn began to bleed through the dark sky. I set the shoebox I'd just wrapped under the tree. I'd gotten up early to wrap Jade's gift. It was the first chance I had since I'd only picked it up the day before.

I was hoping she would like it. I wanted Christmas to be special for her. Since her parents had died in between Thanksgiving and Christmas, she wasn't thrilled about celebrating, and with Savannah recently buried, it was even harder for her to get into the spirit.

I wandered into the kitchen and started a pot of coffee. I still couldn't believe Duke had given me the penthouse. Jade had put her own spin on the decor. Vases of flowers and plants were scattered about. A blanket her mom had crocheted was draped over the leather couch, and decorative square pillows were dispersed on the couch and chairs. The Christmas tree was tucked into the corner near the fireplace.

With Christmas ready to go, I snuck back into bed, careful not to wake Jade. But as soon as I slid into our king-size bed, she rolled over and immediately seated her hand on my groin.

"Merry Christmas, big guy." Her voice was sultry and sleepy. "Where did you go?"

I turned onto my side, found her foot with mine, and rubbed. "I was playing Santa Claus."

She slid closer to me. "The only present I want is you inside me. Or…" She licked her lips. "How about a little oral sex?"

I swallowed, and my cock instantly got hard. "How about both?"

She purred, and that was my cue.

I shed my sweatpants and was on top of her naked body in two seconds flat.

She giggled.

I shoved my cock into her in one fast thrust.

She purred again like a sweet kitten, arching her back. Her nipples were hard and ready.

I latched on to her tit with my teeth. "Best Christmas present." I rocked my hips into her wet pussy.

She pushed on my shoulders. "I want your tongue taking me to heaven and back."

I waggled my eyebrows. "I thought you would never ask." I kissed, nipped, and licked my way down her soft skin. Her nipples were peaks of hard, delectable pleasure.

Her hands latched on to my hair and massaged my scalp, dragging her long nails until she pulled on some strands.

"That's it. Hold on for the ride."

She giggled. "Shut up and eat me."

I chuckled.

She wrapped her legs around my waist and turned us. When I was on my back, she wasted no time sitting on my dick.

"I'm supposed to eat you."

"In a minute." She rode me, rocking her hips. Her tits bounced, her face was flushed, and her eyes were heavy with desire. "This feels too good."

"Fuck yeah, it does. But I want control."

"You'll get your turn."

I knew the perfect position. "Get your pussy up here," I ordered in a tone that was deep and commanding. "Suck my dick while I eat you."

Her green eyes bulged out of her head, but her smile was off the charts.

Once we were in the perfect position, I flattened my tongue on her clit.

She moaned around my cock as she swirled her tongue on the tip, sending jolts of pleasure to my balls.

I threw my head back and growled even louder when she took me deep, the head hitting the back of her throat. I became a madman as I worked until she was panting out breath after breath while she dragged her nails along my balls.

"I'm close, angel. So fucking close." I didn't want any of this to end.

When she sucked hard like she was sucking a lollipop, I was a second away from crashing and diving and feeling that euphoria that came with the best orgasm.

I rolled us around. "I want to be inside you." I wanted to see her go over the edge. I wanted that connection of love and lust as we locked eyes.

We were all arms and legs as we adjusted our bodies until I was buried deep inside her.

"Oh fuck," I said.

She played with herself while I fucked her like a man possessed.

Her breathing grew labored.

Sweat dripped down my chest as I continued to pound into her. "I'm ready, angel."

"I'm almost there." She arched her back, her lips parting in a perfect O. I knew she was sailing into euphoria.

I rocked in then out, watching her moan and tremble. When she squeezed around my cock, that blissful state of orgasm zipped through my body. "Fuuuuck," I shouted.

She ran her hands up my chest. "Look at me."

I didn't know I had my eyes closed. I grinned as I pulsed inside her.

Her hands dove into my hair, and her big green eyes stared up at me. "I love you, Denim Hart."

I pressed my hands into the mattress on either side of her head. "Ditto, angel."

"Best Christmas ever," she said in a breathy tone.

"For sure." I didn't want to tell her the best was yet to come. "Let's take a shower. Then we can make breakfast and lounge around."

"I have something to do first. You shower. Then I'll join you."

I imagined that she had to wrap a gift since I hadn't seen any for me when I tucked her box under the tree. Not that I needed a gift. I had the best gift God could give me—Jade in my arms.

Thirty minutes later after we'd both showered and dressed, we were in the kitchen.

Jade was getting ready to make bacon.

I poured coffee into a cup. "Let's open presents before we eat." I took her hand and pulled her over to the tree.

She lowered herself to the carpet and sat on her heels. "I would like you to open yours first." She snagged the box that she must've put under the tree while I was in the shower and handed it to me.

I joined her on the floor, feeling like we were kids eager to tear into our presents. Then I unwrapped the box that I was guessing had a shirt or sweater in it. But when I finally took the cover off, I cocked my head to one side. "What's this?" I lifted the manila folder out of the box.

"Open the folder," she said.

The paper inside read, "Denim Hart, your murder charge has officially been dropped and your record expunged. Congratulations! Kelton Maxwell."

I'd been waiting for this. Kelton had said it would take some time.

I kissed Jade. "Best Christmas ever."

She smiled from ear to ear. "That was from Kelton. There's something else inside from me."

I pulled out tissue paper to find a square box that looked like it contained some type of jewelry, which I didn't wear. Inside was…

I glanced up at her. "Where did you find this?"

She took the watch out of the box. "I found it in my bedroom a week before you broke up with me. I guess I kept it as something to remember you by."

I had loved that watch. It wasn't anything fancy—a designer knockoff with a silver face and band, but Grace had given me the watch for my birthday one year. She'd saved up her money Duke had given her on occasion. It was more sentimental than anything.

I put the watch on my wrist. "I love it. Grace will light up when she sees this."

Jade tucked her hair behind her ear. "Merry Christmas."

"I have everything I want now. Well, there is one thing I need." I dragged the shoe box to her. My heart ramped up, ready to burst out of my chest.

She tore the wrapping paper off it like a kid in a candy store. Then her eyebrows knitted together when she started pulling out tissue paper after tissue paper until she got to a small velvet box. Her hands shook. "You didn't, Denim Hart."

I took the box from her. "Jade Kelly."

She shook her head. "This can't be happening."

I scooted closer to her until we were knees to knees. "Please look at me."

She lifted her watery green gaze.

I opened the box, not taking my eyes off her. "I've never been surer of us. I've never been happier. I've never wanted anyone as much as I want you. I want you to be my partner, lover, best friend, and mother of my baseball team of kids. But most of all, I want you to be my wife as we muddle through this world and spend every moment making memories. I love you, Jade Kelly. Will you marry me?"

She slapped a hand over her mouth as a sob escaped her. "You can't afford that emerald."

"Angel, that's not the answer I was looking for. But I got a job. Dillon hired me. I'm now officially working on his security staff for the shelter, and his friend Hunt is going to get me into his brother's security firm too."

She blinked away tears. "That's fantastic! But I thought you wanted to go into business?"

"I do, and I will still get my degree, but I have to work." We didn't have rent or a house payment thanks to Duke, but we were partners, and I needed to do my part. "Back to the important question."

Jade took the half-carat emerald out of the box. "Yes, yes, yes." She threw herself at me, peppering kisses on my jaw then lips. "I love you more than you know. My heart has been yours since we met. And I couldn't have asked for a better man to spend my life with."

Now I had everything I needed.

# ABOUT THE AUTHOR

Bestselling author **S.B. Alexander** writes young adult and new adult romances that span the sub-categories of coming of age, sports, paranormal, suspense, and military fiction. Her writing is emotional, angsty, and character driven. She's best known for The Maxwell and The Maxwell Family Saga series.

S.B. or Susan as she likes to be called is a navy veteran, former high school teacher, and former corporate sales executive. She's a lover of sports, especially baseball, although nowadays you can find her glued to the TV during football season.

When she's not writing, she's a full-time caregiver to her soul mate of twenty-one years who got a bad deal in life when he was diagnosed with ALS. Her motto: "Life is too short to waste. So live every moment like it's your last."

**You can connect with S.B. Alexander in the following ways:**
Reader Group: http://sbalexander.com/sbareaderroom
Author Website: http://sbalexander.com
Newsletter: http://sbalexander.com/newsletter
Email: susan@sbalexander.com

**NEVER MISS A NEW RELEASE:**
Follow S.B. Alexander on Amazon
Follow S.B. Alexander on BookBub

facebook.com/sbalexander.authorpage

twitter.com/sbalex_author

instagram.com/sbalexanderauthor

amazon.com/author/sbalexander

bookbub.com/authors/s-b-alexander

goodreads.com/sbalexander

# ALSO BY S.B. ALEXANDER

## THE MAXWELL SERIES

*Upper Young Adult/New Adult Contemporary Romance*

Dare to Kiss

Dare to Dream

Dare to Love

Dare to Dance

Dare to Live

Dare to Breathe

Dare to Embrace

The Kade & Lacey Collection Box Set

Dare to Kiss Coloring Book Companion

## THE MAXWELL FAMILY SAGA SERIES

*Young Adult Contemporary Romance*

My Heart to Touch

My Heart to Hold

My Heart to Give

My Heart to Keep*

## STANDALONES

*New Adult Contemporary Romance*

Unforgettable

Breaking Rules

Rescuing Riley

Holding On To Forever

**THE HART SERIES**

*New Adult Romantic Suspense*

Hart of Darkness

Hart of Vengeance

Hart of Redemption*

**THE VAMPIRE SEAL SERIES**

*Young Adult Paranormal Romance*

On the Edge of Humanity

On the Edge of Eternity

On the Edge of Destiny

On the Edge of Misery

On the Edge of Infinity

The Vampire SEAL Collection

*Coming 2020.

Visit http://sbalexander.com for all future release dates. Please note release dates are subject to change based on reader demand and the author's schedule. Subscribing to the author's newsletter or following her on Facebook is the best way to stay updated with planned new releases.

www.ingramcontent.com/pod-product-compliance
Lightning Source LLC
Chambersburg PA
CBHW021119110726
47900CB00007B/2252